Following a degree in Politics from Manchester University Tamara Kate Jarvis had a successful career in Whitehall before taking a career break to look after her two young children and pursue her dream of writing. 'The Italian Dream' was written as her young son slept and has been a labour of love.

Tamara lives in Hertfordshire with her husband and two children and is currently working on her second novel, 'The Italian Christmas'.

The Italian Dream

Tamara Kate Jarvis

The Italian Dream

Vanguard Press

VANGUARD PAPERBACK

A CIP catalogue record for this title is
available from the British Library.

ISBN 978 178465 038 4

Vanguard Press is an imprint of
Pegasus Elliot MacKenzie Publishers Ltd.
www.pegasuspublishers.com

First Published in 2015

Vanguard Press
Sheraton House Castle Park
Cambridge England

Printed & Bound in Great Britain

Dedications

For my lovely mum. Reminding me to live my life in every possible, wonderful way.

Acknowledgements

I could not let this opportunity pass without mentioning a few special people who have helped to make this book possible.

First and foremost, my Mum. Because when it came to her children she never said never. Because in her eyes there was nothing that I couldn't do. Because of her I believe in me and because of that, I gave it a go. I miss her every second of every day. If she had lived forever I could not have repaid the gifts she gave me.

My husband. Because he sat next to me every night whilst I wrote and he always believed in what I was writing even though he never read it! Because he believes in me and supports me and wanted this for me as much as I wanted it for myself. Because he works hard every day so that I have the privilege of doing something that I love.

My brother. Because it was him who encouraged me to finish and submit the book. Because there is so much of my Mum in him that he made me believe that I could do it too and because I know he asked the Universe for me. And his wife Regina, for being my second pair of eyes. I trust and value her opinion and hugely value her support.

My sister. Because she is always there for me. She understands what I vent about and she lets me do it. Always in my corner and on my side.

My children, everything I do is for them, for once they are here, what is life without them.

My Dad. For his kindness and friendship from the day I was born. Always loving, always caring.

The Jarvis Clan. All of them! For their unwavering belief in me and in the book. And their eagerness to read it. I love them all.

Amy. Her beautiful wedding inspired the book. She always asked about it and always encouraged it.

And finally to everyone at Pegasus, for their hard work, time and patience. For taking a punt on someone who has never put pen to paper before but has always wanted to and hopes to continue to do so for many years to come.

I hope I do you all justice.

Chapter One

'Bye,' I shout over my shoulder as I grab my bag and head out of the front door, shoving my phone in my pocket at the same time.

'Wait, wait!' Andrew bounds down the stairs two at a time and grabs the door before the lock catches, 'No kiss.' He pulls me back through the now open gap and gives me his attempt at puppy dog eyes which just irks me for some reason.

'Sorry,' I shrug in a way which I hope conveys an apology, 'Early start!' I give him a quick peck on the cheek and try to turn back out of the door into the safety of the busy street.

'Oh come on,' he pulls me back again giving me his best smile, 'Surely you can do better than that,' and before I have a chance to say anything he plants a long, wet kiss right on my mouth. I pull away as soon as I can, leaving his lips still pursed in mid air, and resist the temptation to run the back of my hand across my wet mouth.

'Must dash, morning meeting!' I wave my arm behind me in his general direction and jog with pretend purpose to the end of the street before I turn the corner out of view and resume a more dignified stroll.

You might be able to tell that I am not exactly enamoured with Andrew. Don't get me wrong, he really is great, the nicest guy in the world actually. He would pretty much do anything for me. Most people I know think he is quite a catch. And, wet kisses aside, he is. I've been seeing him for about eleven months, ever since my best friend Jen beckoned him over in the pub one evening last August to solve a minor disagreement we were having about whether cruise ships have to carry enough water on board to cater for the staff and passengers, or if they somehow filter the sea water and use that. Andrew couldn't actually solve the argument, in fact he was quite perplexed by the whole debate, but nevertheless he shared our third bottle of wine and ended up walking me home. He was practically carrying me actually but it had been a really busy week at work and Jen can be such a bad influence. When he called me the next day and asked me to lunch I thought it was the least I could do in return for his chivalry the night before. The rest, as they say, is history. I do like Andrew, I really do, but the whole nice guy thing is just a little bit too much for me. There are only so many times the question 'what shall we do?' can be met with 'whatever you would like to do!' Sometimes I just wish he would man up and make a decision. He never stands up to me. Ever. We went to a wedding last Sunday and he asked me to pick up his suit from the dry cleaners on my way home from my Saturday afternoon shopping trip to find a fascinator. Of course, I completely forgot to get his suit. Not on purpose, I just forgot. The problem was that I had picked up my own dress from the very same dry cleaners. If he had done that to me I would have gone mad but he just ruffled my hair in a 'what am I going to do with you?' type way and then stopped off at Next in the morning en route to the wedding to pick up a new suit. I should have been relieved but I found myself silently and irrationally seething the whole way to Oxford. A couple of weeks ago, after work one evening, we had dinner in Wagamamas and I tried to broach the subject of us having a 'bit of a break'. Andrew totally got the wrong end of the stick. He thought that I wanted to go on holiday and got all excited talking about Souks in Morocco and The Spanish Steps in Rome. I just didn't have the heart or the energy to correct him. Breaking up with a nice guy is not an easy thing to do!

Now I find myself constantly fantasising about other men. Not just celebrities, like Ryan Gosling and that guy from the Dolce and Gabbana adverts, everyone fantasises about them. No, I think about the till guy at Austin Reed in Westfield Shopping Centre and the man who delivers the photocopier paper to work every second Thursday. Not that I have ever had any encouragement from them. I don't exactly have men knocking down my door. I spent £150 in Austin Reed last weekend (sensible black pencil skirt for work and quite a pretty white shirt with ruffles down the front, which I could wear with the skirt or jeans, so a good investment piece). Anyway, the point is, till guy barely even glanced at my face when he took my money. Perhaps they don't work on commission but service with a smile would still have been nice, even if he didn't fancy me.

The long and the short of it is that in the absence of anything better (or anything at all really) and in the absence of any bravery at all on my part, we are still together. What's more we will probably stay that way until something intervenes to change the course of our relationship or until I find a little 'gumption' as my granny puts it.

Despite all this relationship drama (or lack of drama, it's quite hard to categorise the situation I am in right now), this morning I am in a seriously good mood! Not because my life is perfect, because quite frankly it's not. I really don't want to sound ungrateful, I know that there are people all over the world who would give anything for a slice of my life, but third world aside, and in relative terms, I'm a long way short of where I would like to be or where I expected to be at twenty-eight years old. But today I feel great. I feel great because I am walking to work on a beautiful sunny morning (which always helps!) wearing my grey 7 for all mankind skinny jeans (it's Friday, 'casual dress' day). My *size 10*, 7 for all mankind skinny jeans by the way. The same ones that I have not been able to wear since last Christmas (it is now July) and even if I say so myself, I actually look pretty good in them. They are not uncomfortably tight around the top of my thighs and I am not wearing a long top because I need to cover my bum. Nope, they fit and they feel great! And therefore, I feel great. I have decided to take great pleasure in small successes and this for me is no small success I can tell you. So today has started pretty well overall. Plus, as I said, it is a Friday.

'Morning!' I cheerfully address no one in particular as I sit down at my desk and switch on my computer. I am greeted by a few barely audible grumbles in return but don't take it to heart. It's a pretty dull office and I am used to being the only one that attempts to make any conversation or bring any kind of joy in. I brought in a plant for my desk a few months ago but was told that I wasn't allowed one due to 'health and safety reasons'. I was asked to remove it 'effective immediately'. I still haven't quite got to the bottom of the precise health and safety issues but suffice to say the plant is now on my bedroom window sill. It was replaced temporarily with my favourite photo of Jen, Fi and me on holiday in Tenerife (circa 1998) but alas that was removed to enable 'hot-desking' should it be required.

My logging in routine is interrupted by the IT manager Neil. 'Sophie, Graham wants to see you in his office.' His dulcet tones are accompanied by an unsmiling face.

'Thanks, Neil.' I smile to no reply. Graham is my boss. He is extremely dull, has a greasy comb over which I can't help but stare at every time I see him, and a grey tinge to his skin. Must be too much time spent in the office – a lack of sunlight, he probably has a severe vitamin D deficiency.

'Morning, Graham,' I knock tentatively on his open door and put a foot inside. 'Neil said you wanted to see me.'

'Come in, Sophie,' Graham gestures to the chair opposite him. Today he is wearing a short-sleeve shirt, which I am pretty sure is supposed to be white but from too much wear is now an off-milk colour and has large yellow stains under his arms. It is tucked into ugly brown trousers which are too short and too tight.

'Take a seat.'

'Great, thanks. How are you this morning, Graham?'

'Sophie, I wanted to see you this morning,' he continues as if I haven't even spoken, 'Because word has come from head office that we are to permanently fill all temporary positions and put an end to any temporary contracts before the end of the summer. We have eight weeks to fill your post. Your work to date has been satisfactory,' he nods at me as if paying a great compliment. 'If you wish to apply for the permanent position you will need to get the application to me within the next two weeks.'

I sit and stare at him for a moment, not really sure what to say but managing to muster something like 'Oh.' My eyes drift to his comb over.

'That's all then, Sophie. You can leave now.' Graham clears his throat obviously wanting me to vacate his office. I stand up and smooth down my shirt which doesn't need smoothing.

'Thanks, Graham.' I turn my back on him and make my way back to my desk feeling a little numb, the happiness I felt walking to work this morning completely disappeared. This job was totally fine as a temporary position, but *only* as a temporary position. There is no way I can work for a stationary supplies company permanently, but then, what else can I do?

Chapter 2

Here's the thing. When I left university with a first class honours in History of Art, I got onto the graduate training scheme at Morgan Stanley (much to my parents' delight). Four years later when I was finally on the verge of securing a full-time, permanent post in asset management, I had just about had enough of the long hours, late nights, all work, no life culture. It was so fiercely competitive and I realised I just didn't care enough about the work to want to compete for it. So I left. My parents were mortified and, to this day, think that I had some kind of nervous breakdown. Fi and Jen, my best friends in the world, said I was the bravest person that they knew, though I'm not sure if that was just misplaced loyalty. I am still swinging in roundabouts to be honest. One minute I feel totally brave and proud of myself but others I can't help but think I have thrown it all away for nothing. I was sure that once I left Morgan Stanley a new career would come to me somehow, something more creative, something I really enjoyed. That the Universe would reward my bravery with the exciting life that I was always supposed to have. So far, though, the Universe has failed to deliver my 'dream job' and I haven't done too well in finding it myself either. I've plodded along with my temp job and I have let myself be fine with it because temping is so, well, so temporary. But permanent, that is another thing altogether. And the scariest thing of all is that I am actually considering applying for the job. I hate this job!! I make a quick trip to the ladies' toilet to take a few deep breaths and run my hands under the cold tap. I check myself out in the full length mirror but even the sight of my legs in the size 10s can't spark a smile now.

Back at my desk I open my emails. I click on the first one from my flatmate, Lucy. I have lived with Lucy for four years – she was on the Morgan Stanley Graduate Programme with me. She was much more sensible than me though and stayed the course. Lucy now works in equities, earns a bundle and has recently started dating one of the partners, Sam. Unfortunately for me she won't be my flatmate for much longer as she is far too successful to share now and has found herself a gorgeous conversion in Fulham. I open her email:

To: SophieDucall@Stationaryisus
From: LucyTaylor@MorganStanley
Hi Soph,
Finally exchanged! Complete in a week! So excited but will miss you sooooo much.
I'm staying at Sam's again tonight as we have a work do this evening but I'll be back tomorrow afternoon. Hope you ok.
Have a good one.
L xx

Ok. So she's finally going. This is not good news. Now I have to find a new flatmate. Still, perhaps it won't be all bad. I can find someone young and exciting who can take me out to the newest restaurants and trendiest bars. I might even be able to put the rent up a bit.

I move down to the next email and click to open it.

To: SophieDucall@Stationaryisus
From: AndrewPorter@RichmondEstates
Hi Darling,
Spoke to Lucy this morning (she popped home before work to pick up a new suit) and she mentioned that she was hoping to exchange today. How exciting for her! How about dinner tonight – perhaps we could talk about who your new flatmate might be?
Love you.

He wants to move in. I'm actually going to have to end it. I can't bear it. I do have to end it, don't I? I don't think I can handle this conversation today. I quickly open a new email and type a message to Fi.

To: FionaChase@condenast
From: SophieDucall@Stationaryisus
Fi... what are you up to tonight? Could really do with a girls' night! Is Jackson home? I can bring white wine and Doritos if you are free!

I click send and only have to wait a moment before the little line at the top of my emails flashes with a response.

From: FionaChase@condenast
To: SophieDucall@Stationaryisus
Hi babe, I'm free! Come over! Jackson in India on shoot won't be back till Monday. Original Cool flavour please. Don't forget the salsa!

p.s. don't bring the wine you brought last time… must have been something about it that disagreed with me, felt horrendous next morning!

p.p.s I can leave early today so come straight from work! xx

Relief floods through me and with a twinge of guilt I open a new message and send a quick mail to Andrew.

To: AndrewPorter@Richmond Estates
From: SophieDucall@Stationaryisus
Hi Andrew,
So sorry, got long standing plans with Fi tonight – thought I had told you?
Call you tomorrow
Soph x

Predictably I get a reply from Andrew immediately.

To: SophieDucall@Stationaryisus
From: AndrewPorter@Richmond Estates
Ok Darling, have fun. Say hi to Fi for me.
Miss you till tomorrow
Andrew x

I open the jumbo bag of chocolate raisins in my desk drawer and eat the whole thing as I scroll through the BBC news homepage for the next half an hour. This is going to be a long day. And I bet these jeans feel tight in the morning.

Chapter 3

Fi is my oldest and best friend, along with Jen. Fi, Jen and I have been best friends since forever. We all grew up together on the same street and even though our lives have taken completely different paths somehow we have managed to stay firmly and happily in each other's lives. Fi is definitely 'the cool one', she is a super trendy, super successful fashion editor at *Glamour* magazine and she really loves her job. Even when we were six and riding our bikes up and down the street Fi was into her fashion, she would always look really cool in things that made Jen and me just look really silly. Fi also has a really great boyfriend who recently moved in with her. Jackson is a freelance photographer who takes really arty black and white pictures of the latest bands and the celebrities 'du jour'. The pair of them travel the world in what seems like an uber-glamorous life but they really are two of the most down to earth people you could ever meet and I love them both. Even if I do admit to being a little envious of the general perfectness that is their lives from time to time.

'Hi Gorgeous,' beams Fi, reaching for the Doritos and the Pinot Grigio as I walk through the door.

'Hey Fi Fi, how's things?'

'Good thanks, babe, I've been styling Heidi Klum today for her first post baby shoot, you wouldn't believe how amazing she looks and she only gave birth six weeks ago!'

'Wow! I love Heidi Klum, is she as beautiful in the flesh?'

''Fraid so, no airbrushing required! Anyway, how's things with you... any news? How's Andrew?'

'Umm good. He's fine. My jobs being made permanent... they've asked me to apply,' I say, taking a glass of the Pinot and the bowl of salsa and curling up in the corner of her huge cream sofa.

'How do you feel about that? Are you going to apply?' Fi asks me somewhat sceptically.

'Oh, Fi, how can I? It's a stationary supplier! I didn't give up a high flying city job to work in an office where the most exciting thing that happens in a week is a top client changing from 160gsm to 180gsm printer paper. I just can't do it!' I groan and mock pull my hair out of my head. Fi rubs my knee consolingly and fills up my glass from the bottle by her feet. Jesus, I drank that glass really quickly!

'I thought I would be doing something so exciting by now, something that would actually impress people when they ask what I do. Something that might actually help my parents forgive me!'

'Well why don't you then, sweetie?' Fi urges in excited tones. 'What is it that you want to do, really want to do?'

'That's the problem,' I shrug. 'I don't know!'

Fi puts her glass down and pulls a smart leather file out of her huge handbag, one of those really expensive Stella McCartney ones that she probably got free through work.

'There was an article in last month's issue about using life coaching to find your dream career. Some kind of career wheel, I think it was. You have to look at all these things, like what you're interested in, what you're good at, what you're rubbish at, etc. and it finds your perfect career for you – ah, here it is!' she pulls the July issue of *Glamour* from a seemingly never-ending pile of paper and pictures. Finding the page with the career wheel, she hands me the magazine and disappears to find pens and another bottle of wine.

An hour and that second bottle of wine later we have a list of careers as recommended by *Glamour*:

Marine biologist
Veterinary nurse
Astrologer
Personal shopper
Travel agent.

A mixed bag to say the least. I did actually want to be a marine biologist once when I was at school but I wasn't really very good at science and to be honest, I'm actually a little scared of the sea now. I mean I totally love to look at it and to be near it, I *always* ask for a sea view when I'm on holiday but over the years I have become a little nervous of actually swimming in it, past my knees anyway. The whole not knowing what is beneath freaks me out a little.

'So what about a personal shopper?' Fi doesn't sound convinced. 'You could work for one of the big department stores and get to check out all the new lines before they even hit the shop floor, or you could set up your own business; mobile personal shopping for women too busy to go to the shops, I've loads of contacts that could help you get started,' she says, clearly warming to the idea.

'Thanks, Fi, but I'm not really sure that I am a "personal shopper"… that sounds much more you than me to be honest. I think maybe putting "fashion" in the "love" box was a mistake, just because I love to browse *Topshop* on a Saturday afternoon it doesn't mean I actually know anything about fashion or how to dress other people.

'Ok, point taken,' Fi concedes. 'So what else is on the list?' she picks up the paper again. 'Veterinary nurse.' She scrunches her face, 'Aren't you allergic to cat hair?'

'Yep,' I nod. 'And horses'.

'Well, I don't really see you as an astrologer either so that leaves travel agent.' Fi raises an eyebrow and smirks, 'I think there is a *Thomson* on the high street.'

'Well, I do love going on holiday,' I smirk back. We were both in silent agreement that loving going on holiday and loving selling holidays were two very different things.

'Maybe that's it though,' Fi jumped up to grab a third (definitely going to feel this tomorrow) bottle from the fridge…

'Oh, don't be daft, Fi,' I shout after her. 'I am not going to be a travel agent, I thought they were all going bust anyway, everyone booking online or something?'

'No,' Fi walks back into the room. 'I mean maybe you need a holiday – you know, a break. When was the last time you got away for a while? You didn't even go away when you left Morgan Stanley, did you?'

She was right, I didn't. It was bad enough that I was going to lose my salary; I certainly wasn't going to blow the savings that I had on a holiday. That would really have tipped mum and dad over the edge! In fact, apart from a weekend in Majorca with Andrew last year, I haven't had a proper break for about three years now. 'I don't know, Fi, a holiday sounds great, but where would I go and who would I go with? I don't think I could stomach a holiday with Andrew at the moment, you are way too busy and to be honest going to India alone to "find myself" just seems a bit sad.'

'Go and stay with Jen!' Fi made it sound as though the answer was staring me in the face. Which, I suppose, it was.

Jen, the third of our three, lived next door to me for ten years until her parents made a fortune from their property empire in the 90s and moved to a beautiful, big house in Surrey. Jen was sent to boarding school, where our friendship grew stronger than ever on account of the fact that she was bullied and absolutely hated it. She came to stay with me almost every weekend whilst her parents travelled the world buying more properties, doing them up and selling them on, making even more money. They were lovely though: so glamorous, so much fun, so lovely to me. I was always their favourite of all of Jen's friends and they stayed in touch with my parents too. The four of them still get together at least a couple of times a year for boozy lunches and dinners. I am one of her family and she is one of mine.

Jen is in Italy doing a cookery course at the Alistair Little Cookery School. This is her latest thing. Since leaving school (Jen never made it to university she was so traumatised by boarding school) she has always had a new dream. First she was going to be an actress, then when she realised she couldn't act she thought she would be a make-up artist but, not really being that artistic, or good at putting make-up on other people, that didn't work either. There was a small stint as a personal trainer when she had a raging crush on the man at the local gym but despite her naturally slim figure, she just couldn't cut the early morning work outs and discipline had never really been her thing, so now she is trying her hand at being a chef. She has visions of grand dinner parties for the rich and famous and maybe even opening her own restaurant one day. Her parents, happy to encourage their only child's latest whim, are more than willing to pay for the best possible training to help her achieve this. As Alistair Little has restaurants at many of the five-star hotels that they have stayed and eaten in over the years, that, of course, was where their girl would go.

'You know what they say,' Fi encouraged. 'A break is as good as a change, or is it a change is as good as a break? It doesn't matter. The point is, why don't you get away from it all for a while and take some time to think about what you want to do in a different environment? What's the alternative? Another crap temp job in the city? Applying for a permanent position at Stationery Is Us? Staying put hasn't exactly done you any favours so far.'

I drain my glass and realise a huge smile is spreading across my face. Fi is right. What is stopping me? I've got savings, I can afford to go and I really could do with a break. 'Pass me the phone,' I grin. 'What time is it in Italy?' As I dial Jen's number my mind drifts guiltily to Andrew. Lovely, understanding, kind Andrew. He will probably drive me to the airport, bless him.

Chapter 4

So just one week, a very disapproving boss and a very understanding Andrew later, here I am in the car on the way to Heathrow. Excited is an understatement. It's a bleak and drizzly summer day in London, which is pretty easy to leave behind. I feel almost reckless at the sudden abandonment of my normal life. I have never just upped and left before and it is quite liberating. OK, so I am not exactly 'jacking it all in' to travel the world, but for the first time in a long time I am doing something just for me and just for the hell of it. It feels good. I haven't quite managed to quash the lingering dullness in the pit of my stomach about the whole Andrew situation but there didn't seem much point in doing anything about it just before I go away and he has been so kind and understanding it would have just been a bit mean. He even offered to come with me, keep me company, but of course totally understood when I explained that Jen might not feel comfortable with us both in her two-bedroom place. 'Check the glove compartment,' Andrew says as if hearing my wandering thoughts. 'Just a few things for the flight.' Opening it I find the latest copy of *OK* magazine and a family size bag of Minstrels. 'That should keep you going for a couple of hours,' he laughs and touches my knee tenderly. In a sudden rush of warmth towards him I cover his hand with mine.

'Thanks, Andrew, that's really thoughtful.' I give him my best 'everything is fine' smile and push the ache a little deeper into the pit of my stomach. 'Just drop me off, the car parks cost a fortune.' I try not to sound too desperate to get out of the car as we pull into the ring road that circles the airport.

'Well, if you're sure, babe.' He pulls in behind a huge people carrier dropping off a young family with a mountain of suitcases and two adults trying very hard to control the wayward cases and what seem like three pretty wayward children at the same time. Revelling already in my freedom I jump out of the car and grab my suitcase and travel wheelie case from the boot. I let Andrew give me a big hug but pull away from the kiss before it gets too passionate. I roll my eyes over towards the wayward children now fighting over who gets to sit on the front of the luggage trolley as if to indicate that we shouldn't get too heavy in front of them.

'Don't forget to water the plants,' I say in an attempt to lighten the mood and skip past any heart-felt goodbyes. 'See you in a few weeks!' I throw another quick peck on Andrew's cheek and, without giving him a chance to say anything else, I grab the handle of my case and head purposefully into the terminal, pleased that Andrew can't see the huge grin on my face or feel the excitement bubbling in my stomach.

I love airports. I love everything about them. The great, big, shiny whiteness of them, the smart uniforms and neck ties on the check-in girls, the big screens full of ever-changing destination names and flight numbers. I love the shopping and the restaurants. It feels like living in a suspended time zone at the airport. A place where spending money on luxury make-up, perfume, sunglasses and the last-minute, must-have dangly earrings from accessorize is fine because it's 'holiday money'. Where drinking full fat vanilla lattes and eating a sticky Danish from Costa Coffee is fine because who watches calories on holiday?

I look at the departures board. My gate opens in half an hour, just enough time to check out the lipsticks at the MAC counter and grab myself that latte and Danish. With the aforementioned goodies in hand I take a seat in front of Gate 15b and watch a long queue form in front of me. I never queue to get on a flight, I don't see the point when I have an allocated seat, I just sit and watch. Airports are the best place to people watch. I love to imagine where people are travelling to and why they are going. Maybe that is what I love so much about airports; they open the whole world to you and all of the wonders that go with it. I notice that the family from the people carrier are on my flight and get lost listening to an argument between the two young boys about who should get the window seat. By the time they have reached the desk, still arguing, the queue has dwindled to the rest of the boys' family and a couple of other single travellers so I jump up and get ready to hand my boarding pass to the pretty young girl at the gate wearing a neck tie.

As the plane climbs high above the grey clouds that blanket the UK and levels in the bright blue that sits above them, I eat the Minstrels and flick absent-mindedly through *OK* magazine. I can see the pictures but I am not reading whatever the latest story about Miley Cyrus is as my mind is luxuriating in the thought of two full weeks in the sun with my best friend. No diets (I didn't even pack my 7 for all mankind jeans), no work, no stress, no boyfriend. I am armed with guide books to Pisa, Florence and Rome (though I think that is actually quite a long way from where I am staying with Jen) and I can't wait. I am excited to have a bit of culture in my life for a change (well I can't sunbathe for two whole weeks). Who knows, I might even be inspired. Perhaps I will fall in love with Italian art and discover a career in curating. I could work at one of the big auction houses where paintings sell for millions of pounds and I would get a whopping big commission for selling them. My flicking and fantasising is interrupted just as I am working out what I would spend my £10,000 bonus on (is an Hermes Birkin still totally out of the question when the money is a bonus?) by two air stewardesses having a discussion about where to find a Twix for the captain who has apparently ordered one along with a cup of tea and which seems to be causing them some problems. I listen to them chatter for a while as they eventually locate a Twix and proceed up the aisle serving the other passengers. When the larger of the two blonde girls reaches me and smiles showing the red lipstick on her teeth, I order two bottles of wine (well they are barely a glass each) and settle back into my seat to enjoy the rest of the flight and resume my imaginary spending spree.

***

Stepping out of a plane into the warm air of somewhere far from home has to be one of my favourite things ever. As I disembark I lift my face to the hot sunshine and feel any last traces of tension disappear. I am fizzing with excitement by the time I get my case from the baggage carousel, which for once isn't the last one out. With 20 kilos of dresses and flip flops dragging behind me I practically run into the arrivals hall. I can hear Jen calling my name,

'Soph! Soph! Can't believe your here! Over here, Soph!' I see her waving frantically as she heads through the doors of 'Tabac' and towards me with an armful of magazines and sweets. I hug her and all of the Tabac paraphernalia hard as we meet at the end of the barriers.

'Oh, it is so good to see you, Jen, you look great!'

'You look great more like! You've lost weight! How was the flight? I'm *so* glad you are here, don't get me wrong, it's great and all, you are going to love it, so beautiful and the weather's amazing, mum said its pretty dismal in the UK at the moment, but it's so great to have my bestest here! I can't wait to show you around.' She is right, I am going to love it, I can feel it in my bones. I link my free arm through Jen's and listen happily as she chats all the way to her car. She tells me about her cookery course, which she clearly loves, and about her friends on the course and in the village. She is obviously pretty taken with one guy on her course called Jake whose name has come up at least three times already.

'Who is this Jake?' I interrupt when I get a second and nudge her in the ribs, 'Someone special?'

To my surprise Jen actually blushes, which I think might be a first! Italy has changed her! 'He's just a guy on my course,' — she is deliberately coy — 'Nothing's actually happened but he is pretty great. He's been in Italy for years so has shown me around a lot. He makes the most amazing chocolate soufflé; he is almost famous for it.'

'He sounds great.'

'Yeah, he is, but like I say nothing's actually happened you know, we're just friends.' I shoot her a questioning glance. 'What!' she laughs. 'It's true! Anyway, enough about me, I haven't stopped talking since you arrived, it's so nice to be able to babble on in English and be understood! What's new with you? How'a Andrew? Is he OK with you being here?'

I am too blissfully happy to get into the whole Andrew debacle now so instead I just skit over the issue quickly, 'Oh, you know Andrew, he's fine with anything I want to do.' She looks at me like only a best friend can, picking up on the tone of my voice, and I know I don't need to say any more.

'Well, this holiday is just about us!' she declares with a smile as we wedge my case into her boot and get into the car. 'The food and wine out here is to die for, you must be able to tell I've put on about ten pounds since I arrived,' she slaps her thigh before turning the key in the engine. 'And tonight I am treating you to the very best of both to say thank you for coming and keeping me company.' She squeezes my arm hard as she turns to look over her shoulder and pulls out of the car park.

I squeeze it back. 'I can't wait.'

Chapter 5

It doesn't take long to get out of the city and soon we are driving along narrow roads flanked by lush green and golden-yellow rolling hills, olive groves and cypress trees. We talk all the way as I take in the beautiful vistas and the amazing sense of peace that shrouds the countryside. It really is truly beautiful. By the time we reach Jen's village the sun is setting and the light is low around us, hovering below a mellow sky that is gradually turning a soft purple. As I get out of the car I can hear crickets singing in the fields behind the house, taking centre stage in the otherwise silent beauty that surrounds us. Jen's home is a very beautiful and rustic cottage, set back from the road with a wide front garden playing host to lemon and orange trees and a beautiful arch of dusky-pink roses growing haphazardly above the wooden front door.

'It's so beautiful, Jen.' I head inside and am met by a large open-plan dining room with huge glass windows overlooking a quaint but mature garden overflowing with plants, flowers and fruits. An oak table dominates the room, making way only for two squidgy-looking terracotta coloured sofas set in an L-shape around a coffee table and a very old fashioned TV in the corner. 'This is great, Jen.' I look around into the small kitchen to the left of the main room which has a stunning view across the fields from the window above an old fashioned steel sink and an incredible old Aga in the corner next to a full wine rack and a large fridge, which I soon find out is also full of wine and little else except the few ingredients that Jen has stocked up on to make us dinner. Fresh pasta, butter, parmesan cheese, cream, mushrooms and pancetta. Cookery school is clearly paying off.

I take my case up to the spare room, which is rustic in keeping with the rest of the cottage but neat and comfortable. It has a larger than single but smaller than double bed with a vase of local lavender on the bedside table and a beautiful view from the window over the fields. It's perfect. I smile and take a deep breath as I wedge my full case into the small space between the bedside table and the old wooden wardrobe at the edge of the room. Jen must have started cooking already as an enticing smell of garlic wafts up the stairs. My stomach rumbles reminding me that I haven't eaten anything except a Danish and Minstrels all day. Jen is waiting for me at the bottom of the stairs with a cold glass of Orvieto which I accept gratefully before following her into the kitchen. I perch on the worktop next to the sink and watch her cook whilst we drink the wine and chat. Dinner is exceptional and what feels like minutes but is actually hours later we head to bed, full, a little drunk and very happy.

***

I wake up early the following morning. Jen is still asleep so I pull on a clean vest and my denim shorts. I scribble a quick note in case she wakes up, and head out to explore the local village. Gloriously the sun on my face is bright and hot even at this early hour. It feels so good that I stop and stand still at the end of the path outside Jen's cottage and put my face to the sky just to feel the warmth of the rays relax my mind and my body.

Fi was right. This doesn't compare to what I would be doing at home right now. The Victoria Line, its seats almost alive with dirt and the smell of a hundred other tightly packed commuters, all in their own hurries, in their own worlds, seems a million miles away right now. I am going to enjoy every moment of this holiday. I breathe deeply and walk on smiling to myself. I am going to forget everything at home and just enjoy myself. I walk down the narrow, dusty roads that are set into the gaps between the rolling hills. The distant view is blurred by the early morning heat waves, rippling its beauty.

As I turn the corner the road opens onto a small piazza with cobbled paving and a scattering of shops set around a square. There are a few tables and chairs set out for tourists to enjoy a cold drink at the end of a long day's walking or sight-seeing. I can see the café (which the table and chairs belong to), a delicatessen with cured meats hanging in the window and a butchers with huge legs of some kind of raw meat hanging up front. There is a patisserie where a young girl stocks the window with some of the most delicious looking cakes I have ever seen and what looks like a newsagents, with papers outside on an old fashioned wooden rack. On walking over I discover that the shop is actually more like a little local store with a strange but wide range of things, Umbria's answer to Tesco Express. I pick up eggs, shampoo, coffee and milk then amble next door to the patisserie for a loaf of freshly baked bread which is still hot to touch and a couple of the strawberry tarts from the window which look too good to leave behind. The bags aren't heavy and I am pretty sure that Jen will still be asleep so I walk on past the village eager to make the most of the precious peacefulness of the morning and the joyous sense of freedom that is coursing through me. It is so liberating to be away from routine, away from supermarket food shopping, broken photocopiers and nagging parents. Away from Andrew.

I walk on up the hill, sweating as it gets steeper and take in the sweeping views as I approach the top. Taking note of where I have walked, just to make sure that I can get back again, I turn right at the top of the hill along an impressive road, wider than those I have been on so far and lined with cypress trees. As I follow the bend in the road, almost out of nowhere I come across a very grand, very old looking house set behind tall, imposing wrought iron gates and an overgrown but clearly once spectacular circular driveway set around what must have once been a large water feature.

The house is beautiful, like something out of an old movie and I stand at the gates quite mesmerised by it. I feel almost nostalgic standing here looking at its neglected beauty, which is silly really because I have never lived — or even stayed — in a house like this before, maybe it is just nostalgia for what must once have been here, for the beauty that must once have been and for the family that must once have shared in it.

I put my shopping bags down for a moment and wipe the beads of sweat from the top of my head and the back of my neck. Even though the bags aren't heavy they have lined the inside of my hands and I rub them before placing them on the large, wrought iron gate which feels surprisingly cool standing in the hot sunshine.

As I lean in to get a better look at this regal place that has clearly been laid to waste, the gate leans with me and I realise the heavy lock holding the two sides of the gate together has given way leaving only a rusting circle of wire looped across the top of the two sides to hold them together. I am so compelled to go inside, I know I shouldn't, but I can't help myself. I push the gate a little harder and it opens enough for me to slip through the hole in the middle. Leaving the bags behind me I cross the threshold and wander around the large, circular driveway. It is overgrown with dry weeds and patches of moss. The stone of the huge water feature has turned green in places and is crumbling in others; a dead frog is shrivelled at the far side. The fountain itself towers over me, three tiers high, the largest at the bottom, almost big enough to swim in (if it was working of course) and the smallest at the top crowned with a single pipe like spout where the water must once have gushed from. The edges are scalloped and the detail in the design is exquisite. As I look closer I can see what look like nymphs and angels carved into the stonework alongside and interweaved with carvings of exotic fruits and plants. The house is a bit like something from the Jane Austen novels I read as a child, perhaps not quite as big but certainly as beautiful as I always imagined the houses to be. Maybe that is where the nostalgia comes from.

With growing intrigue I try the front door but it is shut tight. I'm disappointed but relived at the same time. I'm not sure that I could have stopped myself going inside but I'm already uncomfortable at the intrusion of my exploring — not to mention the trespassing! A stone mosaic path leads around the side of the house and I follow it under an old wooden roof trellis weaved with thick ivy and dripping with the light purple of an incredible wisteria. Large glass and iron lanterns hang from each square of the trellis. Some of them even have the remnants of half-burnt candles melted in their centre. Beyond the trellising an empty but nonetheless grand looking swimming pool with wide, gently sloping steps that lead in from the far end is surrounded by more trellis covered paths, interrupted every few metres with ornate stone statues and smaller fountains.

Beyond the paths, set on its own in a corner plot is a small building. It is a bit like an overgrown version of Jen's cottage and it is the only thing that stands between the empty swimming pool and uninterrupted views of the Tuscan countryside. I stand at the edge of the main house in front of the hole where the pool would once have rippled cool and blue and take it all in, a faint breeze whispers at the base of my neck, it must be that which is making the hairs stand on end. I am not sure how much time passes but as I stand there I imagine how it must once have looked and the family that would have lived here.

I am just picturing an elegant banquet scene with lithe Italian women in beaded dresses, drinking cocktails and smoking with cigarette holders, when a backfiring car makes me jump and brings me back to reality. Suddenly feeling nervous and a little guilty I turn back up the path and walk quickly to the gate where my bags are still sitting on the other side. I pick them up and with a strange mix of adrenaline, elation and sadness I retrace my steps along the road and back to Jen's cottage.

As I approach the cottage I can see Jen in the front garden picking fresh basil for our dinner, homemade pizza! 'Hey, I was beginning to worry about you! What did you think of the village – it's lovely isn't it?'

'It's great,' I agree enthusiastically and before she has a chance to say anything else I tell her all about the house.

'Wow, I've been here ages now and I have never come across that house', she muses. 'Never had a reason to head up that way I suppose. I haven't seen you so excited in ages, Soph; it must have really taken you! Perhaps it's an old ancestral home of yours or something,' she laughs.

I snort in response. 'I don't think so! I can't explain it though, Jen, I really feel some kind of connection to the place, it's really special.'

As I tell Jen about the house and how it made me feel, I try and work out myself what it is that I am so drawn to about it. It reminds me of a piece of antique jewellery, something beautiful and expensive that I could never afford but am fascinated by. Something I would love to know the back story to, a story that would surely be wildly romantic. Jen indulges me as I knew she would.

'You'll have to take me to see it when I get back from class this afternoon. I'll ask my classmates and teachers too, see if I can find out a little more about it or who owns it. You've got me excited now!' she laughs and gets up to put the dough that she kneaded and left to prove earlier in the fridge before leaving for her class.

Chapter 6

Jen is pretty impressed with the house too. Even in its state of disarray, just like me she can see its innate beauty and feel its incredible presence. We walk around it at dusk and sit with our legs dangling over the empty pool as the sun sets in the distance.

'It's so beautiful,' Jen sighs. 'Not just the house, but everything, the setting, the ambience. I can just imagine what it must have been like in its prime. I wonder why it has been left to die like this.'

'I can't imagine,' I agree. 'If this was my house I would never, ever let it be empty. It should be loved and cared for. It could be so beautiful. I almost feel a responsibility to do something about it. I want to take it on. Put the life back into it!'

'I know what you mean.' Looking around at everything wistfully Jen puts her arm around me. 'Let's make it our mission to find out who owns it and why they have left it to rust. I asked this afternoon at college but no-one had a clue. Only one of the teachers even knew that it exists but she doesn't know any more about it than we do. Let's ask around the village?'

'Let's.' I nod and we head back to the cottage where we take out the dough that Jen prepared earlier and work together to make pizzas with beef tomatoes, local mozzarella, large slices of Parma ham and the fresh basil from the garden. As we work side by side creating our own culinary masterpieces we entertain ourselves with ever more outrageous stories about who might have once owned the house: an Italian mafia family torn apart by a rival family perhaps or a wealthy Italian baron who died a single playboy with no-one to leave the house to. The stories go on as we eat the delicious pizzas and share a bottle of Chianti before finally making our way upstairs. I settle into a restless night's sleep and dream of Italian aristocrats and deserted manor houses.

The next day I sleep late despite the warmth of the sun coming in through my bedroom window. When I wake, Jen has already left for a morning cooking class so I take a long shower and make myself a strong coffee before heading down to the village to have a proper look around the shops and treat myself to some breakfast in the café. It is surprisingly busy in the piazza and there are only two small tables left outside the café when I arrive. I sit down at one of them and pick up the small handwritten menu in front of me. A young, nice looking boy, maybe twenty or twenty-one years old, comes out and smiles to acknowledge me before taking the order of a middle-aged couple on the table next to me. They look like tourists from their clothes but the walking map, binoculars and sun hats on their table also give them away. There is an elderly man sitting alone with coffee and cake in the corner; a young Italian family with two beautiful small children, a boy and a girl, eating Paninis and drinking Coke; a couple in their fifties who also look like tourists and a young girl who I recognise from the patisserie drinking an orange juice. She smiles at me as I catch her eye whilst taking in the surroundings. The young waiter comes to my table.

'Hello signorita, what can I get for you today?' His English is heavily accented but easy to understand, which is a relief.

'Hi, I would love a cappuccino please. And some scrambled eggs on toast?'

'Of course,' he smiles. 'And would signorita like bacon with her eggs? The English, they love their bacon,' he laughs. 'You are English, yes?'

'I am,' I laugh too. 'Go on then, I will have some bacon too! Thanks!' My stomach is starting to rumble and the smells coming from inside the café are making me really hungry. The nice boy takes my order inside and I watch as the young girl from the patisserie follows him in with her eyes. Perhaps she has a crush on him. She catches me looking and I smile at her and wave hello. She waves back shyly. Feeling in the holiday spirit I beckon to the chair opposite me and ask her if she would like to join me. We had a quick chat yesterday when I picked up the strawberry tarts, she asked me if I was on holiday and knew who I was talking about when I told her I was staying with Jen. She walks over to my table and pulls out the second chair. She sits down and puts out her hand to me.

'Hello, my name Katarina, did you enjoy strawberry tart?' she asks in broken English, which is nonetheless infinitely better than my Italian.

'They were delicious, thank you. Are you on a break from the patisserie?'

'Yes. In morning we very busy but now not so much until for one more hour maybe. My mother say to take break now so I like sit in the sun for a while.'

'Does your mother own the shop?' I ask.

'Yes, my mother and father. For thirty years nearly, I work only in holidays.'

'So are you at school then, or college maybe?' I ask, enjoying the company.

'Yes. I go college in Florence where I live with aunt for shorter journey. I study art. It is art that I love most, one day I will be painter.'

'Oh, how lovely, what do you paint?'

'Lots of things,' she makes a wide gesture with her arms and looks around her. 'There is much of beauty to paint here.' I have to agree.

As I wait for my food to arrive we chat more and she tells me about her course and the things that she likes to do in Florence. She even offers to take me there and show me around if her mother doesn't need her in the shop.

'We close Tuesday afternoon. If you like, we take the train together and I show you best shops and galleries?'

'That would be so wonderful! Thank you!' I am genuinely touched at Katarina's sweet offer. 'Perhaps if Jen doesn't have college then she can come too?'

Katarina seems happy with this, nodding in agreement as the young waiter comes out again bringing my bacon and eggs with him. 'Another cappuccino signorita?' he asks me as he puts the plate in front of me.

'Oh go on then, yes please!' I tuck into the eggs which are a taste sensation, they are soft and creamy, unlike scrambled eggs I have ever had at home before. The boy says something in Italian to Katarina, who blushes and shakes her head. I try not to watch the two of them too obviously as they talk briefly and concentrate on my food. 'Is he your boyfriend?' I ask once he has gone back inside. Katarina shakes her head.

'Paulo is old family friend. His parents and mine are friends for very long time. He study in Pisa at college but has finished his study now and come home for the summer'.

'He seems very nice and he's lovely looking too.' I smile at Katarina and she smiles back, blushing again.

'Yes, I think he very nice, but I think he has girlfriend in Pisa'.

'Ah well, the summer's a long time over.' I wink at her and cut into my bacon.

'What does this mean?' Katarina looks confused.

'Oh, nothing.' I laugh lightly and listen as she tells me about her favourite shops in Florence and her friend who has a summer job in one of the designer boutiques and can get 15% off the clothes.

After breakfast I wave goodbye to Paulo and Katarina — who goes back to work in the patisserie — and I wander back to the cottage. I take a quick detour past the old house and stop again for a while to admire its broken beauty. Back at the cottage I finish my unpacking. I fold all my clothes neatly in the pine chest of drawers and hang my summer dresses in the small matching wardrobe. Then I sit in the garden and read through a pile of tourist leaflets that I picked up from the café. I am just reading about the latest Canaletto Exhibition at the Uffizi Gallery in Florence and thinking about asking Katarina if we should go when Jen opens the front door and runs straight through to the garden excitedly.

'I've had a brilliant idea!' she beams at me. 'Let's throw a dinner party!'

Chapter 7

'I've got my first proper practical food exam coming up. I have to prepare a three course meal for two of our chefs at the school and a local restaurateur,' Jen explains as she sits down on the grass next to me. 'It would be so great to have a trial run, like live revision, what do you think?'

'I think it's a great idea,' I say. And I do. 'Who would we invite — do you know enough people?'

'Well I can ask my friend Sara, she's the secretary at the cookery school and she's English. She has been such a help since I moved here, helping me find my feet and introducing me to some of the lovely local restaurants. Her husband is Italian and works for the university in Florence so she could bring him too. And I think Jake will come if I ask him. Plus it will give me a chance to show him what I look like when I don't have chef's whites on and my hair in a net! He probably won't even recognise me!' She laughs but I can tell that she is desperate for him to see her looking her best.

'Well that's five, including us,' I count. 'What about Katarina from the village patisserie? I met her today and she was really sweet. And maybe Paulo too, from the café. I think Katarina has a bit of a thing for him, we could play matchmaker! They are a little younger than us but I'm sure they would be good company.'

'Wow! You have been busy, I've only been gone for the morning and you've met half the village! Yes, let's invite them. I think that's a great idea. So that makes seven. Odd numbers are never good. We need another man really, to even out the numbers, but I'm not sure that I want to invite anyone else from my course, I don't want them checking out the competition before the exam!'

We sit in silence as we try to think of a seventh man, which isn't easy for me as I really didn't know anyone at all.

'Perhaps I could ask Alberto,' Jen says finally. 'He lives in the next cottage, about a hundred yards down the road, his family owns the farmland around this cottage and the butchers in the village, he often pops in to check on things. His English is pretty good too.'

'Great, that makes eight, perfect!' I smile, excited.

'Perfect!' Jen agrees, clearly excited too. 'We can move the main table into the garden and there's another small bench-table in the shed at the end of the garden that we can add on to make it longer.' She stands up, 'This calls for a celebration, let's open a bottle of wine and start working out what we're going to cook!'

We sit in the garden long into the night, working out the perfect menu and where to get all of the ingredients. We come up with ideas for decorating the table and the garden, and make a long 'to do' list in preparation.

The next morning, over coffee and some delicious sweet pastries that Jen brought back from school yesterday, I fill her in on my conversation with Katarina and her offer to take us to Florence. 'I think that's a great idea. I have study days tomorrow and Wednesday to prepare for my exam. If I come with you I can get the ingredients for the dinner party that we won't be able to pick up in the village.'

'Great, that's settled then. I'll walk down to the village later and tell Katarina that we can all go. I want to talk to her about maybe going to the Canaletto exhibition anyway.' I hand Jen the leaflet.

'I think I'll leave the gallery to you' — she passes a cursory glance over it — 'But I'll drive in with you to do the shopping. I'll need extra bits for my exam anyway so I can go off and find those whilst you do your cultural thing.'

'Excellent, I'll take that back then.' I laugh as Jen passes the leaflet to me and I tuck it into my bag ready for our trip.

Another sticky pastry (I am so glad I didn't bring those jeans with me!), coffee, freshly squeezed orange juice and a shower later, I pull on a little, yellow sundress, grab the floppy, straw sun hat that has come with me on every summer holiday for the last five years, and make my way into the village with a spring in my step. As I cross the piazza I can see Katarina restocking the front window of the patisserie with the largest meringues I have ever seen, filled with cream and drizzled with chocolate. They look absolutely amazing and, even though it is not possible for me to be hungry, my mouth waters as I watch her squeeze the biggest one onto the end of the row. I push open the door and she looks up as it hits the little brass bell hanging on the corner of the wall.

'Hi, how are you today? Those meringues look great!'

Katarina beams at me, 'Hi! They are my mother's famous baking.' She steps out of the window and returns to a position behind the counter. 'You like one?'

I would like one very much but thinking of my beloved jeans and the sinful breakfast I am still digesting I decline her offer. 'Actually, I want to talk to you about our trip to Florence, if you can still make it? It's Tuesday tomorrow.'

'Oh yes,' her face lights up, 'I am still making it'.

'Great!' I smile at her excitement and broken English, 'I spoke to Jen and she would like to come with us too, she said she can drive us in as she wants to get some shopping whilst we go to a gallery. I was thinking about maybe the Canaletto exhibition. Have you seen it?' I pass her the leaflet and she nods in recognition.

'I have not seen, but I hear it very good. We must go. We must also go to my friend's shop. Do you think?' she asks hopefully.

'I would love to,' I say and Katarina beams again.

'And maybe to my favourite restaurant? Best pizza in Florence, I ask mother if I have morning off so we can have more time?'

'If you don't think she would mind, I think that is an excellent idea, we can make a day of it. If your mother agrees, shall we say nine a.m.? We can pick you up outside the shop.'

'Yes, that work well! I'm excited!' Katarina claps her hands like a little girl.

I tell her about the dinner party and ask her if she would like to come and if she thinks I should invite Paulo too. She is even more excited about this than about the trip to Florence.

51

Before I leave she insists that I take a large slice of panettone with me, then waves with enthusiasm as I tuck it under my arm and walk across the square to the café where I stop for a Diet Coke before the walk home. I sit at the same table as the previous day and let the sunshine bathe my face. It is another stifling day and there isn't a single cloud in the sky, which is a bright, clean azure-blue. Half an hour drifts by as I watch the comings and goings in the small village, then before I decide to head back I ask Paulo if he would like to come to the dinner party. He is surprised to be asked but happy to come. I'm pleased that he seems particularly keen when I tell him that Katarina is coming. I am going to ask him if he has a girlfriend in Florence like Katarina told me but think it might be a little soon to ask personal questions, given this is only the second time I have spoken to him, so I leave it for now. I'll save it for the dinner party!

With time to luxuriate in, I walk slowly back to the cottage via the old mansion house and have another sneak peak around the back. Nothing has changed, still no sign of life. I have a closer look at the small cottage on the grounds but it is locked and the windows are so dusty I can barely see through them. Back at the cottage I pick up my suncream, iPod, a bottle of water and a large towel from the cupboard at the top of the stairs and take them all out into the garden with the panettone that Katarina gave me. I set myself up on the towel in full glare of the sun, put my favourite playlist on my iPod and douse myself in factor thirty, before taking a huge bite of panettone, laying back and closing my eyes. It is absolute bliss. I feel totally relaxed for the first time in ages. So relaxed, in fact, that

I must have drifted off to sleep because the next thing I hear is Jen at my side.

'Soph!' she shouts because she thinks that I am listening to my iPod. The music has long since stopped but her voice wakes me up so it has the desired effect!

'Oh, hi! I was asleep, it's so relaxing here.' I rub my eyes, feeling groggy. 'How was college?'

'Great! We made quiches and goat's cheese and caramelised onion tarts. I thought we could eat them with a nice salad for dinner. I can make some pesto and garlic ciabatta too if you fancy it?'

'Sounds lovely.'

I sit up and pay attention as she chats on. 'I picked up a couple of bottles of the local white wine from the small cheese and wine shop near the catering school too. Shall I open one?'

'Ooh yes, that sounds lovely.' My throat is dry from sleeping in the sun and suddenly I feel really hungry too. 'What time is it?' I ask.

'It's nearly five thirty.' Jen glances at the Rolex on her wrist that her dad bought her on her twenty-first birthday. 'I stayed a little later today to help Jake with his menu for the end of term test'.

'Oh, did you?' I raise my eyebrow at her and she laughs and rolls her eyes to dismiss my teasing.

'He's coming to the dinner party and so are Sara and her husband Michael'.

'Excellent. Katarina and Paulo are coming too. They both seem really excited about it.'

Jen is pleased, 'Perfect! It's happening then! I just need to ask Alberto. I'll pop into the butchers tomorrow.'

She turns and skips inside in search of the bottle opener and I follow her loaded down with my paraphernalia from the garden. As she hands me a large glass of wine I tell her about my conversation with Katarina and the trip to Florence.

'It's all falling into place then,' she says happily. 'We can pick Katarina up in the morning and I will run in to speak to Alberto whilst we wait. Now, I'll just have a quick shower, then I'll make the salad and ciabattas while you have one if you like?'

'Thanks. Perfect.' I take a large gulp of the wine, which is a little warm from the journey home in the back of Jen's hot car. 'Have you got any ice?' I call after Jen's back as she hops up the stairs.

'There's a bag in the bottom of the freezer, babe,' she calls back and then I hear the water bashing down on the other side of the ceiling above me.

***

We sit in the garden to eat dinner. It is still very hot and the sky is turning a deep red in the distance as the sun begins to set over the hills. The food is delicious. Jen is really good at cooking! She seems so happy too. Perhaps she has finally found her niche. Just as she opens the second bottle of wine, now joyously cold after a stint in the freezer drawer, my phone rings.

'Oh God.' My stomach tightens immediately as I see Andrew's name flash on the screen. I watch it for a few moments wondering if I have to answer but knowing that I do, and feeling awful that I have all but completely forgotten about him for the past couple of days. Apart from a text or two when I arrived I haven't even spoken to him. 'I guess I can't avoid him forever…' I look at Jen in the vain hope that she will tell me that I can.

'Oh, put the poor boy out of his misery, just have a quick chat then we can get on with enjoying this wine and we'll work out an exit strategy for you.' She smiles encouragingly and pours me another glass while gesturing to me to answer the call. I dig deep.

'Hi, babe' – I am full of mock cheer – 'How's life in London?'

Andrew rattles on for a while telling me about his work and the new girl that has started at his firm. He is mentoring her apparently, and he takes his role as a mentor very seriously. I cut him off as soon as I can to avoid being dragged into an in-depth conversation about his 'development strategy' for her. 'Sounds interesting, I hope she proves better than your last mentee.' As the words come out of my mouth I immediately wish that they hadn't. Andrew's last mentee had been a rather troubled young man who had joined the firm straight out of university but who clearly didn't want to be there and became a great frustration to Andrew in his attempts to lead him to greatness. Andrew is just about to launch into all the ways that he had tried to help the poor boy and how disappointing it is when people don't follow good advice (I know it is coming I have heard it several times before!), so I try again to stop him in his tracks. 'I'm sure she will be great, she is very lucky to have you. Let me tell you a little about this place to take your mind off work, you would love it here.' I prattle on a little bit about the village, our planned trip to Florence and the dinner party, then promise to call him in a couple of days' time. As I hang up the phone the serenity of ten minutes ago has vanished. I drain my glass and look searchingly at Jen.

'You really must tell him how you feel soon.' She fills my glass again with a sympathetic face. 'It's not fair on him, you know, and it's not fair on you either, you need to move on, find yourself a nice young Italian man,' she winks.

'I know, I know,' I groan, 'I'll do it as soon as I get home. I have to do it face to face.' I grimace at the thought. 'Let's not talk about it tonight; I've had such a lovely day. What do you think I should wear for the dinner party?' I change the subject.

'Ooh, well, what did you bring?' Jen sits forward, she loves talking about clothes. All thoughts of Andrew are forgotten, or at least temporarily pushed back to the bottom of my stomach as we talk through my holiday wardrobe. Although there are definitely a few options; the red shift dress with my gold wedges or the strappy, delicate floral summer dress with the criss-cross back and ruffles at the bottom, we both agree that we should try and get new outfits in Florence and spend a long time discussing the possibilities whilst we finish our wine and pick at the last of the sticky pastries.

Chapter 8

Excited for our trip to Florence, we both wake extra early on the Tuesday morning. After showering and putting on our comfy clothes and flat shoes in preparation for the day ahead, we have a quick breakfast of warm bread rolls from the oven with butter and jam, then jump in the car to pick Katarina up. It is only 9am but the sun is already hot and the car is dusty from driving around the Italian lanes in the heat. Jen switches the air con on and slips in her Katy Perry CD, which we sing along to on the short drive into the village.

When we arrive, Katarina is already waiting outside the patisserie. She looks very pretty in cut-off denim shorts that show her slim legs, a white shirt tied at the waist, white pumps and her long, dark hair hanging loose down her back. Jen stops the car and, with a quick wave to Katarina, runs into the butcher's to invite Alberto to the dinner party.

'Good morning! I look forward very much to today. I hope you enjoy!' Katarina is clearly excited as she stoops to get into the back of the car.

I smile at her warmly: 'We're excited too!' I tell her and it's true, I am excited. I have loved my first few days in the cottage and the village but it feels great to be getting out for the first time.

Jen gets back into the car. 'He's not there, away for a few days apparently. Never mind, I ordered the meat anyway.' She looks behind into the back seat: 'Morning, Katarina, are we ready for the off?' Katarina nods.

'Let's go!' I say. 'Jen and I are going to try and get something to wear for the dinner party. I hope you know some good places?'

'Oh yes. I know many.' Katarina claps her hands together and tells us about her favourite shops and where we should go first. We chat happily for the hour-or-so drive and, as we approach the city, Katarina guides us through the area that she is clearly familiar with. She takes us to park at a place called Piazzale Michelangelo. 'It is walking for about twenty minute from here but it is best for parking and nice place to see city too,' she explains. She isn't wrong. As we get out of the car the view across the city is spectacular.

'Oh wow!' I take a deep breath as I look around. 'This is so beautiful. So...' I search for the right word but the only thing I want to say is 'Italian', as if I had been expecting something else! But it is quintessentially Italian, everything I expected Italy to be, the jade green river glistening in the city sun beneath the grand bridges arched across it, hugging it to their legs. What seems like hundreds of churches and historical monuments and an array of multi coloured slatted roofs and domes scattered across the city. There is so much to see, I find it impossible to believe that you could ever run out of things to see and do here. We amble down the steps from the car park, along the river and across one of the stunning bridges into the buzzing city streets where tourists and locals mingle together, scooters buzz around the old stone streets and students ride their bicycles along the pavements.

Katarina takes us to a lovely shop-lined street, full of designer boutiques selling clothes, shoes and leather goods. We walk about halfway down and she stops outside a smart shop window with exquisite jewelled kaftans hanging on mannequins.

'This is it! My friend's boutique. We go in?'

'It looks great!' I smile and gesture at her to lead the way. Inside, the air conditioning is on and is a welcome relief to our warm skin. I look around, impressed by the sheer number of dresses that line the four walls. They are hung according to colour and what a wonderful array of colours it is. Alongside the creams, peaches, silver and gold nestled together at one end are lemons and sunshine-yellows, then corals, pinks and fuchsia, before turquoise, mint, emerald-green, baby-blues and navy, then finally rich purples, and softer lilac and violet. It is a real feast for the eyes. Jen and I exchange a glance and I can see that she is impressed and eager to rifle through the loaded rails.

Katarina's friend greets us warmly. 'I am Rosa, please, look around, try anything you like on.' She gestures to two small cubicles covered by thick cream curtains at the back of the shop.

'Look at this one, Soph.' Jen is already pulling out a cream coloured, floor length chiffon dress with an asymmetric shoulder strap covered in tiny crystals and gold beading. It has a delicate sweetheart neckline and a thick band of crystals around the waist.

'Oh, Jen, it's gorgeous!' I gasp.

'You have to try it on, Soph.' Jen hands me the dress to hold, 'It's perfect for you!'

'It is gorgeous, a little dressy for the dinner party though, don't you think?'

'Hmm, perhaps a little,' Jen relents. 'But you have to try it on anyway. You're not limited to buying clothes for the dinner party! Treat yourself!'

I look at the dress in my hands again. It is so delicate and beautifully made, 'It can't hurt to try it on!'

Rosa takes the dress off me and hangs it in the dressing room while I keep browsing the rails. As Rosa and Katarina chat behind the cash desk, Jen and I pull out dress after dress before settling on a further three or four each to try on. Katarina and Rosa take great pleasure in watching us come out in each of the dresses, they make us twirl around and have fun putting various accessories on us to complete the looks.

'*Try the blue one on, Jen,*' I shout across from my changing room.

'*It's on, I'm coming out now.*' Jen shouts back and I hear her pull across the curtain rail. I open mine to see her in the short, midnight-blue, halter-neck dress with a flirty skirt that swishes as she walks. It is backless except for a wide column of sheer navy chiffon from the neck to the top of the skirt. It looks wonderful on her olive complexion and slim figure, accentuating her small waist and long, slim legs.

'You have to have it!' all three of us say at the same time. With the help of the girls, I choose a sweet coral, strapless,empire line, dress that sits just above my knees at the front and swoops to just below them at the back. It fits me beautifully, showing my toned arms and my slim shoulders and back whilst skimming nicely over my curvier hips and thighs that are definitely rounder than they were just a week ago! Fun and flirty, summery and not too dressy, it's perfect for a dinner party! Jen is standing at the cash desk with her blue dress in hand and I have tried on all but one dress, the cream, one-shoulder number. I pick it up again and feel the beadwork.

As if she can see through the curtain I hear Jen's voice: 'Try on the cream one, Soph, I have to see it on you'. I slip out of the coral dress and put it to one side, then step into the soft chiffon, taking care not to pull at any of the beading or snag the material on my jewellery. It feels amazing on, it hugs and skims my body in all the right places. I step out of the changing room and the three girls turn from their conversation to look at me.

'Oh wow,' Jen gasps.

Katarina puts her hand to her mouth and whispers, 'You look so beautiful, like a movie star.'

'She is right,' Rosa chips in. 'You look the best that I have seen in that dress. It is like it is made for you!' I blush at their compliments and walk over to the full length mirror in the middle of the shop. I'm not sure about a movie star, but even I am taken aback by my reflection. It really does look like the dress is made for me. And it feels so good on, heavy enough to hang right, clinging in all the right places but not uncomfortable. It is luxuriously soft and sheer. I love it. Really, really love it.

'You have to have it.' Jen stands next to me.

'I know I do,' I agree. 'How much is it?' I'm too scared to look at the price tag that hangs from the beaded strap on my shoulder so Jen picks up the thick cardboard tag and turns it around to face her. Her face falls.

'It's 1000 euros — but I still think you should have it,' she adds hastily, trying to compensate for her obvious disappointment. 'I mean, it's definitely an investment piece. Don't you think girls?' She turns to Katarina and Rosa who nod fervently.

'Definitely,' they chime in unison.

'1000 euros! Jen, I can't! I wouldn't even have anywhere to wear it! Maybe if I had a really special event or something, but I can't possibly justify 1000 euros on something that I might never even wear. I can't justify the money even if I did have somewhere to wear it. I have never spent that much money on anything, except my flat and car!'

'But, Soph–' Jen starts to protest but I stop her in her tracks.

'Honestly, babe, I can't. I love it, I really do, but I just can't'.

I look at my reflection again in the mirror. I wish I hadn't even tried it on now. 'Perhaps if I ever get married.'

I take a last wistful look and twirl then reluctantly return to the dressing room to take it off. Sadly, I hang the dress back on the rail then pick myself up and pay for the lovely coral dress, at a much more sensible 70 euros. With our dresses in hand we leave the shop and stroll on through the streets, stopping to look at the handmade shoes and smell the fresh lavender outside the perfume boutique. As it approaches midday Katarina takes us to her favourite restaurant, a small, buzzy place that spills out onto a pretty square set around a large fountain with tiny, ornate churches on two of its corners. The waiters are fast and friendly, bringing us iced-water, breadsticks and a bottle of wine. Jen and I have a large glass each, whilst Katarina has half a glass with fizzy water. The cold wine tastes so good; our shoulders visibly drop as we relax at the table and read the menus.

'The pizza here is the best in Florence!' Katarina hands us a separate piece of laminated paper with the longest list of pizzas I have ever seen.

'Pizza it is then!'

I eye the list hungrily and settle on a Fiorentina, which apparently is the house special and has ham, spinach, garlic and olives. Jen chooses a Calzone and Katarina a Margherita with fresh basil. We chat happily until the food arrives, mulling over the bits that Jen has to buy for the dinner party and trying to decide whether to get rosé, red or white wine. We have just decided on rosé for the starter, a red Montepulciano for the main and a nice dessert wine for the pudding, when the waiter comes over with our food. My pizza is huge and doughy and dripping in fresh mozzarella. It looks absolutely delicious and tastes even better than it looks! We barely speak as we eat the food, it is so good!

'I am fit to burst,' I sigh heavily as I take my last mouthful and put my knife and fork down next to each other on my plate, admitting defeat to the last quarter of the pizza.

'Me too.' Jen has also left a large piece of Calzone. We look over at Katarina who smiles sweetly as she places her knife and fork together on her empty plate.

'Where do you put it all?' I laugh. 'How on earth can you eat so much and stay so slim!'

Katarina laughs too and rubs her flat belly. 'I love my food! Must be an Italian thing!'

'And she works in a patisserie,' Jen shakes her head in wonder.

'Bitch,' Jen and I mutter in unison and we all burst into laughter, including Katarina who takes the last slice from my plate just to prove her point. We finish the wine slowly whilst we digest our food and build enough energy to get up from the table. Jen and I pay the bill to thank Katarina for showing us around and we get up and go off in our separate ways, agreeing to meet again later. Katarina links her arm into mine and leads me across the square towards the Uffizi Gallery, pointing out churches and places of interest along the way.

I am blown away by the gallery. The Canaletto exhibition lives up to all of my expectations. After two hours we have barely touched the surface, it isn't nearly enough time. We scour the halls as quickly as we can whilst still trying to pay due respect to the incredible works of art around us, taking in Botticelli, Giotto, Leonardo da Vinci, Cimabue, Michelangelo and Raffaello to name just a few! We are barely even halfway through everything that we want to see by the time that we have to leave to meet Jen. We run to have a glimpse of the *Madonna with Child and Two Angels* on our way out. I have to see if it before I leave. I studied the picture at university and I have always wanted to see if it is as beautiful in real life as I have always imagined it to be. It is. As we stand admiring the Madonna I tell Katarina the famous story behind the painting: 'The picture was painted by Fillipino Lippi. He was a monk who fell in love with a nun called Lucrezia Buti. They had a passionate, secret affair for years and eventually were both forced to give up their religious votes because of their love for each other. Many believe that this is Fillipo's picture of Lucrezia and their two children'.

'She is beautiful,' – Katarina is memorized by the painting too– 'So graceful'.

I smile, 'I know. Many artists have modelled the women in their paintings since on the Madonna. I love her'.

We stand for a few minutes longer looking at the cherub-like children and the sweetness of the composition before Katarina looks at her watch.

'We must go now! Really! We already late for meet Jen.'

'It's such a shame, I wish I could stay longer, I didn't expect there to be so much to see, I don't know why!' We walk quickly out of the gallery and back towards the square where we had lunch.

'We can come back,' Katarina comforts me. 'Yes definitely, I would love to go to the Academia and see Michaelangelo's *David*,' I tell her.

Katarina looks at me, 'How do you know so much about art?' she asks.

'I studied History of Art at university,' I tell her.

'You are an expert?' she looks so impressed and I don't want to disappoint her but alas I am not an expert, just a lover!

'Not quite. But I am interested in it and I really enjoy it,' I tell her. 'To be honest, I have forgotten a lot of what I learnt, it seems so long ago now, but you never forget to love beauty when it is in front of you and the stories will always fascinate me.'

'Will you tell me some more stories, about your favourite paintings?' Katarina asks.

'Of course!' I promise, but before I have a chance to say anything else we hear Jen call us from across the square.

'Soph! Katarina! Over here!' She is standing next to someone who is dressed as the Statue of Liberty on top of an upturned milk crate. We wave and walk over to her.

'Wow, that person must be so hot!'

'I think they crazy!' Katarina snorts. 'They student try to make money'.

'There must be easier ways!' I throw a euro into the bucket next to the milk crate, which can't have had more than a couple of euros in total in it. The statue moves in a gesture of thanks and attracts a small crowd of tourists. Katarina and I help Jen to pick up her shopping bags and we walk together across the river and back to the car.

'Did you get everything you need?' I ask Jen.

'Nearly, I'll go to the village tomorrow to pick up the meat from the butcher's and that will be everything. How was your day? Did you enjoy the gallery?'

'It was great, I just wish we had more time, I didn't expect there to be so much to see!'

'You will have to come back, when we don't have bags of fresh langoustine cooking in the heat!' Jen lifts one of the carrier bags and I can see the little black eyes and blue faces of the langoustine poking out of the paper that they are wrapped in.

We load the bags into the boot and are glad to sit down in the car and turn the air conditioning on. As quickly as they did on the way in, the roads change from the busy city traffic to the quiet country lanes and, in no time at all, we pull up again outside the patisserie in the village. Katarina gets out of the car full of 'grazi's' and excitement for the dinner party the next evening.

Back at the cottage we quickly put all of the ingredients for the dinner party into the fridge, open one of the bottles of rosé that Jen bought to go with the starters (for tasting purposes only, of course!) and slump across the sofa, exhausted from the day's activities. Too tired and full from lunch to eat a proper meal, we make do with left over quiche and crisps before falling asleep mid-conversation.

Chapter 9

We wake up to the sun streaming through the large French doors at the back of the house. 'I can't believe we fell asleep on the sofa! My neck is so stiff!' Jen groans as she pulls herself upright.

'I know,' I groan back, lifting my head off the arm and squinting in the glare of the sunshine. 'We didn't even drink that much, did we?'

'Not at all–' Jen looks over at the single bottle of wine sitting on the coffee table with at least a glass left in it– 'That's barely two glasses each.'

'Excellent!' I jump up and she looks at me strangely. 'That means we can't be hungover!' I explain my enthusiasm, 'So let's get up and get this place ready for a dinner party!'

The menu for the dinner party is:

- Langoustine wrapped in Parma ham, pan fried in garlic butter

- Slow roasted lamb shanks with rosemary and shallot parmentier potatoes and baby carrots

-    Homemade Cassata and shortbread

-    Coffee and sweet pastries

Having eaten our current stock of sweet pastries, Katarina has promised to bring some with her so that Jen can focus on cooking the three courses that she will also be presenting at her end-of-term examination. The langoustine will be easy and can be done once the guests have arrived, but the lamb needs prepping and putting in the oven for at least four hours beforehand and the Cassata needs making first thing so that it has time to freeze. Jen gets to work quickly on the Cassata whilst I take her car into the village to pick up the lamb from the butcher.

The butcher, Alonzo – Alberto's father – is in his late fifties. He is portly, red-faced and incredibly friendly. He greets me with open arms when I tell him who I am, and takes great pleasure in taking out the lamb shanks to show me how good they are before wrapping them up for me and putting them in a huge plastic bag. Back at the cottage, whilst Jen prepares the lamb for the oven, I tidy and clean. I get the small table from the shed at the end of the garden and wash it down with buckets of soapy water, then leave it to dry in the afternoon sun. At about four p.m. Jen and I drag the large dining table out into the garden and set the two tables up next to each other. We cover them in thick white table cloths and put out the plates, cutlery, water and wine glasses before filling the remaining water glasses with flowers from the garden and lining them down the centre of the tables. We place a row of tea lights between the flowers and put the left over ones in empty jam jars scattered all around the edge of the garden. It is simple but stunning. The garden looks like a fairy dell, I can't wait for dusk to fall to see the candlelight in full effect. The table is so inviting I almost don't want to ruin it by putting food on it!

'It looks great, doesn't it?' Jen asks, getting a little nervous as the time for guests to arrive approaches.

'It's beautiful,' I say emphatically. 'Now let's get ready!'

I am ready first and go downstairs to check on the lamb and open the red wine to let it breathe. A few minutes later Katarina arrives with the sweet pastries.

'Thank you so much,' I say as I take the plate from her and welcome her into the cottage. 'Come through, can I get you a drink?' As we walk towards the back doors Jen comes down the stairs, resplendent in her new blue dress, full bouncy hair and perfect make up. 'Jen, you look beautiful!'

'Thank you!' she beams at the praise. 'Hi, Katarina, thank you so much for bringing the pastries.' She eyes the heaped plate in my hand.

'Oh, you are welcome, you look bella, bella!' she whirls her hand above Jen's head to get her to spin around.

'Gorgeous! Jake is one lucky man!' I wink at her.

'Is Jake your boyfriend?' Katarina asks.

'No!' Jen laughs. 'Not yet anyway!' I nudge Katarina and she giggles.

By seven fifteen p.m. the rest of the guests have arrived and the cottage is full of conversation and laughter. Everyone has a glass of wine in their hand and is looking forward to the food.

The smells wafting through from the kitchen are divine. I leave the happy chatter of the main room to ask Jen if she needs help with anything and realise that Jake is already in the kitchen helping her to wrap the langoustine in Parma ham as she warms the garlic butter in a pan.

Jake is literally tall, dark and handsome. He must be at least 6ft, perfect for Jen's 5'10 frame. He has a smooth olive complexion, wavy dark hair and is certainly handsome. Jen has always gone for the archetypal good looking man. She was into Jordan from New Kids on the Block (while I was obsessed with Joey) and she fancied Howard from Take That (first time around!) while I was into Mark. We both had a raging crush on Johnny Depp when he was all chiseled jaw and had Kate Moss hanging off his arm, but then so did all of our friends at the time. I also had a strange crush on Phillip Schofield during his broom cupboard years, so my taste was varied to say the least! Jake certainly lives up to that archetypal handsome image. With large, round, brown eyes a straight, strong nose and a sculpted jaw. He is definitely Jen's type. Strangely he is not my type at all, but in real life I have never really gone for the obviously handsome type. It's probably a self-preservation thing, because I never thought the really good looking boys could ever fancy me back (and they usually didn't, Jen and Fi had much more success in that department than I did). It wasn't really until Andrew that I even had a proper boyfriend, not a serious one. But let's not think about Andrew tonight. Jake moves confidently around the kitchen, encouraging Jen and helping where he can, he seems to really like her and it is lovely to see Jen finally in her element. In an environment she really fits in and wants to be a part of. It makes me want to be a part of it too.

At seven thirty p.m. on Jen's instruction, I usher everyone into the garden and we take our places at the candlelit table. There are lots of 'ohhs' and 'ahhs' in appreciation of the setting as we walk outside, and even more when Jen and Jake carry through two huge platters of langoustine and place them in the middle of the long table.

Everyone eats hungrily, using their hands and licking the garlic butter off their fingers.

'This is divine,' Michael, Sara's husband, pulls the head off another langoustine and places it on top of the already large pile on his plate. 'Cooked to perfection,' he makes a circle with his thumb and finger to illustrate his point.

'Thank you.' Jen takes the compliment graciously and asks Michael about his work at the university.

'I'm a lecturer on art' he explains. 'I specialise in Italian Renaissance artists and of course Florence is the best city in the world to study this!' he smiles.

'Soph studied History of Art at university!' Jen looks down the table at me. 'She went to a gallery just yesterday with Katarina.'

'Which one?' Michael asks, now looking at me too.

'The Uffizi, to see the Canaletto exhibition,' I tell him. 'I've always loved the Madonna with Child and Two Angels. It didn't disappoint!'

'It's an excellent exhibition,' Michael agrees. 'And a beautiful picture too, you have good taste! If you are interested in seeing more I can let you have the details of some of the smaller exhibitions that I know about. They are less well advertised but just as wonderful, I have some good contacts in the city.'

'That would be wonderful,' I gush, slightly in awe of Sara's husband. The conversation flows easily and, if it is possible, the lamb shanks are an even bigger success than the langoustine. Everyone waxes lyrical about the way the meat falls off the bone and the rosemary infuses the gravy. I have to admit to feeling quite proud of Jen as we enjoy her wonderful food, outside in the warm, fragrant evening under the mildness of the Tuscan night sky. By the time the Cassata comes out everyone is high on happiness, full of good food, fine wine and fun conversation. It is lucky that Jen's closest neighbor is a hundred yards away as the din from the gathering must have drifted in the warm air far down the road. Fuelled by the wine I ask the table if anyone knows anything about the abandoned house up the lane. I look hopefully at Michael, thinking that his local knowledge might come in useful, but alas, he can't tell me anything meaningful. Paulo looks up from the far end of the table.

'You mean the old Russo house?' he asks.

'I don't know, the house up the lane to left of the cottage, on for about a mile around the bend, with large iron gates.' I try to describe it as best I can without giving away quite how much of it I have actually seen.

'Yes, that is it, the Russo house, I do not know the owner, but I hear the story from my father, he tell me that the house was owned by Rialto Russo.'

I sit forward and encourage Paulo to continue.

'Rialto is the son of a very wealthy Florentine with high connections. He hand the house to his eldest son as a gift when he turn twenty-one.' The table had gone silent, taken in already by Paulo's story. 'Legend has it,' Paulo continues in his strong Italian accent, 'That Rialto fall in love with local girl, she work in the village shop, called Lucia. He marry her against his family's wishes, which were for him to marry the daughter of another wealthy Florentine family. His family are very hurt and angry. They disinherit their son. They cut him off and leave him only the house, where he live with his young wife. My father say that soon they expecting a child but before it is born Rialto dies in terrible road accident. He leave Lucia pregnant and alone. The Russo family blame Lucia for taking away their first born child and ultimately for his death. The house still legally belong to them so still angry at their son for his betrayal and grieving for his loss, they evict his wife and their unborn child.'

'What happened to Lucia and the child?' I ask. 'And what happened to the house, why is it empty now?' The questions spill out quicker than I realise and poor Paulo has trouble trying to work out what I want to know. I repeat myself, slowly this time, and Paulo answers but he doesn't know very much more.

'I am not sure, to be honest, as far as I know Lucia move back with her family in the village and have baby but I do not know where they are now.'

'And the house?' I ask, wanting to know more. 'Why would they go to so much trouble to get it back and then just leave it?'

'I don't know,' Paulo shrugs, probably wondering why on earth I am so interested in the old house on the edge of his village that I hadn't even seen before this week. 'I think perhaps they are so heartbroken by the death of Rialto that they cannot bear to be near the house. They leave it to ruin, just like their lives are ruined by the forbidden relationship and the tragedy that befell it.'

'Wow. That is so heartbreaking, so much heartache for so many people, I don't know who I feel worse for.' I am overwhelmed with sadness for the doomed young couple, for the family who lost their son to pride, for the beautiful house laid to waste and for the poor child who would never know its father. Conversation carries on around me whilst I mull a hundred thoughts and questions in my head.

'Soph,' Jen touches my arm, 'Are you ok?'

I come to, suddenly very aware of myself and my beautiful surroundings.

'Of course, sorry, let me help you clear.'

We take the pudding plates inside and Jake helps us to carry out the rest of the dessert wine along with a huge pot of steaming coffee and the sticky pastries. Everyone is fit to burst and little else gets eaten as the evening draws to a close, but conversation and laughter lingers as the coffee is drunk and no one is in a hurry to go home. I can see Katarina and Paulo leaning in to each other at the end of the table and talking in whispers. Sara has her head on Michael's shoulder as he finishes her pudding and from the corner of my eye I can see that Jake has his hand gently lying across Jen's knee under the table. It is a picture of contentment. It is so lovely to see and yet somehow, amidst the perfectness of the evening, I feel just a little sad. For a second I even think it might be nice to have Andrew here, just so that I don't feel the 'being on my own' part so much, but I know deep down that I don't want him. It might have been nice though, I think, to have my own Paulo, Michael or Jake. Just for tonight.

Chapter 10

By two a.m. Jen and I are finally alone again in the cottage; everyone has left full of praise and thanks for a lovely evening. Jake is the last to leave, helping us to bring everything in from the garden and to ensure that all of the candles are out before we lock the back doors for the night. Sensing a moment is approaching, I say my goodnights and leave him and Jen to say goodbye in private, also leaving the plates, glasses and cutlery in great piles in the kitchen to tackle in the morning. I fall asleep almost as soon as my head hits the pillow and wake up in exactly the same position only a few hours later. I know it is early by the position of the sun which is still low and weak in the sky and the fact that I am still utterly exhausted. My stomach is still full from last night's excesses and I am in dire need of water and paracetamol!

I stumble downstairs, trying not to wake Jen and search around for the bottled water. I groan audibly as I take in the state of the kitchen, there is no way that I can face it yet. I definitely need more sleep and rehydration before I can do anything else. 'Where is the bloody water?' I open the back door and check around the table to see if we left any bottles outside. No luck. 'Damn!' My throat is so dry it is practically closing and the dull ache in my head is fast turning into a strong pounding. I tiptoe back up the stairs and push the door to Jen's room just a crack to see if there is a bottle by her bed. There isn't! We must have drunk it all last night. This is bad, really bad. There is no way I am going to be able to get back to sleep without some fluid in me!

Perhaps there is some juice left in the fridge. I go back into the kitchen, trying not to look at the teetering piles of washing up waiting for us, and open the fridge door. It is full with left over langoustine, lamb and pastries but nothing to drink. Not even a pint of milk! There is half a lemon in the fridge door which, in desperation, I consider squeezing into the water from the tap but I really don't think I can handle an upset stomach on top of a hangover so, more than a little reluctantly, I go back to my room and pull on the dress that I was wearing last night with my flip flops. The village shop it is. I grab my wheelie case so that I don't have to carry the heavy water bottles back, and set off.

As I walk out of the front door I kick something with my foot and the resulting crashing and clinking of glass seems to go on forever as wine bottles fall in a domino effect down the path. 'Great!' I mumble and reel off a few profanities as I chase an errant bottle to the end of the path and stop it just before it crashes into the gate at the end. I stand the intact wine bottles back up (all twelve of them) and quickly sweep the remaining broken bits of glass up with a dustpan and brush. No wonder I am hungover, the seven of us must have got through nearly fifteen bottles last night and I am pretty sure that I had more than my fair share of them! Pathway finally clear, I head into the village, for the first time not relishing the sun on my face but wishing instead for a little cloud cover. My headache does ease a little as I walk (even if my scorched throat doesn't) and I remind myself to be grateful again that I am walking to the village with my hangover and not on the Victoria Line on my way to work! Perhaps I will treat myself to a magazine and set up camp in the garden with some mindless entertainment for a few hours. I pick up four bottles of water, *Now* magazine, a couple of cans of Diet Coke, a fresh loaf of bread and a packet of paracetamol. Outside the shop door I promptly drink half a bottle of water and take two of the tablets. I soak up the fluid like a parched plant, luxuriating in the cold water as it streams down the back of my throat, feeling every drop until my stomach is full from it.

The village is quiet, no sign of Katarina or Paulo. To be honest, I am grateful not to see anyone. I realise I haven't even brushed my teeth or hair in my rush to get some water inside me. In fact, I haven't even looked in the mirror. God knows what the lady who works in the shop must think of me. The crazy, dishevelled English girl with a lovely dress, flip flops and a wheelie case!

Feeling slightly revived by the water, I decide to walk the long way back to the cottage past the mansion house. Now I know a little more about its back-story I desperately want to see it again in its new light. Now that I know the story, it makes sense that the house looks so sad, like it is grieving for its lost family. I am longing to see it again. As I walk the now familiar road past the cypress trees, pulling my little wheelie case behind me, tuning out the clattering of the wheels against the cobbled paving stones, I am surprised to see two people standing in front of the house. A tall, slim, well dressed woman in a black suit with very high pointed heels and long curly dark hair is standing holding onto the large front gate, as if she has just pulled it shut. She is talking to a tall, slim man who has his back to me. They are engrossed in their conversation and haven't noticed me walking up the road despite the noise from my case. The woman has a large, brown envelope and a pink folder in her hand. She takes out some papers and hands them to the man who has now turned around to stand opposite her and is facing in my direction. He has a beautiful combination of olive skin and dark blonde hair. He has a lovely face, which is ruined only by its solemn stance. They make an attractive couple. I slow my pace as I grow closer to them. I feel a bit awkward for some reason, like I shouldn't be there. I can't stop and look at the house whilst they are standing in front of it but it's too late to turn around and walk in the other direction. I am so close to them now they must have heard or seen me, even if they haven't acknowledged me.

I start to regret taking my usual detour today. Why didn't I just go home and get back into bed? There is nothing for it, I will just have to keep walking, I have no idea where the road leads to or how far it goes but what else can I do?

As I approach the couple the man looks up from the paperwork in his hands and momentarily his eyes meet mine. They are dark and brooding, quite beautiful actually. He doesn't smile, his eyes drop to my case and linger on it for a while before briefly turning back to my face.

'Morning!' I try to sound jolly but feel ridiculously self conscious and wish with everything in me that I had at least looked in the mirror before I came out and brushed my hair, or my teeth, preferably both. Although perhaps it is a good thing that I don't know quite how awful I look.

I can feel the heat rise in my face and curse my traitorous cheeks which must be practically glowing by now. The handsome man says nothing. He just nods his head in a grave manner and gives me a look bordering on disdain before returning to his conversation, speaking in fast Italian. Feeling like a prize plum and about one foot tall, I scuttle on past them making an unfathomable amount of noise and wishing desperately that I didn't have the bloody wheelie case with me. I keep walking up the hill until it dips again and I am finally out of their view: now what? I could keep walking but I have no idea how far the road goes or where it will lead me to, and I am starting to feel weak in the strong morning sun. My hangover is coursing through me and I don't think I can walk much further but I can't exactly turn around and walk back past them again.

'This is ridiculous,' I scold myself out loud. 'Just turn around and walk back down the road. You can be back at the cottage in bed in twenty minutes. You don't know them and they don't know you! Who cares what they think?' Yep, still talking to myself. Out loud. But despite my own protest I just can't bring myself to walk past them again. I really shouldn't care. He is clearly just a very rude man with no manners whatsoever, even if he is gorgeous.

I put my case down on the edge of the road, take out the open bottle of water and the *Now* magazine and sit down. I am going to have to wait it out; they can't stay there all day. I'll sit here for ten minutes and then head back. They look like they were on their way out rather than in, so hopefully they would be long gone in a few minutes. I sit on the case mulling a million thoughts in my pounding head. Who are they? What do they want with the house? Why is he so rude? Why does he make me feel so small? Why does he have to be so damn good looking? My stomach is churning and I can't tell if it is the result of last night's excesses or something else. I feel uneasy. I have no claim on the house, I haven't even been inside it for goodness sake, but somehow I feel attached to it and I really don't like the thought of other people being interested in it. I am just starting to feel a little sick when I hear a car start up. Excellent. They are leaving. I stand up and pick up the case ready to head back down the hill. As I do so, to my horror, I see the car travelling towards me. It never even crossed my mind that they would be coming back this way and now I am going to look like a right fool! The car moves up the hill slowly towards me, the woman is driving and as they pass me the man shoots me a slightly bemused but still disdainful look. Bastard. I pick up my case and walk quickly back down the hill, trying to look like I have a purpose. I get back to the cottage in record time and crawl straight back into bed, desperate to start this disastrous day again!

Chapter 11

I wake again much later, feeling considerably better, and look at my phone. It is just gone three p.m. No wonder I feel better, I've slept for hours! I can hear Jen moving around downstairs so I get out of bed and go down to tell her about the morning's escapades. I grimace as the memory of the couple at the house floods back. I can be such an idiot sometimes.

'Afternoon,' Jen greets me as I walk into the kitchen.

'Hi! Jen I can't believe you have done all of this, you should have waited until I got up so I could help you!' The kitchen is gleaming, no sight nor sound of a pot, plate or glass.

'Oh, don't worry about it!' Jen is cheerful and doesn't seem to mind at all. 'I've been up for a while now, thought I would make a start and it actually hasn't taken too long at all. How are you feeling?'

'I'm OK, a little fragile perhaps,' I smile. 'I had a great time, it was such a lovely evening and, Jen, your cooking was amazing. Really, I was so impressed.'

Jen smiles widely. 'Really? Thanks! I think everyone else enjoyed it too. Sara called this morning to say thanks and that they had a great time. And Jake just text me too.'

'Oh, yes!' I remember that I left the two of them alone downstairs when I went to bed last night. 'What happened with Jake? You two certainly looked quite cosy last night. It is obvious he likes you!'

Jen beams. 'Really? Do you think so?'

'Of course, he was all over you last night and he couldn't do enough to help.'

'I know,' Jen pauses, clearly for effect. 'And he kissed me!' she squeals and grins widely.

'When? When I went upstairs? I want all the details!' I am almost as excited as she is.

'Yep, we finished clearing up for a little longer and then when he went to leave he said what a great time he had and he kissed me.'

'A proper kiss?' I have to check.

'Yes!' Jen laughs. 'A proper kiss! I was a little drunk so I don't remember everything exactly, but I remember that it wasn't awkward or embarrassing, he just held my face and kissed me.'

'Is he a good kisser?' I have to ask that too, though by the look on Jen's face I already know the answer.

'He's great!' she grins. 'He said he's wanted to kiss me for ages!'

'Ahh, that is soo cute!' I decide there and then that I really like Jake and I am so happy for Jen, the drama of my morning has gone from my mind and I am caught up in her happiness. 'So what did he text?' I ask, eager to know everything. She hands me her phone with the text message already on her screen:

Thanks for a great night.
Everything was perfect.
See you tomorrow. x

'Everything was perfect,' I read out loud. 'That is so nice! I'm assuming he isn't just referring to the food!'

'I hope not! I really like him, Soph. I'm nervous about seeing him at college tomorrow. It could all be so different in the cold light of day!' Jen bites her lip like she always does when she's nervous.

'But you always see him at college and it's always fine,' I try to reassure her.

'Yes, but I don't always see him when the last time I saw him he kissed me!'

'It will be fine,' I soothe. 'Just be how you always are with him, don't make it awkward, let him bring it up if he wants to. Just be the same as you would be any other day.'

'You're right,' Jen nods, 'I just hope he doesn't regret it!'

'He won't! Stop worrying about it!' I chastise her kindly, 'Now how about something to eat?' I ask. 'I'm starving.'

'Good idea, so am I. What do you fancy? We haven't much in. Left over lamb and langoustine...' Jen looks up from the fridge.

'I don't think I can face that, hon. Not that it wasn't lovely,' I add quickly so as not to hurt her feelings.

'Don't worry,' she laughs at my obvious concern, 'I can't stomach that this morning either — here.' She hands me the plate with the left over pastries on it and opens the freezer door. 'There's a couple of ciabattas left in here. How about I make a pizza with the cheese and ham in the fridge? I think there's some tomato paste in the cupboard. Then we can get started on the pastries!'

'Sounds yummy,' my stomach starts to rumble. It is almost half past three! And I haven't eaten a thing. 'What can I do?' I ask.

'Nothing, babe, maybe just brew some coffee?'

'I'm on it,' I reach for the bag of coffee beans in the cupboard above Jen's head and get to work.

Not long later we are sitting in the garden, immaculate again after last night's chaos, eating homemade pizza and drinking strong coffee. 'That's better,' I sigh. 'I think I'm starting to feel human again!' I reach for a pastry and sink back into my chair feeling relaxed.

'Me too,' Jen picks up the last pastry. 'Although to be fair, I don't think I drank as much as you did! I was so busy in the kitchen that I didn't really get a chance until much later on!'

'The curse of the host!' I laugh. 'Although I bet you are grateful for it today.'

'I am,' she agrees. Jake and I counted about fourteen bottles when we put them outside last night.'

'Oh, that reminds me!' I grimace again, remembering the bottles that I kicked over as I left the cottage this morning. 'I got up early and went to the village to get water.'

'What? This morning?' Jen asks, bemused.

'Yes! I didn't want to wake you but I was gasping and we must have drunk all of the bottles last night, so I went into the village to get some.'

'You're mad!' Jen points inside to where six bottles of Evian are stacked up between the end of the sofa and the wall. 'There's loads of water!'

I groan and put my head in my hands. 'I don't believe it. How on earth did I miss that? I could have avoided everything!'

'What do you mean?' Jen asks. 'What could you have avoided?' she looks at me questioningly and I tell her the whole story about the couple at the house, how rude the gorgeous man was and how I made a complete fool of myself. By the time I have finished the story Jen is laughing pretty hard. 'That is so funny! I can't believe you just waited there, they must have wondered what the hell you were doing!'

'I know, I know,' I groan again. 'I wasn't thinking straight, I was tired and hungover and he is so handsome it totally threw me. It didn't even cross my mind that they would drive back that way!' Jen is still laughing at me, clearly revelling in my shame.

'You should have asked them about the house, tried to make conversation.'

'He didn't really look like he was in the mood for talking,' I say honestly. 'And anyway, he's Italian and you know that my knowledge of the language is pretty much limited to "ciao" and "gratzie".'

'Hmm,' Jen ponders. 'I wonder what they were doing there.'

'Me too, perhaps I'll go and talk to Paulo again tomorrow, see if he can find out a little more from his parents.'

'Good idea. What else do you want to do next week?' Jen asks. 'After my exam on Tuesday I have the rest of the week off. We start level three next Monday for four weeks and then that's it. End of the summer, end of cooking school. It's going so fast.' Sadness flashes across her face just for a second.

'What will you do when it ends?' I ask.

'I don't know yet, I don't really want to think about it until I have to! Let's just make sure that we have some fun before you have to go. Time is flying!'

'I know!' I agree. 'I can't believe the first week has already come and gone, I can't bear to think about going home! I start to reel off a list of things I would like to do: 'I'd love to go back to Florence, maybe go to some of the galleries that Michael mentioned last night. And Pisa, I would love to go to Pisa. I've loads of leaflets inside that I picked up from the village café, I'll grab them later and we can work out a couple of trips together.'

'Good idea,' Jen smiles. 'I have to go back to Florence tomorrow after college too, to collect fresh ingredients for my exam on Tuesday. Do you want to come with me? We could have dinner there if you like?'

'Oh, that would be lovely.' I am excited already about the prospect of going back to Florence.

'Great! Remind me to take the freezer bags so that we can store the langoustine in them, then we can take our time, stroll around the shops and find a nice place to eat.'

'Perfect,' I say. I am looking forward to it already.

Chapter 12

The next day I spend the morning at the cottage, pottering around, reading my book and doing some research on Jen's laptop into things to see and do in Florence and Pisa, as well as some of the other surrounding areas. I am finding so much it is going to be really difficult to choose what to fit in to the time I have left. I can't believe that a whole week has gone by already.

Andrew texted me this morning. It just said *'Only a week to go, can't wait to see you!'* My sentiments could not have been more different, I think sadly and cruelly. But it is true. I don't want to go home in a week and I don't want to see Andrew. But what other choice do I have? I push the negative thoughts from my head with great mental force and return to my list:

- Visit Saturnia thermal baths
- Wine tasting in Chianti
- Visit Versilia / Maremma beaches
- Leaning tower of Pisa
- Gucci outlet in Florence
- Academia / Pallazzo Vecchio — speak to Michael re: other galleries

- Prada outlet in Florence
- Tarot Garden in Capalbio
- Armani outlet in Florence.

That is a lot to do in a week. I refine the list and try to be ruthless, like when cleaning out my wardrobe at home, only keeping on it the things I absolutely have to do:

- Visit Saturnia thermal baths and Maremma beach — one trip
- Wine tasting in Chianti
- Leaning tower of Pisa
- Gucci, Armani and Prada outlets in Florence — one trip
- Academia / Pallazzo Vecchio — speak to Michael re: other galleries
- [Tarot Garden in Capalbio] if time left at the end of the week!

Not exactly great strides forward, I admit. I'll talk to Jen and see what she wants to do. Perhaps that will help me narrow things down. Jen will be home soon so I go upstairs to get ready for our trip to Florence. I am really looking forward to a nice meal out and an evening stroll around the city. After showering and washing my hair, I pull on a pair of cream, wide-leg trousers that are loose enough to be comfortable in the heat, but smart enough if we end up somewhere nice. After a little deliberation I plump for a pretty nude camisole top to go with them and my flat gold sandals from Accessorize. I am just heading back down the stairs as Jen walks in the door.

'Hi! How did it go with Jake — was everything ok?' I hardly need to ask, Jen is beaming from ear to ear!

'Great! It wasn't awkward at all! My stomach dropped when he walked in but he came straight over to me, gave me a kiss and asked when he is finally going to get to take me out to dinner!' She lets out an involuntary squeal of delight.

'See. I told you. That's amazing, hon, I'm so happy for you!' I jump off the bottom stair and give her a hug.

'Thanks, you're the best!' she hugs me back. 'I told him that we should have dinner next week, to give me something to look forward to after you've gone. I'm not wasting a single second of the time I have left with you!'

'You didn't have to do that!' I say, though I'm secretly pleased that I am not going to have to spend an evening home alone.

'Of course I did,' Jen admonishes. 'And now I have to get ready quickly so that I don't waste any time tonight! Just give me ten minutes to try and make me look as lovely as you do!' I laugh as she takes the stairs two at a time. I pour myself a small glass of wine from the open bottle in the fridge and take it with me outside the front of the cottage.

Whilst I wait for Jen I stroll down the path taking in the beautiful flowers and colours in the front garden and the incredible views down the lane and across the Tuscan hills. It really is beautiful here, so calm and peaceful. I feel so relaxed and at ease with myself and my surroundings as I take in the incredible vista and sip my cold wine in the warm, late afternoon sun. In less than ten minutes Jen is downstairs looking gorgeous in a simple white shift dress, flat sandals and sunglasses. We jump in the car and head into Florence in high spirits. En route I tell Jen all the things on my list and we try to work out what we should squeeze into the next seven days. 'Definitely the designer outlets,' Jen says with predictable enthusiasm for shopping. 'We can make a day of it, splurge on ourselves.'

'Agreed,' I nod, and mentally tick that one off the list.

'And I think we should do the beach and the thermal baths,' Jen decides. 'I've been here for nearly two months and I still haven't seen the beach, I would love to do that!'

'Me too,' I agree again. 'Done.'

'Tell me the other things again.'

I think back to the list. 'The Palazzo Vecchio and the Academia,' I tell her.

'I'm not sure I even know what they are,' Jen cuts in pretty quickly. 'Why don't you do them whilst I am at college tomorrow?'

'Maybe,' I think about it. 'But that would mean coming back into Florence again, wouldn't it? How would I get in?' I ask.

'You could get the train,' she suggests. 'Let's think about it, what else is on the list?'

'Wine tasting, Pisa and the Tarot Garden,' I mark them off on my fingers.

'Right.' She thinks for a second, 'I say we shop first, kind of a celebration for the end of my exam tomorrow, then we can reward ourselves for our hard day's shopping at the beach and baths and we can relax to get over our exertions at the end of the week with a little wine tasting in Chianti in the evening'.

I nod beside her in agreement.

'Then you can choose between Pisa and the Tarot Gardens on your last day,' Jen goes on, 'Though if you want my opinion, I think that everyone should see the leaning tower of Pisa before it falls over!'

'It's not going to fall over!' I laugh.

'How do you know?' she is laughing too.

'Well I don't really!' I admit. 'But I am pretty sure that someone would do something about it if they knew it was going to fall and squash a hundred tourists! I'm even more sure,' I add, 'That you just want to get out of going to the Tarot Gardens!' Jen has never understood my love of art, not that it matters in the slightest.

'OK,' she admits, 'You got me, but I also think that not going to the Tarot Gardens is an excellent excuse for you to come back before I finish school at the end of the summer!' She looks at me and raises her eyebrows in half hope, half question.

'Well I would certainly love that!'

'So we have a plan?'

'We have a plan,' she nods.

All the best laid plans…

***

This time we park in a little side road close to the shops that Jen needs to visit. We get the shopping done quickly and take it back to the car, leaving the fresh shellfish in the freezer bags in the boot. Pleased with ourselves for finishing everything we need to do, we set off for a stroll around Florence before dinner. We walk past the entrance to the Renaissance Bardini gardens and I tug at Jen's arm: 'Let's walk through the gardens, pleeease.' I plead as I sense her reluctance. 'We don't have to look at everything, but let's just take a stroll through'.

I pull out my guide to Florence. 'It says here that if we walk through the gardens we can get to the San Niccolo neighbourhood, "the perfect place for a meal or drink." I read aloud from the book.

'OK then,' Jen relents. 'A nice walk before dinner will probably do us both good.'

We walk through the impressive entrance in front of a beautiful rose garden. The smell is exquisite. It just sits in the still air, like it is being soaked into the warmth around us. I feel my heart swell as I take in the beauty. Even Jen is impressed by the grandeur of the terraced lawns, which are decorated with elegant statues. 'I wonder who the statues are of?' she asks as we stroll around aimlessly but contentedly.

'I don't know.' I look in the guide book but can't find anything that specific.

'Wouldn't it be amazing to have a statue made of you?' she muses, running her hands along the arm of an incredible woman made from white stone and covered in intricately-carved draping, standing delicately like a ballerina. We wander for a while without much purpose except to take in the beauty of whatever we pass. We come across several impressive fountains, a small canal that reminds me of the Japanese gardens I have seen in pictures and on the TV but not yet in real life, a tempietto and hundreds of beautiful colours from the flowering roses, irises, hydrangeas and other flowers that we don't know the names of. An elderly couple walk ahead of us holding hands and, as we approach a grand staircase, the man puts his hand on the small of the lady's back to support her up the stairs as he uses his other hand to hold one of hers aloft, guiding her upwards.

'That is so lovely,' I sigh, gesturing at the couple.

'I know,' Jen agrees. 'I hope that I still hold hands with whomever I marry when we're an old couple.' We stand and watch the couple move up the stairway, encouraging and smiling at each other as they do. The gardens lead us out onto a picturesque cobblestoned street called Via San Leonardo. We negotiate the cobbles, both glad to be wearing our flats, stopping occasionally to take in the breathtaking views across the city. As we approach San Niccollo Square the atmosphere changes. The peacefulness of the walk from the gardens is replaced by the bustling of the main square, packed with restaurants and bars where tourists and locals spill out onto the streets.

We head into the throng of people looking for a place to stop and eat, much in need of resting our feet and filling our now rumbling tummies. We pass a row of lovely little artisan shops and follow a wide pavement off the main side of the square. Jen stops after a few steps to look at a menu outside one of the more popular restaurants and, as she does so, something catches my eye in the window of the building next door. It is an old, elegant building that dominates the road. In the middle of the very large window is something I recognise. I walk to get a closer look and with every step I am more convinced, it is the Russo house. Right there in the middle of the window standing on a large, old wooden plinth is a framed photograph of the house that I have fallen in love with. There is a light attached to the plinth so that the picture stands out from the darkness behind it. Below the light a large gold plaque holds a thick ivory card which reads:

Rare auction opportunity
18th Century Russo Family Residence
Guide price in excess of 950,000 Euros
Sale takes place August 12th

Please enquire within for more information

I stare at the picture of the beautiful house that I have become so familiar with and have fallen so in love with. It looks wonderful in the picture, though it still doesn't do it justice. My head is suddenly filled with a thousand thoughts that I can't quite decipher. The house is for sale and for some reason this simple news has knocked me for six. As I stare into the window, Jen walks up beside me.

'Soph, I've been calling you, what are you looking at?' She follows my gaze. 'Is that your house?' she asks, knowing already that it is. I nod, still not sure what to think or say. 'It's for sale!' she states the obvious.

'I know,' is all I can say.

'Wow, what a coincidence that you should come here and see this after admiring it all week, there's a ring of fate about it, don't you think?' She looks at me.

'What do you mean, how can this be fate? It just means that someone else is going to buy the house.' I tear my eyes away from the picture. 'Come on Jen, I need a drink.'

We take a table in the small restaurant next door and are both quiet as we read the menus and order bruschetta, pasta and a bottle of Gavi. I know that Jen is desperate to talk about the auction but she bides her time. The waiter arrives with the wine and pours us both a large glass. I gulp it gratefully and immediately I feel slightly calmer.

'So?' Jen looks at me and waits for me to say something.

'So what? What do you want me to say?' I ask her.

'Well, what do you think about the house? It's for sale, for goodness sake. I mean you have been to look at it almost every day this last week. You talk about it all the time. You've asked my friends about it. You said it yourself, it's your dream house. You feel attached to it.' She is looking at me intently.

'I know I've done and said all those things,' I concede. 'And I do feel some kind of affinity with the place, but that doesn't mean anything. Anyone would fall in love with it, it's so beautiful. But it's not as if realistically it could ever be mine.' I take another large sip of wine.

'Why not?' Jen asks matter of factly.

The privilege of the wealthy is that nothing ever seems out of reach to them. Almost anything is possible. I love that about Jen, she is always inspiring and encouraging me to do things I probably otherwise wouldn't do, but life is easier for her.

Sometimes the line between fantasy and reality, or maybe more accurately possibility and probability, is more blurred for her.

'Did you see the guide price?' I ask, actually wondering if she has.

'I know it's a lot of money, but it is only a guide, it might not even go for that.' Jen sounds hopeful.

'Even if it doesn't go for that much, there's a whole list of reasons why I can't buy that house, Jen.' I reel them off. 'For one, even if it was half that price, I couldn't afford it. Two, even if I could afford the house, I could never afford to renovate, decorate and furnish it. Three, even if I could do all of those things, which I can't, I couldn't possibly afford to live in it! I don't have a job here and I don't speak Italian, which removes almost any possibility of me getting a decent job here so I couldn't pay a mortgage or a bill in a flat, let alone an 18th Century manor house that costs nearly a million euros!'

Rant over, I drain my glass and soften my voice. 'Sorry, Jen, I know you're only trying to help, but honestly, this just isn't something that can happen for me. I don't even know that I would want it to happen, what would I do alone in a beautiful, big house in Tuscany? Especially once you've gone!' I smile in resignation. We are distracted for a few moments as the waitress brings over our food and refills our wine glasses. When she leaves I pick up my fork and start to eat but Jen sits very still and looks at me from across the table.

'My turn to lecture.' She has her serious face on, which I very rarely see so I listen carefully. 'I understand that things come easier to me, Soph, I really do. But I wasn't born with a silver spoon in my mouth and nor were my parents. You know that. I've watched them earn everything that they have now by taking risks, following their dreams and investing wisely. I have learnt a lot from them over the years and I see a lot of them in you.'

I stop eating. 'What do you mean?' I ask.

'You want more from life, Soph,' Jen explains. 'Why did you quit your job at Morgan Stanley if not because you wanted to follow your dreams, to do something exciting, get off the treadmill and be your own person? That is what my parents wanted. And that's what they did. I remember when you were thinking of leaving your job. It was them that you turned to for advice, because you knew that they would understand in a way that your parents wouldn't. You're like a second child to them, Soph, and they have had a part in your upbringing too. I think that's rubbed off on you and I think that you owe it to yourself to do more with your life than working in a stationary office. Or any office, for that matter, if you don't love it, because unless you do love it, you gave up a great career for nothing.'

I smile at Jen with genuine love and affection for her.

'You're right. I've never quite looked at it like that. I do admire your parents and in many ways I aspire to be like them. I so want to do something amazing with my life and I do love that house very much. But none of that changes everything that I said earlier. I still have to live. I need to earn that life like your parents did. I still have to be realistic, Jen.'

'I know that, Soph,' Jen looks frustrated. 'I'm not suggesting that you just "buy the house" but perhaps this is what you're meant to do with your life. You've been thinking and searching for nearly two years now and you aren't any closer to knowing what you want to do. Well, perhaps fate has handed you an opportunity. A business opportunity.'

'Go on...' I am interested in what she can possibly be thinking. 'The house is a wonder,' — she is getting more animated now — 'It is in a stunning location, easily accessible by road and air from abroad and there is so much to do around it that we can't even fit the activities into two weeks,' she laughs, remembering our conversation this morning. 'It is also big and in an established tourist area, an area of outstanding natural beauty, it would make such a wonderful hotel, a luxury, traditional, Italian manor house set in the heart of the Tuscan countryside, less than an hour from Florence. It has a pool and a guest house. It's perfect!' Her voice is getting faster and louder as she gets caught up in her own excitement. 'Oh, just think about it, babe, the only other places to stay locally are small B&Bs and guesthouses, my parents have to stay over half an hour away from me when they come for the weekend just to get something that suits their taste. The grounds are so amazing, it would be perfect for weddings, and I could do cookery weekends. The possibilities are endless!'

I have to admit that it all sounds wonderful, so wonderful that I am actually getting drawn in by the idea and by Jen's enthusiasm for it. 'It would make an exceptional hotel,' I agree. 'It's totally the perfect place and cookery weekends are such a brilliant idea! Does that mean that you would stay in Tuscany?' I ask Jen, as if I have just decided to go ahead and buy the house, which of course I haven't.

'Well, actually, I was going to talk to you about that.' Jen looks a bit unsure of herself all of a sudden.

'About what?' I ask.

'About the fact that I am thinking of staying,' she explains. 'I've fallen in love with it here and I've been thinking about trying to find work for a while once I finish school. In one of the restaurants or cafés, to get some experience. Then maybe after a while I can set up something on my own. I really think I've found my niche.' She looks at me waiting for a reaction.

I'm surprised. 'I wasn't expecting that,' I say honestly. 'Why can't you get experience in London?'

'I can, but I'm not sure that I want to. Don't get me wrong, I miss you and Fi desperately, but everything just feels so right here. I love the Italian way of life, the Italian cooking, and the weather. I am picking up the language. And now I have Jake too,' she smiles as she says his name. 'Well, maybe anyway!'

'I had no idea you feel this way, Jen. If it is what you want then I am so happy for you! It's great! I've missed you so much though, it will be unbearable having to go back and knowing that you won't be coming home in a few weeks!'

'But that's just it!' Jen grabs my hand over the table. 'You don't have to go! I'm serious, Soph; this house could be an incredible investment, a great business, a great adventure! And we could go on it together!'

'You mean, buy the house together?'

'Why not?' Jen is almost out of her chair now. 'I know it's your dream, but we could work on it together, you could run the hotel, the business side of things and I could run the kitchen. I know I still have a lot to learn but with the right help and training I could do it, I know I could!' She tightens her grip on my hand. 'I really think we could do this.' She is so earnest it is hard not to take her seriously. 'Will you at least think about it?' she asks, full of hope.

I am having trouble processing all this. Other people do things like this. Other people take risks and follow their dreams and live amazing lives. Other people find ways to work out the impossible. But can I? 'I will,' I nod and squeeze Jen's hand back before I can talk myself out of it again. 'I promise I will think about it.' After all, what harm could thinking about it do?

Over another half a bottle of wine (for me), tiramisu and strong coffee which stretches out for a good couple of hours, we talk at length and uninhibitedly about our dreams, what we could do, what we might do, what we want to do. As I relax and allow myself to dream it feels like the possibilities are endless and, maybe actually possible. We are the last to leave the restaurant. We link arms as we walk out and go back over to look in the window of the auction house again before making our way back to the car. My eyes linger on the 950,000 euro guide price but I put it to the back of my mind. I can think about that in the morning when I am armed with paper, pen and a large dose of reality. It's a fair way but we reach the car in no time, caught up in ourselves and our conversation. By the time we get back to the cottage I am exhausted by the wine, the food, the excitement and the journey. It's late and Jen has her exam in the morning so I wish her luck and we head straight to bed, vowing to talk about it all again the next day.

Chapter 13

By the time I get up the next day Jen is already long gone. I am groggy and still overwhelmed by the events of last night. In the harsh light of day the excitement has subsided and reality has set in again. Even with Jen's input, the likelihood of me being able to finance a share in the house, in the business, is pretty limited. Plus, we have no idea who or what we are up against. We haven't even seen inside of the house, it might be a complete wreck! There is so much whirring through my mind that I decide to go for a walk into the village and have breakfast at the café. I need some fresh air and to fill my stomach before I can think properly. I pull on a pink sun dress and my dark glasses to hide the bags under my eyes, the result of a restless night, then on the way out of the door I pick up Jen's pad and a pen from the table so that I can work through some numbers if I feel up to it once I have eaten.

The village is quiet and the café is empty except for one man sitting in the corner with his back to me. Across the square I can see Katarina standing in the doorway of the patisserie helping an elderly lady with her bags. I wave at her and she beckons me over.

'Hi! How are you?' she asks.

'I'm good, thanks.' — I hope I sound more energetic than I feel — 'I just came in to get some breakfast. Would you like to join me?' Some company might be a good thing, buy me some time before I have to start thinking seriously about things.

'I must work' — she looks disappointed — 'but I have a morning off tomorrow, I think maybe you like to see another gallery?' she sounds hopeful.

'I would love to' I say honestly. 'But I have plans to go shopping tomorrow. You're welcome to join us, though I think we'll be gone most of the day.'

Katarina looks disappointed again and tells me that her mother won't allow her to have another whole day off so soon.

'Well, perhaps we can have lunch or breakfast later in the week?' I suggest to placate her and it seems to work. 'I'll pop in after breakfast for a few bits.'

'OK, enjoy!'

Katarina turns back through the door of the patisserie but before it closes she leans back outside and lowers her voice, 'There is very handsome man in café, he come in here earlier and he is very dreamy!' She mock swoons and I laugh at her as I set off back across the square. I take a small table in the corner and put my pad and pen on it. Paulo comes out and looks happy to see me, he smiles widely and thanks me again for the dinner party before insisting on getting me breakfast 'on the home!'

'I think you mean, *on the house*,' I smile at him fondly. 'That's so kind of you. Thank you!'

He blushes at his mistake but smiles too and takes my order of poached eggs on toast and a milky coffee. Once he is back inside I pick up my pen and start to doodle on my pad. The clink of a cup on a saucer reminds me of the man sitting at the corner table, now facing in my direction, and I look up to see if he is as handsome as Katarina has made out. As I do, I meet his gaze directly. He must have been looking right at me. He is startlingly handsome but also uncomfortably familiar. It takes me a few moments to realise that he is the man I saw outside the Russo house a couple of days ago. He is staring at me with cold, beautiful eyes. I smile at him nervously. I don't want to hold his gaze but I can't look away either. His mouth doesn't move at all, it's like he is looking straight through me but, at the same time, I can't help but feel that his coldness is directed right at me.

I drop my eyes to the table and doodle again to distract myself. My face is burning. I can feel my cheeks getting redder by the second. Damn cheeks. Damn him. Why does he make me feel so small? And how can he possibly hate me so much? He doesn't even know me! At worst he might think I am bit strange for hanging around outside old houses with a wheelie case but surely that doesn't warrant such contempt. I keep my eyes down and wonder what on earth I could have done to upset him so much and why he has to be so ridiculously gorgeous when he is clearly such a horrible man. It isn't fair to bless such good looks on someone who doesn't have the good grace to carry them off.

After what feels like an age but is probably less than five minutes, Paulo comes out with my eggs on toast and some bacon on the side. 'The English, they love the bacon!' he winks as he puts it down in front of me. I am hungry and grateful for the good food but I just feel so self conscious now. I don't like eating in front of people at the best of times, let alone when they are extremely handsome, very horrible and staring at me. I am sure I can still feel him watching me but I'm too scared to look back up in his direction. Those eyes would probably burn me if I met them again. I look resolutely down and eat as delicately as I can. I am just finishing my plate when I hear a chair scrape. I look up. The man picks up a smart, tan case and walks away from the café, around the corner, out of sight. As I watch him go it dawns on me that the reason he was at the house the other day is probably because he is thinking of buying it at the auction. He must have been looking around it before the sale. Perhaps the lady with the folder is an estate agent or maybe she works at the auction house. Perhaps he thinks I am a competitor bidder, maybe that's why he hates me so much? Definitely an overreaction if that is the case! Maybe I am a competitor bidder! I look at my pad again. It is covered in 3d squares, stars and flowers. I pull the first page off and write 'Money' on the top of the next page and underline it twice. I do have some money, I saved every month of the four years that I worked at Morgan Stanley and, for the last ten years of my life, my parents have put money into premium bonds for me on my birthday and at Christmas. Plus I have my car and flat. My parents encouraged me to buy as soon as possible once I started earning and I managed to get on the property ladder before the market went crazy. I looked into selling when Lucy told me that she was moving out and I couldn't believe it when I got the agents' valuation. Thanks to a massive surge in London property prices, I've made over £100,000 in the last five or six years, without doing a thing! Plus I still have the small amount I originally put down as a deposit (which my parents so generously helped me with) and I've been paying the mortgage off for a few years now, so I definitely have a reasonable amount of equity in my flat. Still, it can't be enough for me to be a viable partner in the house. And even if by some crazy chance it is enough, can I really risk it all on a dream? I write everything down:

Money
Savings: £15,000
Car: £4,000 (ish... needs a good clean!)
Premium bonds from parents: £10,000
Flat: Maybe £150,000 left over if sold for full whack (also needs a good clean!)
Contents of flat: About £3,000 max if everything decent is sold and Andrew doesn't ask for his half of the TV and DVD back!
Giant plastic Coke bottle: About £400
Current account: About £600

Total: £183,000

One hundred and eighty-three thousand pounds. It is strange seeing my entire financial worth in black and white. I am not sure if I am pleased that I have that much money to my name or if it makes me feel quite inferior. My whole life to date adds up to less than £200,000, without a house or a car!

Regardless, at least it makes one thing very clear: I can't afford to buy the Russo house! Even if Jen does invest with me, I am still over £300,000 short of my half of the asking price and I haven't even thought about the thousands of pounds that we would need for work on the house once it is bought. I can't imagine the prospect of me getting a mortgage for that amount of money is great. Especially given my payslips from Stationery Is Us don't exactly make exciting reading material and I doubt I'll even be getting those for very much longer. I've known it all along really. I don't think I ever really believed that the house would be mine or that my life would really take such an amazing turn. It had been nice to let myself dream for a while, but now I wish I hadn't. The disappointment is more bitter than I had expected it to be and suddenly the reality of not owning the house, of that future not existing for me, is too painful to think about. I turn my pad over and think about what is left for me back at home. My flat, Fi, and my other friends and family, I smile at the thought of them. Andrew and Stationery Is Us, both things that I know can't stay in my life but I have no replacement for. And that is it. I will go home in a few days' time after a truly wonderful holiday. I will finish things with Andrew, get a new flatmate and then I will hand my notice in and force myself to find a new job. Perhaps I will try and get myself a high-earning position again, at least that way I can put aside more money and maybe one day, next time, the dream won't pass me by. Two years from the biggest decision of my life and I have come full circle. Back to where I began.

Resigned to my fate, I am heavier in the heart than when I had arrived in Tuscany but at least I know what I am going to do when I get home. I pick up my bits and head back to the patisserie where I buy a large cream pastry to soak up my sorrows on the way home, and some fresh bread for breakfast the following morning. I agree to meet Katarina for lunch in the village before I go home and tell her that I want to hear all of the news about her and Paulo, at which she blushes and promises to tell me everything.

For the first time, I don't walk home past the Russo house. I can't bring myself to look at it today, not now that I know I will probably never see it again. It might only ever have been a dream but it is still a dream crushed. And crushing it is. I mull on my thoughts as I walk back to the cottage and I start to think about my cousin's wedding last summer. I'm not sure how I end up thinking about it, my train of thought has disappeared behind me, but it ends up at their wedding ceremony in the small church in my aunt and uncle's village in the Cotswolds. They had Corinthians 13:13 as their bible reading, my aunt stood at the front of the church and in her very best voice she told us all that:

'Three things will last forever — faith, hope, and love — and the greatest of these is love.'

How close hope and dreams are, I think. Surely dreams are just a manifestation of hope. So perhaps hope doesn't last forever. I breathe the sweet, warm air deeply into my lungs and close my eyes, lingering in my moment of sadness. When I open them again I see the incredible beauty all around me. My thoughts have blinded me to my sight for the past few minutes and I am amazed again at my beautiful surroundings. They are still as beautiful to me as the day that I arrived.

'For God's sake, Sophie,' I chastise myself out loud, 'Get a grip, here you are in the most perfect place for just a few more days and you are wasting time on a dream that never was. And a pretty short-lived one at that.'

I rally myself and force a smile. Perhaps dreams just change and so hope takes a new direction. I just need a new dream. I feel pretty exhausted by the time I get back to the cottage. I put the pad and pen back on the table as I walk in the front door, take the bread to the kitchen and go outside into the garden with the cream pastry that I have been too distracted to eat on the way home. I am just biting into it when Jen walks into the garden.

'Hi!' she has a huge smile on her face. 'Caught you in the act!' she laughs as cream oozes from the end of the flaky pastry parcel and drops into my lap.

'You have!' I speak with my mouth full, 'I'm glad that you have! It is so good I would eat the whole thing myself if you weren't here!' I laugh and hand her the pastry. 'Try it,' I urge. 'It's delicious!'

'Oh, go on then.' She takes a huge bite and gets cream all over her chin as it spurts out of the end. 'It can be my reward for producing a masterpiece meal this morning.' She wipes her chin and licks the cream off her finger.

'It went well then?' I take the pastry back. 'I knew it would of course!'

'Brilliantly,' she confirms. 'Cooked to perfection according to my teacher. And now I have the rest of the week to spend with you. Good times!' she reaches to take the last bite of cream cake from me. 'Plus, Jake came to meet me from the exam, as a surprise. He said he just wanted to see how it went and to see me!' she is barely able to keep the joy out of her voice.

'He luuurves you!' I sing jokily, just like I had when we were children, and we laugh at the memory.

'What did you do this morning?' Jen asks as she goes inside to make herself some lunch.

'*I had breakfast at the café,*' I shout after her. 'And popped in to see Katarina — there is fresh bread inside!' I follow her in. 'I saw that man again at the café.' I wince at the memory.

'What man?'

'You know, the gorgeous, horrible one from the Russo house.'

'Oh! That man!' she uses exaggerated tones. 'Did you speak to him, find anything out about him?'

'No, but I can confirm that he is indeed gorgeous and indeed very horrible. I have no idea what I have done to upset him but I must have done something. He was shooting daggers at me across the café, yet Katarina was waxing lyrical about him, said he was nice as pie to her in the shop, so it must be something about me that he doesn't like.'

'Well, I say forget him!' Jen is indignant on my behalf. 'You are probably imagining it anyway, what possible reason could he have to dislike you? And if you are right and he doesn't like you, then he's an idiot! But talking of the Russo house', she changes tack, 'Once I've eaten why don't we sit down and work out some numbers. We should go to the auction house too and

111

get the details, ask them to show us around the house. We need to know exactly what we are taking on and how much work is involved'. I try to cut in before she goes too much further. I open my mouth but the words just don't come out. 'I'll call my parents this afternoon too,' she goes on. 'Get some advice and talk it through with them. I mean, this is a pretty big deal really. Well, huge actually! I have thought about it almost non-stop since we talked last night and I really think we can do this. It's the perfect solution for me and wouldn't it be great, me and you working together?' She looks up from her sandwich finally and she can tell that there is something wrong. 'What is it?' she asks. 'You haven't changed your mind, have you? You were so sure about it last night.'

'I know I was.' I hate disappointing her like this. 'I do think it would be perfect for us. For me. For everything! Perfect. But that's what I did at the café this morning: I worked out my finances. And they don't look good, Jen. Even if we went 50:50 I'm not even close to being able to afford it.' I pick up the pad from the other end of the table and put it down next to her. 'See?' I let the numbers do the talking. Jen looks at the paper.

'This doesn't look too bad! You've more money than I have!' She laughs. 'If I could match this figure we would have more than enough to put down a decent deposit. I'm sure we could get a mortgage with the right business plan in place.'

'I don't want to be the bearer of bad news,' though I knew I was about to be, 'But I don't think that any bank is going to lend us nigh on a million euros when we don't even have any experience!'

'Don't be so defeatist!' Jen jumps up. 'With a great business plan I think we could get the money. I'm sure my parents will act as guarantors if they know we are serious. We would have to prove it to them though, and to the bank.' She pauses. I think she is waiting for a response but I don't know what to say. She looks at me intently. 'I think this might be one of those all or nothing moments, Soph. Every bone in my body tells me this is right. I think we should give it our all, what do you think?'

Things are changing so fast, I have just started to get my head around saying goodbye to the dream and here Jen is putting it right back on the table in front of me. I sit down slowly and take the pad back off her; I look really hard, straight through the numbers, as my head whirs with the confusion. Can I really do it? Give up everything? My beloved flat, my home, my life in London? Risk it all on a dream? I put the pad down and look at my best friend sitting opposite me, willing me to go with her. I had done it once before, given up everything and I had been waiting for this ever since. What choice did I have?

Chapter 14

With no time to lose, we start work straight away. Jen phones the auction house and arranges a viewing of the Russo house the following day at ten a.m. The auction is to be held in exactly one week and one day. There is so much to do in that time I am not sure that it is even possible. Ever the 'can do' girl, Jen rolls up her sleeves, picks up her trusty pad and writes in big black letters at the top of the first clear page: '**TO DO LIST**'.

She reads out the things that I need to get started on as she writes.

'First things first, you need to cancel your flight home and speak to your boss. And you should probably speak to Andrew too.' She sounds apologetic.

'So far this list isn't looking great for me! Can't I do something else?'

'Well, you can start putting the business plan together, we are going to need the very best of your Morgan Stanley training on that one.' She nods authoritatively at me

'That sounds better, that I can definitely do.'

'Unfortunately,' her apologetic face is back, 'You can't really do that until tomorrow when we have seen the house, know what work we need to do and can start doing some basic costing. So I'm afraid that you still have to cancel your flight, call your boss and call Andrew first.'

'Well, I can make a start on the business case at least, set out the template, and work out our finances in more detail.'

'Good idea!' Jen agrees. 'Make those three calls first and then you can crack on with it.' She is relentless. 'I'll start doing some research on the going rates for other hotels and B&Bs locally as well as cookery courses and wedding packages etc. help us to work out if and how we might actually make some money out of the place, put the business into the business plan!' She jumps up and switches her laptop on then hands me the phone. 'Like a plaster,' she smiles. 'Just rip it off!'

I can sort my flight out later so I call my boss first, probably the easier of the two calls I have to make. He is predictably unexcited about speaking to me and lets me know in no uncertain terms that he is not able to authorise any additional leave for me and that he expects me back at work on Monday morning. 'Given that we are presently sifting for the post I think that is the most expedient option for you,' he says pointedly.

'That's fine,' I respond calmly.

'See you on Monday then.' He is terse in his reply.

'No.' I am outwardly calm but raging inside. How dare he threaten me with my job. And why on earth have I wasted so much time and effort working for this thankless man? 'I mean fine, I won't come back at all. Good luck with the sift. Please accept this as my formal resignation.' I put the phone down, leaving him still spluttering at the other end of the line. 'Now that feels good,' I grin at Jen triumphantly.

'See. I told you! Good on you! It's only taken you two years to do the right thing,' she laughs.

'I don't think the next call is going to feel so good.' I look pleadingly at her.

'Well, you have two options. You can either tell him the truth or you can just buy yourself some time. It's up to you but I know what I would do.' What Jen would do and what I would do are usually two very different things. The truth is I just don't have any idea what to say. I'm not sure that I am ready to tell Andrew everything that is going on, it is all still so uncertain. What would I say? 'Hi Andrew, I've decided to buy a huge, derelict house in Tuscany, move here, live in it and try and turn it into a successful hotel, even though I have zero experience and very little money. I'm selling my flat and everything in it and probably won't ever see you again. Hope you don't mind!'

No. The truth just isn't going to work. Biding my time it is! 'Here goes.'

I dial Andrew's number and he answers before I hear a second ring. It doesn't help that he is clearly so excited to hear from me but bless him, as expected, he is super happy for me when I tell him I am having a lovely time and really want to stay a little longer.

'I'll miss you dreadfully of course, darling.' He is so sweet to me. 'What are you going to do for another week, anything fun planned?'

'Oh, you know,' — I cross my fingers behind my back — 'Just check out the area, get to know it a bit better, it will be lovely just to spend some more time here with Jen. It's so beautiful. Jen is even thinking of staying on once her course is finished,' I tell him. At least I have managed to avoid telling him an actual lie, even if I haven't quite told him the truth. After a drawn out, lovey-dovey (on his end) goodbye, I put the phone down and breathe a sigh of relief.

'You're going to have to tell him at some point you know, even if we don't get the house!'

Jen is right. 'I know, I know, but I can't think about it this week. I need to focus on getting everything done we need to do. When we have an outcome I can talk to him properly and fairly.' I am so relieved just to have bought myself a little time.

'What about your parents?' Jen reminds me that I haven't even spoken to them since I have been here.

'Oh, blimey! I didn't think of them! This has all happened so quickly!' I feel the panic rising again.

'Don't worry,' Jen soothes, recognising my reaction. 'Let's just see how this week goes, see the house and work everything out before we tell people anything that we don't have to. No point worrying people until we actually know what is going to happen.' By people she means my parents. She knows them well and knows as well as I do that they won't see this opportunity in quite the same exciting light that we do.

'Good idea.' I am truly grateful that I can put that phone call on hold. 'Now let's get to work!'

We work all afternoon, me setting out the business plan template, filling in the details where I can and working out what else we need to know to fill in the rest. Jen gets started on some research; she speaks to as many hotels, B&Bs and guesthouses as she can. She finds out room rates, food and drinks prices. She compares the properties' styles, sizes and facilities, looks online at wedding packages and other special packages or services that are offered. Every few minutes she pipes up with a new idea.

'What about wine tasting weekends?'

'Great! You would have to make sure you leave enough for the guests though!' I laugh and she throws a pen at me.

'How about yoga or meditation breaks?' she offers as she peruses the website of a health spa in Assisi.

'Sounds good!' I indulge her. All ideas are good ideas at the moment and we can work out what we are actually able to do once we have seen the house. It is hard not to be taken in by her excitement though. I envy her her evergreen optimism. 'Try and find out how booked up some of these places get, what their capacity is at different times of the year and also look up food and drink suppliers, try and get some costs,' I rattle things off as I think of them. The more we do, the more we realise how much we have to do.

'Why don't we phone Fi?' Jen suggests several hours of research later. 'Find out how much the glossy travel magazines in her publishing house charge for advertising.'

'Yes! Good idea,' I agree.

And so the list goes on. We work long into the night, stopping only to open a bottle of wine and to eat some pasta that Jen rustles up with homemade pesto and parmesan. I am excited, overwhelmed and exhausted. At two a.m. we finally go to bed to catch a couple of hours' sleep before we set to work again in the morning and before we finally get to go and see inside the Russo house. God willing, it might even soon be our house.

Chapter 15

By nine thirty a.m. we are already waiting outside the Russo house, eager to get inside and look around. With half an hour to kill before the representative from the auction house turns up, we walk around the side and explore the back again. It is still as enigmatic and entrancing as it had been the first time we saw it. We are just exploring the pool area again when we hear a car pull up and stop in front of the house. We exchange an excited glance; both of us fit to burst.

'This is it!' I grab Jen's hand and after a deep, calming breath we walk as professionally and confidently as we can back around to the front of the house. A slim lady with curly, dark blonde hair gets out of the car with a folder in her hand. As she turns to face us my stomach plummets. 'Oh no,' I groan quietly.

'What is it?' Jen whispers, looking worried.

'It's her! The lady I saw outside the house with the handsome man. She must have been showing him around.'

'Oh, don't worry about that now. She probably won't even remember you! Come on, just be confident. It's fine.' She pushes me gently forward. I can feel my face burning as I walk with as much poise as I can muster and put out my hand.

'Hi. I'm Sophie,' I offer. 'Nice to meet you.'

The lady smiles and shakes my hand 'Gina. Nice to meet you too.' Her handshake is firm but she lets go quickly and after a quick introduction to Jen she takes a large bunch of keys from her jacket pocket and walks us up the front drive, past the giant fountain to the grand front door. She doesn't say anything and I know that Jen will just think that I am being paranoid, but I'm sure that she recognises me. I'm sure I saw a little smirk on her face as she introduced herself. Before she unlocks the door she opens the pink folder that has been wedged under her arm and takes out several sheets of paper that include the house details, auction rules and regulations. She hands them to us and then puts the key in the giant, steel lock on the great, oak, double front door.

'Follow me, ladies.' Gina turns the lock and pushes one side of the giant door open. 'This is the entrance hall and lobby. Beautiful isn't it?'

And it is. The house is as beautiful on the inside as it is on the outside. The entrance hall is wide and airy with incredible large dome shaped windows to each side, which the bright sunshine streams through, picking out thousands of dust particles that float around us and glisten as they hang in the air. Around the windows the walls are the same large stonework as is on the outside of the house and they match the floor.

'The floor is made from original flagstones imported from Rome,' Gina tells us in her thick but corporate accent. 'And the ceiling is hand carved from oak beams'.

Jen and I look above us and see the most stunningly intricate carved beams criss-crossing above our heads along the entire entrance hall. I gasp at the beauty of the workmanship. The house just gets better from there on in. Beyond the entrance hall is a very formal, large room to the right. It is empty inside but for an outstanding fireplace made of green marble and wrought iron that dominates the far wall. The rest of the walls are covered in thick, light but rich green wallpaper with a raised paisley style print that is in incredible condition considering the age of the house and is framed by wide, ornate cornicing.

To the left of the entrance hall is an oak panelled library with shelves on all walls but one, which is covered in a rich red and gold paper. There is a ladder attached to the shelves on the left hand wall and chandelier hanging from the centre of another ornate plaster ceiling. Most of the shelves are empty but a few books remain on the far wall. I walk across the room to look at them more closely. The titles are written in Italian so I can't work out what they are, but they look old and well read. I run my hand along one of the shelves; it is dusty and marks my fingers. I am desperate to give the place a good clean.

In front of the library and the formal room with the fireplace, is a large dining room which spreads to both sides of the entrance hall and across the width of the entire house. At each end of the room there are large French doors (or the Italian equivalent perhaps!) that reach from floor to ceiling and fill the room with light right through to the middle. Through the doors on the left hand side I can see the patio with the trellising and lanterns and through the doors on the right views of the rolling Tuscan countryside beyond the trellised walkways and statues that surround the swimming pool. It is a grand and imposing room but somehow despite the grandeur and its emptiness it is still warm and inviting. Beyond the dining room is by far the most beautiful room in the house. We walk through double doors set in the middle of the back wall into a second room that runs alongside the dining room and is exactly the same in size and shape but is decorated with expensive looking primrose yellow wallpaper on the wall that meets the dining room but is almost entirely glass windows across the other three walls. The incredible grounds and the vista beyond is visible from all sides. Huge domed windows, larger versions of the ones in the front hall, stand beside more floor to ceiling glass, oak framed doors that open out onto what would once have been manicured lawns around the swimming pool. The windows and doors are all framed by incredible draping in primrose yellow taffeta and a cool, blue silk with scalloped and beaded edging. They are elegant and exquisite to the eye and I am pretty sure that once the dirt and dust has gone they would be in excellent condition too.

To the side of the dining room and the morning room, almost separate from the rest of the house, is a large, open plan kitchen with a huge, wooden block workspace in the middle of the room and an old fashioned wood burning stove on the far wall. Lines of copper pots and pans still hang along the length of the ceiling and below them the shelves are still full of glasses in every shape and size imaginable.

Jen gasps as we enter the kitchen. She walks quickly from corner to corner, end to end, taking in every inch of it. She lifts her hand and lets it run along the bottom of the copper pans, making them swing above her head.

'Soph, this is incredible. The space is amazing. I could do so much in here.' She comes over to me and grasps my hands in hers. 'It's incredible, isn't it? The whole place, it's just perfect'.

'It's perfect!' I agree, thrilled that Jen loves it as much as I do. 'Perfect in every way.' At each end of the entrance hall, in front of the library and formal room and before the dining room, two sweeping staircases of black and white marble curl up the sides of the house flanked by heavy wooden balustrades. At the top of the stairs there is a large master bedroom at the back of the house with a bathroom, dressing room and a huge balcony beyond another set of French doors. There are two further bedrooms, smaller but both with sweet balconies that open out to the back of house. On the other side of the corridor, facing out over the main driveway, there are five further bedrooms, all a good size and all beautifully decorated, albeit a little dated and dusty. There is also a large, second bathroom that looks like something out of a period drama. It has a huge, free-standing, roll-top bath with gold taps and yet more beautiful windows overlooking the grounds.

We walk around the whole house once and then again, taking it all in. Gina shows us a vast wine cellar underneath the house which, sadly, is empty of wine but would make amazing storage for food and drink as well as linens and all the other things that we would need to run a hotel. In general the whole place is in great condition. It could definitely do with modernising in parts, but I love the authenticity of the original features and furnishings. The strong Italian sun has faded many of the silks and some of the walls. It is easy to see from the large dark patches left where pictures must have once hung. The whole place is in desperate need of a good clean but otherwise the house is immaculate. Gina shows us around the grounds again and inside the small but sweet and well-proportioned cottage at the edge of the estate. Once we have seen everything we sit at one of the tables on the large terrace outside the morning room and Gina talks us through the details from the auction house, the necessary information for the auction itself and gives us a chance to ask some questions. Jen and I are so taken in by what we have seen and so eager to get started on planning for the auction that we can barely think of a question between us so Gina leaves us her card and tells us to ring if there is anything else that we want to know.

Once she has left we walk back to the village to have lunch with Katarina as I have promised. She is happy and chats away about the date that she has with Paulo that evening, what she is going to wear and how she is going to do her hair. We join in with her excitement and try to match her enthusiasm but we are desperate to get away and to talk about the house. We eat quickly and make our excuses. Luckily Katarina has to get back to work in the patisserie so we both give her a hug and wish her lots of luck for her date which she promises to tell us all about.

'Oh God, I hope she doesn't think we were rude, I don't want her to think we aren't interested in her and Paulo,' I say to Jen as we walk home.

'Oh, I wouldn't worry, she is so caught up in her date and her own excitement I doubt she would have realised if one of us had actually got up and left!' Jen laughs. 'I'm happy for her though, they are so sweet together. Did you see how she blushed when he served our food?'

'I know, too cute.' I have grown really fond of Katarina and I am thrilled that Paulo has finally asked her out but I can't concentrate on anything but the Russo house and the task ahead. Now that I have seen it I am even more in love with it. I just can't imagine it not being ours.

The auction is in seven days and there is so much to do we literally don't have a minute to waste.

'Seven days is not long.' I am thinking out loud but Jen is clearly thinking the same thing.

'I know,' she looks serious. 'There is so much to do.'

'Have you still got the "to do" list?' I ask her.

Jen pulls it from her bag, unfolds it and reads aloud, 'First things first, we need to get some quotes for the work on the house. I scribbled a few things as we went round, I think the main things are the modernising of the kitchen; adding en-suites to the four bedrooms without them, if you think we should, perhaps changing the main bathroom into another bedroom if we do; furnishing and decorating where we need to; then obviously all of the outside work: the lawns, pool, fountains etc. I mean, they are all filthy.'

126

I nod to each item as she talks through them: 'We are lucky really, according to the auction survey it is structurally sound and as it is a protected property we can't really do any major building work or reconstruction anyway. It's in great condition, just a little unloved.' I pull a sad face and Jen smiles at me.

'Well, we can definitely fix that! Sara's father runs a building company in Florence, I can ask him to recommend people to give us some rough quotes for the work once we've decided exactly what needs doing.'

'Great!' I'm relieved that we have somewhere to start. 'Once we have some ball park prices we'll just need to work out how to pay for it all!' I laugh nervously at the thought. 'The auction guide says payment is due within six weeks of the sale, that doesn't give us long.'

'It doesn't,' Jen agrees, 'But hopefully we can get a bank to agree to a loan in principle based on the calculations in the business plan and then if we get the house we'll have to put everything in to selling our own properties as soon as possible. It shouldn't be too difficult; they're both in great areas.'

'I hope so! We'd better get an appointment at the bank as soon as possible.'

As I speak the words I realise that this is going to be difficult. 'Jen, neither of us can speak or read Italian well enough to deal with the Italian banks, we don't even have Italian back accounts. I don't think we'll be able to secure a loan whilst we're over here.' Jen doesn't seem fazed. 'Yes, I thought of that, I think that we should go back to London, just for a day or two and try and secure everything with my bank manager. Then we can get our places valued too and you can even speak to Andrew, if you can face it.' I frown at the thought but it does make sense. 'And,' she goes on, 'I thought I would speak to my parents, see if they will act as guarantors on the loan. Then worst case, if my bank won't buy into the business plan, perhaps we can go to the family bank?' I know that Jen doesn't really want to have to do this and I'm touched that she is even considering it.

'That's a good idea,' I agree with her, 'but we should send your parents the business plan too, so they can see how serious we are.' Jen seems happy with this.

'Let's get to work straight away, then I'll call them when we have a draft that I can fax over to them from the village. They're in France at the moment at the summer house but Dad has an office there I can send it to.'

'That's settled then.'

As we walk the last few hundred metres up the road we divide up the rest of the jobs on the list. As I am in charge of writing the business plan and so have to wait for the building and decorating quotes, I am given the job of arranging flights home and meetings with the bank. I decide to call Andrew too and tell him that I will be coming back a little early and want to see him. I won't tell him I'll be leaving again after a day or two. I will deal with that when I have to.

We work late into the night again and all through the following day. Through the wonder of the World Wide Web we send enquiries and get rough estimates for much of the work that we think we will need to do. We price up furniture and kitchen equipment, swimming pool cleaning, filling and maintenance and send quote requests for building work and landscaping. Sara's dad pulls in some favours for us and manages communications with builders, plumbers and electricians who speak very little English and who are probably reluctant to quote for such big jobs without actually seeing what is involved.

Before we know it, four days has passed and we have barely left the cottage except for food and drink supplies. My arms and fingers ache from the writing and typing and we are exhausted from the emails, phone calls and research. Jen has told Jake our plans and he has stepped in, delivering fresh pasta and pizzas for us in the evenings with some much needed wine and coffee. Last night he even cooked for us at the cottage and for the first time since we have started work, I had an early night and left him and Jen to enjoy some alone time together downstairs. I could hear them laughing together as I drifted off to sleep, exhausted from the days exertions. I don't know if he stayed late and arrived again early in the morning or if he stayed all night but I am guessing from the smile on Jen's face and the spring in her step that it is the latter.

By the end of the following day I have finished the business plan. It is very rough around the edges with regards to the numbers but I have no other choice. We have done everything that we can and I am actually really proud of it. It has been nice to really apply myself to something again. I haven't worked so hard on anything or tested my brain so much since I left Morgan Stanley and it feels good. It feels especially good because I am doing it for something that I really believe in. Something I am passionate about. Now it is in the hands of the bank manager.

We are due to fly home in the morning so Jen calls her parents whilst I go into the village to fax them a copy of the business plan and pick up some food from the café for the three of us for dinner.

'How did it go with your parents?' I ask her as I walk in the door, with a bottle of wine and two of Paulo's pizzas. Jake takes them from me and sets them out on the table with a salad that he has made.

'Really well,' she takes the wine and opens it. 'They were a little taken a back at first, I'm pretty sure that they thought I was joking to begin with, but when I explained everything to them and read out some of the numbers they could tell we are serious. Dad asked a lot of questions and I think he is quite impressed with how much we've done. He has agreed to be a guarantor if we need him to be.'

'That's amazing.' I give her a big hug and for the first time I really believe that this can happen for us. With guarantors like Jen's parents on our side, the bank is bound to lend us the money. We clink glasses in celebration and sit down to a well deserved meal before an early night, for me at least, in preparation for the early flight.

Chapter 16

If Jake stayed again he is gone by the time I get up in the morning. We leave early for the airport, excited but nervous. I am keen to do what we have to do and get back again as soon as possible. Our flight back to Italy is at eleven a.m. on Friday morning and the auction is seven p.m. in Italy. We should have plenty of time but I know I won't be able to relax until we are in the auction house and have won that bid! Our appointment with Jen's bank is at midday tomorrow so we have the whole day ahead of us to ourselves. This is lovely for Jen, she is going to catch up with Fi for lunch, sort out her flat a little and get a valuation from the estate agent to help make the business plan as accurate as possible. I need to do this too but there are two other things weighing much heavier on my mind, my parents and Andrew.

At the airport we have cappuccinos and cheese and ham toasties from the coffee shop whilst we wait for our flight to be called and I grab a mascara from the Lancôme counter in duty free. Mine is running pretty low and I can justify it because airport money isn't real money. I know that I should be putting everything aside for the house but mascara is one thing that this girl definitely can't live without! It's pretty much a shopping essential, especially with the lack of sleep I have had this week! Then again, I think as the pretty young girl at the till scans the mascara and asks to see my boarding pass, perhaps if I am make-up free when I see Andrew later he might be pleased when I break up with him and make it a bit easier on me!

The flight is quick and uneventful and we both grab a couple of hours much needed sleep. We don't have luggage to collect so we walk straight through into the arrivals hall where Andrew is waiting with flowers.

'There he is.' Jen's voice is full of pity for him. 'Be gentle, he looks so happy to see you'.

'I know,' I grimace. 'I wish he hadn't insisted on picking us up, this is not going to be fun. I can't believe he's brought flowers'.

Jen rubs my arm quickly before we reach the end of the barrier and steps ahead of me to give Andrew a quick hug.

'Great to see you, Andrew, thanks so much for picking us up'.

'Of course, it's good to see you too, Jen, and I have missed my little Soph so much, I couldn't possibly wait any longer to see her!'

Jen smiles at him and I know that he doesn't pick up on her apologetic look. He turns and gives me a hug.

'How's my girl?' He lifts me off the ground as much as he can when hindered by a huge bunch of roses.

'I'm good.' I wriggle out of his hold. 'Thanks for coming!' I try to sound cheerful but I know I am failing miserably.

'Don't be silly! Darling, you look so tired, did the flight take it out of you?'

'Must have done,' I say feebly. 'Shall we go?'

'Sure.'

He picks up my bag and leads the way to the car. The journey home is awkward. Andrew asks a hundred questions about what we have been up to over the last two weeks and Jen and I answer them clumsily. Not wanting to lie but not telling the truth either.

We drop Jen at her flat and the moment I have been dreading arrives all too soon, Andrew and me alone in the car. As we wave goodbye to Jen he lowers his hand and puts it on my knee.

'I'm so pleased to have you back. It feels like you have been gone for so long!'

His voice is so warm and tender. I know I can't keep the facade up much longer. He is still speaking but I have zoned out, whatever he is saying and I cut him off mid sentence.

'Andrew, we need to talk.' I say it more firmly than I intend to and feel bad already.

'That sounds ominous!' he laughs nervously. 'Is everything OK?' We have just pulled up outside my flat. I take off my seat belt and turn to face him.

'The thing is, something has happened in Tuscany, something potentially amazing but I'm not sure what it means for us'.

This is a bit cowardly, I know it is. I know I should just break up with him here and now for no other reason than because I don't love him and I don't want to be with him. But this way feels so much kinder, and easier. I tell him all about the house and how I have fallen in love with it. How I think that, finally, I have found what I want to do with my life but that it means living and working in Italy. Andrew is clearly shocked. He sits back in his seat and looks straight ahead, over the steering wheel, he breathes deeply. For a while I think he might cry and I hope desperately that he doesn't.

'I'm not sure what to say,' he manages eventually. 'I'm happy for you, darling, of course I am.' He turns to face me and takes my hands in his. 'I know how long you have waited to find something that you really want to do and I'm so pleased that you have. I guess this is just a big shock, I wasn't expecting it. This is going to be really hard.'

'I know.' I try to sound soothing and stroke his hand gently. 'You will be ok, Andrew'.

'I will' he nods his head. 'But I will miss you dreadfully.' He pauses then adds with a little more resolve, 'Still. We can make this work. In the short term at least, we can commit to flying back and forth. It's not exactly that far and flights are so cheap if you book them in advance. Then, if you get the house of course and everything works out, if business is going well, we can think about the longer term then. I've always wanted to go to Italy. I might be able to arrange to take some time off work or I could even learn Italian and find work over there with you.' He is looking almost pleadingly into my eyes, 'What do you think?'

I stumble over my words as I try to think of something and again I take the cowards' way out. 'Thank you for being so supportive and so positive about everything. You are such a lovely man, I really don't deserve you.' I mean it as I say it. 'But I can't impose on your life that much. If we do get the house, the building and renovation work is going to take up nearly all of my time, weekdays and weekends, so even if you do come to see me I will barely be able to spend any time with you. And I doubt very much that I will be able to find the time to come home, at least until the house is up and running and that could take months.'

Andrew goes to say something but I stop him. 'Andrew, I know you are trying to work this out for both of us, but I can't ask you to fly back and forth when I can't do the same for you. And I can't take you away from your career. You love it too much and you are so good at it. You love your office and your colleagues. You have friends and your family here. I care for you too much to expect you to sacrifice so much.' I am surprised to feel myself welling up but I realise that I will be sad to say goodbye to Andrew for good. I don't love him, but I do like him. He is good company and he has been so good to me. I think I might actually miss him a bit when he's gone. Andrew clearly takes the tears for more than they are and he envelops me in a huge bear hug. He holds me tight for a long time without saying anything.

'Let's not make any decisions now,' he says finally. 'It is so lovely of you to put me first and care so much about what makes me happy.' I swallow guiltily as he speaks. 'But you make me happy, Soph, and I don't want you to forget that.' Tears are actually falling now, but I think this time it is because I feel so awful about being such a coward to such a lovely person. 'Go back to Italy, do what you have to do, make this a success for you and Jen and we can talk about us when you're ready.'

Andrew pulls away from me and the conversation is over for now. I know I shouldn't but I nod in agreement and, with a last kiss on the cheek, I leave Andrew in the car and go into my flat to gather my things and start planning for my new life. Perhaps I will email Andrew when I get back to Italy and set things straight.

The estate agent comes to my flat a few hours later and confirms what I already know about its value. Then I pack a few boxes for shipping to Italy if we win the Russo house. By three p.m. I am absolutely shattered and the last thing I want to do is face my parents. This day has been emotionally draining enough already. I have to do it though. I considered waiting to see the result of the auction but on balance I decided that they might struggle even more to come to terms with what I am doing if I have gone ahead and done it without even telling them about it first. So at three thirty p.m. I jump into my car and drive the forty minute journey to their house. They are thrilled to see me and both hug me hard at the front door. We sit at the kitchen table and mum makes me a cup tea and gives me a giant slice of fruit cake, which I devour hungrily. I haven't eaten since the airport this morning and mum's cake is the best. I reach for another slice and muster up the courage to tell them about the house, the auction and all of our plans.

Against all odds, mum and dad are actually amazingly supportive. I think that they are relieved that I am finally doing something with my life, although I can tell that dad is worried. He asks a lot of questions about the money and it takes me a long time to reassure him that we have it all worked out properly. He has never been one to get into debt. He doesn't even have a credit card. The thought of borrowing such a huge amount of money is completely alien to him. 'What if it doesn't work out, love?' he asks carefully. 'You'll have no flat, no car, no job and huge debt. What will you do then?' He keeps his voice soft and I can tell he doesn't want to upset me; it makes me feel so much love for him.

'Dad, please don't worry,' — I try to sound reassuring — 'If we get the house, and it's still a big if, we will make it work. And if something happens and it doesn't work, then we will still have it as capital. It won't all be lost.'

I realise that I am trying to convince him and me at the same time. I don't know how much I managed to reassure him but he smiles all the same and wishes me luck. They both offer to do anything they can to help and then the talk moves on to the potential for holidays in Tuscany with Jen's parents, and wine tasting weekends with their neighbours, Sheryl and Bob. After another cup of tea we all hug again and I promise to call once we have seen the bank manager and as soon as the auction is over.

They wave me off happily at the front door and I feel a huge swell of love for them as I drive away from the house. I hadn't realised just how important their support was to me but now I feel like a great weight has been lifted off my shoulders. It feels really great to have told them everything and to know that they are rooting for me. Despite my exhaustion, I am buoyant again after the disappointment of my conversation with Andrew. On the way home I pick up a bottle of wine and an oven pizza from the Tesco Express at the top of my road. I slump in front of the TV and eat and drink the lot before falling fast asleep.

At eight thirty a.m. Jen is knocking on my front door. I have been up for two hours going over the business plan and I am pretty sure that I know it inside out now. In our best suits and heels we head to the bank on Clapham High Street. The bank manager, Mr Irwin, is a portly man who, judging by the crumbs on his tie and black suit jacket, has just had his breakfast. He dusts them off with one hand and puts out the other for me to shake. After introductions he leads us into a little office off the main floor. Once there he gestures at us to take a seat and he sits back in his chair on the opposite side of the desk.

'So, Miss Ducall...' He interlaces his fingers and places his hands on top of his round stomach, 'Tell me your idea and how I might be able to help you with it.'

I stand up and straighten my jacket, ready to give our pitch. Mr Irwin clears his throat and interrupts before I get my first word out: 'There is no need to stand up, Miss Ducall, this isn't school, please, sit.'

'Of course,' I sit back down, embarrassed.

He has thrown me right off course, my cheeks are burning and everything I planned to say goes right out of my head. I fumble my way through the pitch, missing whole sections and muddling others. Defeated already, I stop talking and hand Mr Irwin the business plan.

'Please,' I plead, 'Just look at the numbers. They make sense, I promise they do.'

Jen starts to talk through some of our plans for the house but, once again, Mr Irwin stops her before she has a chance to get going.

'I think I've heard enough, thank you, girls.' He sounds just like my old head teacher. 'Please give me a moment to look over the numbers.'

We sit in silence for what feels like an age but is probably less than ten minutes. When he is ready, Mr Irwin puts the business plan on the table in front of him and sits forward in his chair, pulling his jacket together over his stomach. 'Miss Ducall, Miss Phillips,' he sounds formal now, 'I have looked carefully at the numbers and I have listened to what you have to say.' He turns his gaze to me. 'Although I admire your ambition and I think that you have put together a reasonable plan, I'm afraid that on the basis of the limited information in front of me and your limited experience in this field, I am not able to support a loan of such magnitude. I do wish you every luck in your endeavour though.' And that is it. He stands up and holds his arm out towards the office door. 'It was very nice to meet you,' he ushers us out.

I can't believe that is it. It is over. All that work, all that time and effort and he has thrown it all out in less than ten minutes. He didn't even ask us any questions or read the whole plan. I am crushed and I feel awful to have let Jen down so badly. If I hadn't messed up so much in the beginning this might not have happened. As we walk out of the bank and back onto the High Street, I turn to her. 'I am so sorry, this is all my fault. He completely threw me at the beginning and I just lost my way. Everything went out of my head. Please don't hate me.'

'Don't be silly.' Jen's voice is soft and I can tell that she isn't cross with me. 'It wasn't your fault, Soph. I don't think it would have mattered what you said, I'm pretty sure he wasn't going to lend us the money anyway. It's too much and he doesn't know us well enough. He didn't take us seriously, did you hear him call us "Girls"? I knew then that he wouldn't lend us the money.'

I am placated that it might not all have been my fault but still devastated that we didn't get the money. 'So what are we going to do?' I ask. We go into the Starbucks on the High Street and sit in the window with hazelnut cream lattes discussing our options.

'To be honest, I really think that the only option we have now is to try my parents' bank,' Jen suggests. 'At least they know me and they know that my parents will guarantee the loan. That has to mean something. I don't know what else we can do.'

'It's your call,' I say, 'But I agree, I'm not sure there are any other options if we are going to go ahead with all of this.'

'What do you mean "if"?' Jen looks worried. 'Are you having second thoughts?'

'Of course not! Not at all. You know how much I want this. I'm just a little dispirited I guess.'

'Don't be.' Jen takes out her phone and calls her parents' bank manager. They are on first name terms and chat happily for a few minutes before she gets down to business. I watch anxiously trying to work out what is happening on the other end of the phone and I am distressed to see Jen's face fall. She bites her lip as she listens to whatever is being said.

'OK, thank you, I really appreciate it, George. We'll be round soon.' She ends the conversation and switches her phone off.

'He'll see us?' I ask as she hangs up.

'He will,' she nods. 'But he is out of the office for the rest of the day and fully booked for tomorrow.'

My heart jumps and I try to stay calm. I don't need to remind Jen that the auction is tomorrow evening. 'He says if we can get the business plan to him in the next twenty minutes that he will look at it tonight and then see us at eight a.m. tomorrow.'

'eight a.m.' I try to sound calm now. 'But our flight is at eleven. Will we make it?'

'We'll have to.' Jen is matter of fact. 'We'll get everything ready so that we can go straight to the airport from the bank. He has a nine a.m. meeting after us, so worst case we should be on the road by then.'

I am relieved to get another chance but more than a little panicked by how close this is going to be. Still, Jen is right: what choice do we have?

We go via my flat to collect my things and back to Jen's so that we can leave together in the morning. I practise my pitch for an hour after dinner before Jen sends me to bed.

'You need to sleep! You know everything, you know you do, you just need to relax. It will be fine. George is lovely.'

She is right. George is lovely. He meets us at the bank door at eight a.m. and shakes our hands warmly. Inside he gives us tea and biscuits and takes us to the brightly coloured sofas at the far end of the main floor. I needn't have worried about the pitch as I didn't even have to do it.

'Your business plan is good,' he tells us as we sit down. 'There are a few holes but nothing that I am too worried about. I spoke to your father last night,' he looks at Jen, 'He has great faith in your idea and he has agreed to act as a guarantor to a loan should you need one. Obviously he will need to come in and sign the papers with you but I'm sure that we can arrange that.'

'So, are you saying that you will lend us the money?' Jen asks George directly.

'That's exactly what I'm saying,' George smiles widely at me. 'If you get the house at the auction within the allocated financial boundaries then, with your parents' guarantee, we would be happy to lend you the money. Congratulations!'

He laughs at the shock on our faces and shakes our hands again. Then Jen gives him a hug and he laughs again. He looks like he might even ruffle her hair for a moment, but instead he looks at his watch and clears his throat. 'Right, ladies, I believe you have a plane to catch and I have a meeting to get to.' He hands Jen a pile of papers. 'These set out our loan terms and conditions, repayment terms and requirements, interest and some calculated examples etc. Read it all carefully and we can talk again after the auction.'

He walks us back to the front door and we both thank him again. 'Good luck!' he calls after us as we jump into our waiting taxi.

Once inside we both scream and hug each other, we are practically jumping on the back seat. The driver is not impressed.

'Belts!' he booms in a surly voice over his shoulder. I look at the clock above the radio in the front of the car, eight forty-five a.m. 'Put your belt on, Jen, we have to go and buy a house!'

Rush hour traffic is a nightmare. The car crawls along, taking twenty minutes just to get outside of Clapham. As the minutes tick by, faster than they ever have before I am increasingly jittery.

'Stop moving your knees, it's driving me mad!' Jen puts her hand out to stop the movement.

'Sorry.' I put my feet firmly flat on the floor of the taxi. 'I can't believe this traffic; we are never going to make it.'

'Don't say that,' Jen looks at her watch. 'We've an hour before check-in closes, it should only take us forty minutes from here, and it'll be fine'.

Fifty-five minutes later we drive up to the airport concourse. 'The traffic in there's a nightmare, I'll drop you here and turn around.' Our surly driver, who has been tutting and heavy breathing the whole journey as if the traffic is our fault, pulls the car to the side of the road just in front of the last roundabout before the main airport ring road. 'You can walk the rest of the way.' He looks over his shoulder at us.

'No!' I cry. 'We only have five minutes, take us to the front. Please.'

'Will probably take longer in the car, there's been some kind of problem this morning, the queue is backed right up'.

'Sod it.' Jen opens her car door, 'Let's make a dash for it'.

She practically throws some money into the front of the car to pay the driver and we get out of the taxi and run as fast as we can towards the main airport building our cases flying behind us.

By the time we reach the departures hall we can barely breathe, I think I might actually throw up. I have never run that fast in my life and my chest is heaving. Jen is coughing and trying to catch her breath next to me. I can see her searching the terminal for our check in desk. I scan the giant departures board for our flight.

'Soph, look at the time, its 10.35, I don't believe it, we're too late.' Jen is looking at the giant clock hanging in the middle of the terminal. 'What shall we do?' I can hear panic in her voice for the first time and for once it is my turn to be calm, I've just found our flight on the departures board,

'Don't worry, the flight is delayed,' I tell her just as an announcement comes over the tanoy system:

'All flights are subject to delay and disruption due to unforeseen problems with the computer systems. We currently have engineers working on the problem and hope to get it sorted as soon as possible. Please keep checking the departures boards for the status of your flight. We apologise for the inconvenience.'

As it turns out there has been some kind of IT crash across the airport and most of the check-in systems are down. Nearly all of the flights have been delayed and some have been cancelled. Luckily ours is still going.

'It says here departure is expected at 12.05, that will be fine. Let's sit down and get our breath back, I need a drink!'

For once, I mean water, I am gasping from our Olympic sprint. I could probably do with a trip to the ladies too, I'm sure that I look a complete wreck now. Via the toilets (where I do what I can with a hairbrush, mascara and bronzer to limit the damage caused to my face and hair by the unexpected exercise) we set ourselves up on a small table in the corner of Prêt A Manger until our check-in desk opens again.

By midday, after water, Diet Coke, two bags of popcorn and a granola bar, the departure board is still saying 12.05 but there is no sign of movement at the check-in desk.

'What are we going to do? It's two p.m. in Italy. Even if we leave in the next half an hour we'll be cutting it fine and it doesn't look like that is going to happen, we haven't even checked in yet, let alone gone through security and got on the actual plane.' I can feel the panic rising again.

'Don't worry,' ever calm and practical Jen has an idea. 'I'll phone Jake and see if he can take our place at the auction, just in case we don't make it.'

She takes out her mobile and, as she is dialling Jake's number, four ladies in orange uniforms walk past us and take their places behind the check-in desks for our flight. The sign above them flicks to 'check-in open'. I pull at Jen's arm and point at the desk.

'It's open!' Jen clicks her phone off and we run to the front of the check-in desk before anyone else can get there.

We look at our watches every few minutes until we are on the plane and then every few minutes until it starts to taxi. My stomach only begins to unknot when we are finally in the air and on our way back to Florence. I sit back and physically feel my body unclench. It is two p.m. in England and we are due to arrive just before six p.m. Italian time. That gives us an hour to get off the plane and to the auction house. It is still going to be close but there is nothing that I can do to make this part of the journey go any faster so I sit back and relax.

A large air stewardess with bright red lipstick makes her way up the aisle with the drinks trolley and reaches us far too slowly. 'Can I get you anything?' she asks when she eventually reaches our row and leans over the arm of my seat.

'White wine!' Jen and I say in unison. We look at each other and laugh. The stewardess smiles but is clearly quite bemused by our delirious-like state. She passes us both a small bottle of white wine with a plastic cup.

'That will be £6.00 please.' I hand her the money and open the wine gratefully.

'Cheers!' I knock my cup against Jen's.

'At least we don't have hold luggage.'

I can tell that Jen is thinking about what is going to happen when we land. 'We can get straight off the plane, run through as fast as we can and jump in a cab. We'll make it.' I sound more confident than I feel.

'Fingers crossed!' Jen gulps her wine.

The plane lands as expected just before six p.m. It taxis slower than is even possible, on what must be the longest imaginable route to arrivals, before coming to a complete stop. The minute the seat belt signs go off, we stand up and take our cases from the cabin hold above us. We wait impatiently for the plane door to open and as soon as it does we are off the plane and running as fast as we can to passport control. In our first spot of luck since the journey began there isn't queue and we go straight through into the arrivals hall with barely a glance from the nice young man checking the passports. We get out of the airport and into a taxi in less than five minutes.

Predictably, the traffic in Florence is not good and we weave slowly through the mass of cars, jerking about, stopping and starting but not getting very far. I stare at my watch the whole way, willing the hands not to move. Jen and I don't speak the entire journey. There is nothing to say now. At 6.55 p.m. the car pulls up outside the auction doors. We made it!

'Thank God!' I jump out of the car and pay the driver with a huge tip. 'Quick!' I help Jen out of the car. 'We have an auction to win!'

Chapter 17

We push the heavy door to the auction house open and run through the entrance hall, our travel cases crashing along behind us. An impeccably-dressed young woman is sitting at a desk outside the main auction room. She smiles sweetly at us as we stop just before we crash into it. She quickly checks our names off the list in front of her and hands us each an auction guide. I push the doors into the main hall with more force than is necessary and we burst into the room just as the bidding is about to begin. The commotion as the double doors swing back from my herculean push and hit the walls behind them is exaggerated by the silence in the room.

A hundred heads turn in our direction, a mixture of surprise, humour and annoyance on the sea of faces. My face, already red from running, must be positively puce by the time we manage to find two free seats next to each other and make our way over to them, still rattling our suitcases behind us. I sit down and lift the case onto my lap. I unzip it as quietly as possible thinking that right now I would actually quite like to climb inside it and disappear. The auctioneer clears his throat and speaks in Italian as pictures of the Russo house are shown on a large white screen behind him.

'Carpe diem!' Jen whispers and squeezes my hand. And so it begins.

The bidding starts slowly at 500,000 euros. For the first thirty seconds or so there aren't any bids at all.

'I knew it!' Jen is fidgeting in her seat trying to contain her excitement. 'Shall we bid?'

'I don't see why not.' I put my hand on her elbow and push it gently to indicate that she should raise her arm.

I've never been to an auction before. Not a real one anyway. I do remember going to a charity auction once when I worked at Morgan Stanley, but most of the lots consisted of barely-dressed men, so I'm not sure that I can count that as actual experience of how these things work. Now that it has started, I am realising that Jen and I should probably have had a plan of action before we came in. The closest we have to one is an agreement that we have to get the house and that we can't spend more money than we have, which I suppose is a good start at least. In the absence of any plan, I am thinking that now is as good a time as any to bid so as Jens arm is still pushing back against my right arm, I raise my left one high in the air.

The auctioneer nods at us and repeats the sum to confirm my bid. Once again most of the room has turned to look at us, eager to see who has opened the bidding. I feel quite grown up bidding in a real auction for a real house and probably for the first time ever I don't mind everyone looking at me.

The bidding goes up to 550,000 euros and this time an arm is raised quickly by a middle-aged man wearing a suit and sitting to the far right of us. A telephone bidder takes it to

600,000 euros, then the man in the suit and the telephone bidder take it in turns, one after the other, until the price has reached 900,000 euros. I have barely had a chance to raise my arm again and as the number continues to climb I start to get a sinking feeling in my stomach. Jen squeezes my hand super tight and I can see that she has her fingers tightly crossed. I cross mine too. Please let the bidding stop now.

The auctioneer calls out 950,000 euros and there is a lull in the room. Perhaps someone is listening to me. I cross my fingers even tighter, and my legs, just for the hell of it. The auctioneer repeats the price for the second time and looks between the two bidders currently in contention.

I hold my breath not wanting the silence around me to break. Jen nudges me.

'This is our chance!' she whispers. I raise my arm again and catch the auctioneer's eye. He nods at us again. I squeeze Jen's hand so tightly with my other arm that I am sure I must be cutting off her blood supply. She doesn't say anything though. I think she might be squeezing my hand back just as tightly as I can't actually feel it now.

The bidding is with us now at 950,000 euros.

The auctioneer looks around the room for one million euros. One million Euros! This is insane!

He repeats the amount for the second time. I realise that I am still holding my breath and take a gulp of air before I pass out. I close my eyes and I can hear the auctioneer repeat the amount for the third time. I squeeze my eyes tighter. I can't believe this is going to happen.

I wait for the sound of the hammer to fall but instead I hear the auctioneer's voice again.

'One million euros, I am bid,' his voice booms across the room.

I open my eyes and my mouth, breath pours in but disappointment is seeping out of every other pore.

'I am looking for one million fifty thousand.' The auctioneer scans the room.

That's it. It's over. I think. Jen and I look at each other, silently asking the same question, desperate not to lose the house.

'Can we do it, just one more bid?' Jen whispers. To my surprise I think I can see tears in her eyes. Before I can answer the auctioneer speaks again: 'One million fifty thousand, I am bid. Thank you.'

If we could have gone for one more bid we certainly can't now. I scan the room to see who the auctioneer is looking at.

The arm still being held aloft is dressed in an immaculate beige suit and white shirt with small gold cufflinks poking out of the top. I follow the arm down and with surprise I realise that I know the face. It is the handsome man that hates me. I don't know why I am so surprised, after all that must have been why he was looking at the house, because he wanted to bid for it. As he lowers his arm he looks to his right, probably to watch his competitor bidder. He must feel me staring at him because he turns his head a little further and catches my eye. He looks at the auction guide with our auction number on my lap and as a telephone bidder takes the next bid of 1.1 million, he immediately raises his hand to outbid at 1.15 million.

Now we are definitely out of the race. There is no way that Jen and I can possibly go that far over our limit. I am completely and utterly dejected. I can't believe that our dream is over before it has even begun. I am cross with myself. I feel stupid for ever believing it. I wish that we had never let it get so far because right now I am more crushed than ever. I blink back the tears that are quickly forming in my eyes. The noise of the auction is muffled behind my thoughts but I know that the number is still going up. I scan the room to see who else is bidding for my beautiful house but the room is still and quiet except for the murmurings coming from the row of auction staff talking quickly in hushed tones on the telephones. It is from here that the bidding reaches 1.3 million. I turn back to the handsome man to see if he will bid again. He is so beautiful it's mesmerising just watching him. He seems calm but I can make out a slight frown as the auctioneer confirms the price from the telephone bidder and I notice that his right foot is tapping up and down fast beneath his chair.

An elegant, elderly lady, who must once have been as beautiful as he is handsome, puts her hand on his arm and speaks into his ear. As he turns to look at her I can see his face more clearly and I am shocked by his pained expression. His obvious anguish makes me forget mine for just a moment. If he wasn't so horrible I might feel sorry for him. The auctioneer is looking at him now too, waiting for a response. The handsome man puts his hand over the elderly lady's which is still on his arm. He looks directly at the auctioneer and shakes his head. It is difficult to see him now because he is staring straight ahead, calm again and barely moving. The auctioneer closes the bidding to a telephone bidder at 1.3 million euros. That is it. It's over.

Jen puts her hand on mine and squeezes it gently. I squeeze hers back and quickly wipe away an errant tear that has escaped and is rolling down my cheek. Everyone is moving around us but I have barely noticed.

'Come on, Soph,' Jen tugs gently on my arm. 'Let's go'.

Still holding hands we stand up, gather our things and follow the crowd out of the auction room. Neither of us speak. I don't think that either of us know what to say. There is nothing to say really. We are still trying to process what has happened and I can't quite put the disappointment into words. I am not ready to be mollified or jollied yet and I know that Jen isn't either, though I know too that we will be, eventually. The noise around us is loud and the hall outside the auction room is still buzzing from the excitement of the sale. A small crowd of people has gathered just inside the main entrance where there is a heightened fervour.

As we pass, Jen and I crane our necks to see into the throng of people, but whoever is in the middle is being accosted by too many people in the auction house uniform and men in formal suits.

'That must be who bought our house.' Jen still refers to it as ours which just makes me sadder.

'I thought it was a telephone bidder,' I say, though I am past caring now, I just want to leave. As we make our way back through the front doors of the auction house and into what is still bright sunshine outside despite the late hour, I take Jen's arm and look down the street in search of a taxi.

For a second I think I hear someone call Jen's name. I look at Jen and she is looking around as if she heard it too. We both turn back to face the auctioneers but can't see anyone.

'It must be someone else.' I turn back again.

'Jen! Jen!'

There it is again. This time it is much clearer and it definitely sounds like it is directed at us. It is coming from just inside the door of the auction house, amidst the big throng of people.

We look again to see who on earth can be calling Jen's name and from the middle of the crowd a small, familiar face comes through, still shouting and waving frantically in our direction.

'Jen! Over here.'

'Oh my god! It's your mum. It's Pauline!' I scream, shocked but thrilled to see her. We run over and she throws her arms around us both at the same time.

'Girls!' she shouts despite being right next to us now. 'My lovely girls!'

We hug her tight until Jen pulls away first.

'Mum! What are you doing here? I thought you were in France!'

'We were, darling! We flew in this morning to support you at the sale but we didn't make it in time. Our plane was delayed and we only arrived a few minutes ago.'

'Oh Mum! That's so lovely!' Jen gives her another hug. I am tearing up again at the gesture and she pulls me back into the hug with them.

'You're so amazing to come and support us but we didn't get the house. You came all this way for nothing!'

Now I feel just as disappointed for Pauline as I do for Jen and me. Pauline steps back and looks at us both.

'You are such clever, wonderful girls,' she smiles indulgently at us. 'I have something to tell you'.

Jen and I look at each other then back at Pauline, confusion on both of our faces.

'Is something wrong, Mum?' Jen sounds concerned.

'On the contrary, darling.' Pauline is grinning like a Cheshire cat now. 'I need to tell you that the house was bought by a telephone bidder.'

'We know that! Soph just told you that, Mum!'

'I know you know that but what you don't know is that the phone bidder was actually two bidders. It was Daddy and me.' She waits for a response but Jen and I are still trying to digest what she has said. We stand in front of her in shock.

'*You* bought the house? I don't understand!'

Pauline takes one of each of our hands. 'Darlings,' her voice is soft now, 'Daddy and I got your business plan two days ago. We read it carefully and we think that it is brilliant. Daddy is so proud of you both. We talked about it and we have decided that we don't want you to have to borrow from the bank. We want to do this for you.'

'You bought us the house?' I ask in utter disbelief.

'Not exactly, we have loaned you the money for the house. The house is yours. But we want you to stick to the business plan and when you start generating money, then you can pay us back, slowly and without interest. You can still use the money that you were going to put up from your own savings for the refurbishment and building work. This is your house, your business. We just want to help you get started.'

By the time she has finished speaking I am fit to burst. My stomach is in my throat and my feet are flipping all over the place. I don't know whether to cry or scream or be sick. I do the first two. Jen and I both scream and my tears are falling freely now. We throw our arms around Pauline again and we all cry with happiness, shock, utter amazement and sheer joy. Pauline rubs our backs like only a mum can.

'We are so proud of you. We just know that you can make this work. Daddy is inside now signing all of the papers. Come and see him.'

She leads us back into the auction house. The throng is starting to clear and we can see Jen's Dad shaking hands with the auctioneer and holding a large wad of papers along with the auction guide. When he sees us he excuses himself from the multiple men in suits and strides over to us arms open wide. Jen hugs him tightly and kisses him on the cheek with force then I do exactly the same.

'Thank you, Frank. Thank you so, so, so, so much, I can't believe you have done this for us! This is amazing.'

He puts his hands on my shoulders and looks at me intently. 'You did this. You and Jen had a great idea and have put together an excellent business plan. I am proud of you both. You deserve this. It's not a handout though.' His voice is firm now.

'Mum told us everything, Dad, we know,' Jen tells him. 'It's the most amazing thing you have ever done for me. For us. Thank you so much!'

'You're welcome.' Frank dismisses the thanks with a wave of his hand. 'I guess these belong to you.' He reaches into his open briefcase on the large table next to us and pulls out a set of keys. Jen takes them and looks at them in awe. This time we hug each other, long and hard. And jump a little and cry some more.

Once we have all calmed down, Jen's parents have a few more formalities to complete with the auction house and some papers to sign so Jen and I wait in the foyer for them. I put my wheelie case on the large table where Frank's briefcase had been and unzip it so that I can pack in the large wads of papers, contracts and of course the keys. As I do so Jen and I talk excitedly about getting started on the refurbishment.

We are deep in conversation and almost ready to leave by the time I realise that the handsome man is standing in the doorway watching us. As I look up from my case I catch his eye, he looks angry and sad at the same time and it makes me want to speak to him. I am just about to walk over when a car pulls up beside him, driven by the elderly lady who was sitting next to him during the auction. He looks at my case and his gaze lingers on it, just as I remember he did when we were outside of the Russo house only a few days ago. The Russo house, I have to stop calling it that now! It is my house! Mine and Jen's! I shiver with excitement as it hits me all over again.

The excitement is quickly quelled by the look on handsome man's face. He stares at me, full of hate, before

157

stepping out of the entrance and into the waiting car. I feel winded by his reaction, it is definitely personal, heartfelt even, standing so close to each other in this confined space there is no mistaking it.

'Wow,' Jen brings my attention back. 'What was that look for! Who was that?'

'That was him! Handsome man.'

'Oh!' She is surprised. 'He really is handsome, but what the hell have you done to upset him so much? He looked like he wanted to hit you or something!'

'I told you! That's what he was like last time. I don't understand it! He doesn't even know me!'

At least I know I'm not going mad, he really doesn't like me, but I'm totally at a loss to think of any reason why.

'Too strange,' Jen is clearly at a loss too. 'But hey, don't think about it now. It's time to celebrate!'

She picks up the large bunch of keys, throws them in the air and catches them twirling around at the same time. Jen's parents walk out of a side office and back into the main foyer just as we are doing our celebratory twirling and laugh indulgently at us. 'Business women in the making!' Frank puts his arms around our shoulders. 'But still my little girls! Shall we go and celebrate?' As if he has to ask!

We spend the rest of the evening sitting outside the same restaurant that Jen and I ate in the first time we had discussed the possibility of buying the house. When the first bottle of champagne arrives Frank takes it from the waiter to open and pour, he hands us all a glass and raises his for a toast, 'To my girls and their adventure.'

'To making dreams come true,' I add, and we all clink glasses and get a little tearful again. We eat and drink to our hearts content.

We talk constantly, loudly, excitedly and over each other all the time as our ideas spill out. Pauline tells us about their nightmare journey of delays to Italy and how they had to join the auction by telephone from the car on the way to the auction house.

'Why didn't we think of that?' Jen and I raise our glasses to the miracle of mobile telephones and tell our own story about nearly the missing the auction. Then we thank our lucky stars for the way things have turned out. And we thank Jen's parents, again and again and again.

'It wasn't just the flights that nearly prevented us from winning the auction,' Jen's dad tells us over coffee and liquer. 'There were some pretty strong rival bidders in there. I had a limit of course, for a moment I thought that one of them was going to go all the way.'

'Who were the other bidders?' I ask. 'Do you know?'

I am thinking of the handsome man but Frank, of course, doesn't know that. 'Well, there was you two of course!' He laughs. 'Then I thought our main rival was going to be Mediterranean Dreams.'

'Mediterranean Dreams, the holiday company?'

'That's them, you know them then?' Frank asks.

'Andrew and I went to stay in one of their hotels in Majorca last year,' I explain. 'Why would they want to take on the Russo house?'

'Well, they are pretty big in the Spanish market; my understanding is that they are looking to expand in Italy. I've a close friend in the business and he warned me that they might be interested in the property.'

'I wouldn't have thought the manor house was up their street, most of their hotels are big and modern aren't they?'

'That's right,' Frank nods, 'but more and more they are specialising in smaller, quirky places. I imagine they planned to buy the manor house and, keeping within building regulations, totally modernise it. Sort of old on the outside, new on the inside, kind of old age meets space age'.

'That's awful! How could anyone want to do that to our house?'

Jen pours herself another limoncello from the bottle on the table and pitches in: 'I know the company; I stayed in a converted monastery in the Andalucian Hills when I was travelling a few years back. It was quite incredible really, but pretty awful too. From the outside it looked just like the monastery probably always had, but inside it was all Bang and Olufson and up-lighting. The foyer looked like something out of Star Trek.' I shiver at the thought of someone doing that to my beautiful house.

'Well, now I'm even more pleased that they didn't win the auction. What about the other bidders?' I ask, trying to sound nonchalant. 'Do you know any of them?'

'I'm not sure about any of them really, love. There was a gentleman in a beige suit who was bidding. He asked the auctioneer to introduce me to him, hung around until I had signed the papers.'

'What did he say?' I am eager to know more about him.

'Not a lot really, he just shook my hand and asked me to take good care of the house. A bit strange really.'

'Did he speak English?' I ask.

'Yes, very good English. You seem very interested in him, Sophie. Why do you want to know so much?' he grins at me as if he already knows the answer.

'Oh, it's nothing. I'm just interested, you know, in who else wanted the house.' I know I am speaking too fast and Frank laughs.

'He was a very handsome man.' Pauline looks at me from across the table and raises her eyebrows.

'Was he? I hadn't really noticed.' I look at my plate and concentrate very hard on my half-eaten truffle. I can tell they are all smirking at me and I am blushing so I'm pleased when the waiter comes over with the bill and diverts everyone's attention.

We leave the restaurant late and get a taxi back to the cottage. Jen's parents are going to stay in Jen's room tonight before booking into a hotel tomorrow. They are staying on for a few weeks to help us start work on the house. I offer my bed to Jen but she won't think of it and is happy to take the sofa. Pauline sits between Jen and me in the back and we fall asleep on her shoulders before the car has even left Florence.

Chapter 18

Despite my exhaustion I am awake at nine a.m. on Saturday morning, even asleep I'm too excited to stay that way! I can hear movement downstairs and the smell of bacon and toast is wafting through my open door. Jen and her parents must be up too. From the corner of my eye I see my phone flash on my bedside table. Six messages. Six! Word must have got out. The first message is from my mum:

Congratulations again, darling. Daddy and I are so proud of you. Can you give me a call when you are up... lots to sort out this end! Love Mum. Xx

Mum always signs her text messages with her name, even though she knows I know the messages are from her.

The second message is from Andrew:

Darling, I spoke to your parents this morning! They told me you got the house! I'm so happy for you. I understand that it was all a bit manic so you couldn't call me yesterday. Give me a call later when you get a chance. Love you. xx

I flick past that one quickly and try to ignore the spasm of guilt in my stomach. I'll text him back later. The next is from mum again:

Mum again, darling, I forgot to say that Andrew called this morning. I told him about you getting the house. I hope that is OK? Perhaps you could give him a call too when you get a second. He seemed a little sad. Love Mum xx

Another guilt spasm. Next message:

You did it! I can't believe it! Just spoke to Jen and she told me everything. Amazing... I've decided to take some credit for this, for convincing you to go to Italy... you owe me a huge drink! I'll come to see you soon so that you can buy me one! I'll call you later. Love u lots! Xx

It is so true! Who would have thought that Fi convincing me to come and see Jen for a fortnight would end up like this! I can't wait to show her the house! I decide to call her after breakfast and scroll down to the next message. It's from my phone company, informing me of my phone bill for the month. I move straight past it to avoid seeing how much I owe them. The last message is from Jen:

Get up! Breakfast is cooking and we have a lot to do! xx

I don't need asking twice! I pull my pyjama bottoms on over the pants that I slept in last night and throw a t-shirt on.

I don't even remember getting into bed but clearly I at least managed to take my clothes off, even if I hadn't put anything on! I skip down the stairs into the sitting room where Pauline is setting the table for breakfast.

'Morning!' I cross the room and give her a kiss on the cheek. 'Did you sleep well?'

'Good morning, darling, we slept wonderfully thank you. Don't worry about us being in your hair too long though. We have booked into a hotel on the edge of the village. Won't it be nice when your place is up and running though? Something a little more luxurious, eh,' she smiles and winks.

I laugh, still delirious at the thought of it all! Me owning a luxury hotel! Well, a luxury hotel in the making anyway!

In the kitchen Frank is wearing Jen's apron and turning bacon in the pan. 'Morning, love, just getting it crispy, won't be long.'

Jen leans out from behind the fridge door where she is getting out the orange juice. 'Hey! How is my business partner this morning?'

I squeal, 'Argh! Business partner! I still can't believe it!'

'I know!' She passes me the orange juice, 'I woke up this morning wondering if it was all a dream! I actually had to think about it for a few minutes before I realised I was on the sofa and it has all really happened! I thought we could take mum and dad to see the house after breakfast. What do you think?'

'Definitely — I can't wait to see it again too!'

'Perfect. Sit down, babe; we'll bring the food through.'

Jen and Frank follow me in with warm ciabatta, crispy bacon, scrambled eggs and an amazing hollandaise sauce that

Jen has made from scratch. It is absolutely delicious. Perfect to set us up for the busy day ahead.

We leave the plates on the side, eager to get to the house and show Jen's parents around. They have seen all of the pictures but they don't do the place justice. I can't wait to show them how incredible it really is, for them to see all of our ideas in context.

Frank and Pauline are just as excited. Frank pumps ahead of all of us, taking long strides and making admiring noises at the beauty of the surrounding countryside while we walk behind to keep a pace with Pauline, who is significantly smaller than Frank with much shorter legs! Frank reaches the gates first and stands back from them with his hands on his hips. He is smiling as we approach just a minute or so later. He spreads his arms wide to the sides as if trying to fit the whole house in front of him into the outstretched space. 'It's magnificent, girls!'

I grin at Jen and feel the familiar rush of excitement that I get every time I approach the house. 'Don't keep us waiting then,' he chides. 'Let's see the place!'

He takes Pauline's hand as Jen opens the gate and I notice that he gives it a little squeeze as he does. In turn, Pauline rubs her other hand over their entwined ones. It is such an innocent and automatic gesture; I feel a wave of affection for my best friend's lovely parents. I have often thought over the years that I want to have a relationship as happy as theirs when I grow up. I guess I am grown up now and there is no sign of it yet, but at least it makes me certain that I am doing the right thing by breaking up with Andrew. I would hate to spend my life wishing I loved my partner as much as other people loved theirs. Feeling envy at the sight of all those special little moments that should really only make you feel good about life.

'Are you coming, love?' Frank turns to me as they walk through the gates.

'Of course.' I grab his free arm. 'I can't wait for you two to see it properly. I really hope you love it as much as we do'.

'Oh we will, darling.' Pauline reaches across Frank to touch my arm, 'I love it already. This fountain is magnificent, look Frank; it's just like the one at the Hotel d'Cap.' Hotel d'Cap is the hotel next door to their rather impressive villa in the South of France. I went there once for dinner with them when Jen and I spent a weekend at the villa. It is a very grand and opulent, boutique style hotel with a Michelin star restaurant and prices that make your eyes water. I remember the fountain, now Pauline mentions it; it is lit up from every angle so that the water is like a streaming river of gold pouring over the top of a huge urn. It is stunning. I make a mental note to talk to the landscape gardener and the electrician to see if we can get lights fitted inside the fountain. I'm lost again, musing as to whether different coloured lights will look tacky or not when I realise that everyone has gone inside. I head towards the front door and I can hear Pauline cooing at the domed windows before I get there.

'Gosh, these are divine, such special features.'

The 'ohhs' and 'ahhs' continue as we walk through and Pauline admires the silk curtains, oak book cases and the luxurious wall paper.

'This is all exquisite.' She is standing in the morning room and the sun is streaming through the windows hitting the primrose of the heavy silk draping above them.

'What do you think about the fabrics, Mum?' Jen asks. 'Do you think they can be salvaged?'

Pauline pulls a chair across the room and stands on it to reach up and touch the scalloped edges of one of the curtains. She lifts them to look behind and turns the edges over in her hands, examining the craftsmanship.

'They are hand stitched,' she says quietly, to herself I think. 'Stunning.' She looks down to Jen and me, now standing below her. 'They will need a good clean and a little bit of repair work here and there, but I'm pretty sure that they can be restored. It will need to be a professional job. You will need to find a specialist in antique fabrics. They are very delicate'.

I make another note, this time on my note pad as my head is filling up way to fast. I walk on through the house with Pauline whilst Jen takes Frank to see the kitchen. Pauline is confident that a lot of the original features can be restored with careful cleaning and repair work, and that is pretty much the theme for most of the house actually. I am so eager and anxious to start work I want to get a bucket and sponge and start right here and now but I know it is pointless to clean before any of the building work is done.

'Should we take the curtains down, then?' I ask Pauline, as she examines another set in one of the bedrooms.

'Well, they will need to come down before any of the work starts but I would leave it to the professionals, dear, they probably have special packaging and protection they can use.

We will need to get the walls covered too and have the chandeliers taken down and restored,' she goes on, and I jot everything down as quickly as I can so that I don't forget any of it. We meet Jen and Frank at the top of the stairs and Frank talks us through some of his ideas for configuring the bedrooms and bathrooms to make the most of the space. It is really great to get advice from people who really know what they are talking about. We listen ardently and I write down as much as possible. I am getting more and more nervous about how we are going to manage all of this work with our limited experience and even more limited Italian so I am grateful and relieved that Frank will be here to support us and to cover for Jen whilst she is at college. They have made a living of buying places and renovating them so I know that they are going to be a godsend. After several hours in the house writing lists, drawing up plans and discussing ideas for layouts, furniture and decoration, we finally head outside to walk Pauline and Frank around the grounds. They are as impressed by the outside as they are by the inside.

'It's really smashing, girls.' Frank pauses at the end of the pool when the tour is over. 'I can just imagine how it will look when it's finished.'

'Thanks, Frank.' I smile at him. 'For everything.'

'Now, no more thank you, girls,' he smiles back. 'The best way to thank me is to crack on and get this place finished!'

We all agree that we should turn the cottage in the grounds into a private living area for Jen and me but that we will stay at her rented cottage until we can make the one on the grounds liveable, when I will move in and Jen will stay where she is until her contract runs out at the end of the summer.

By the time we have seen, discussed and dissected everything, it is early afternoon and we are all hungry again.

'How about grabbing something to eat in the village? Save you cooking tonight, love,' Frank pats Jen on the shoulder. 'The hard work starts tomorrow, then it will be packed lunches and sandwiches on the run. Make the most of it!'

'Good idea!' Jen agrees. 'I'm starving and we've nothing in the cottage anyway!'

We walk together into the village square where it is a busy afternoon and tourists stroll around the shops and sit at the cafe drinking cappuccinos, eating pizzas and paninis. Katarina comes bounding out of the patisserie door and runs across the square to us calling at Paulo to come with her. They reach us at the same time, just as we arrive in front of the café. Katarina throws her arms around me excitedly. 'We hear! We hear!' she shouts loudly in my ear. 'You get the house! I am so excited! So pleased! So now you stay here in Tuscany forever!' She pulls away from me and throws her arms around Jen. Paulo is a little cooler but he kisses us on both cheeks and seems genuinely happy for us.

'How did you hear?' I ask, delighted by their reaction.

'We meet your parents this morning.' Paulo shakes Frank's hand and kisses Pauline on both cheeks as well.

'Hello again,' Frank kisses Katarina. 'We met this lovely young girl when we picked up the ciabattas this morning and this nice young chap gave us a coffee on the house! Thanks again,' he nods at Paulo.

'Of course,' Paulo smiles. 'And now you must come and eat on the house too, to celebrate.'

'Oh, Paulo, that is lovely but we couldn't possibly!'

He interrupts my refusal: 'Of course you can. It is my gift to my new neighbours. I don't take no for an answer.' He leads us to a big table right on the edge of the square.

'Honestly, Paulo, you must let us pay for lunch.' Jen is insistent but not as much as Paulo.

'No. You repay the favour when you have your own restaurant.'

'Agreed,' Jen and I say in unison and giggle, still in disbelief that we are going to have our own restaurant.

'I think I have the better deal!' Paulo laughs and hands us his menu to look at. Katarina runs back across the square to the patisserie where a group of tourists has gathered outside the window, no doubt admiring the fresh fruit tarts that are piled up next to my favourite cream meringues. Frank orders a bottle of Orvieto and toasts us all and the house once again. I sip the cold wine, enjoying it immensely in the hot afternoon sun. We pick at garlic olives in oil and giant Canellini beans in tomato sauce while we wait for our food to arrive and we talk through some specifics about who will do what over the next couple of days. We are deep in conversation and people are coming and going around us all of the time.

It isn't until my calzone arrives and I sit back so that Paulo can place it in front of me, that I realise there is someone new on the table next to us. The man has his back to us but I have seen that back and the beautiful dark blonde hair that brushes the nape of his neck before. He is wearing a crisp white shirt hung loose over a pair of navy chino shorts and I can see his tanned legs and navy driving shoes under the chair. It is the handsome man. The horrible, handsome man.

Paulo comes to take his order, a Peroni and something else that I don't understand. I hear his smooth, deep voice as the effortless Italian falls off his tongue and I know for sure it is him. I wonder if he has seen me or recognises us and suddenly I am very aware of myself.

'Are you ok, dear?' Pauline asks me across the table. 'You have gone very pale all of a sudden.'

'Oh, sorry, I'm fine.' I lower my voice not wanting to draw attention to myself. I look over at Jen, 'It's him,' I mouth quietly. 'Handsome man.' I roll my eyes in his direction so that she can follow my gaze.

'Oh!' she manages to exaggerate the word without making a noise. 'I wonder what he's doing here?' she whispers. 'Why don't you go and talk to him?'

'No!' I baulk at the idea. 'He hates me!' I raise my voice to a little above a whisper.

Frank and Pauline are watching us, clearly confused. 'Who hates you, dear?' Pauline asks. I shoot a look at handsome man quickly to see if he has heard. If he has, I can't tell. Still in whispered tones, I tell Pauline and Frank a quick version of events to date. By the time I have finished they look even more confused.

'How can he hate you?' Frank's voice is its usual booming self. 'He doesn't even know you! That's ridiculous. Go and speak to him, love.'

'Shhh, Dad,' Jen nudges his arm. 'He's right there!' She points at handsome man's back which looks a little stiffer than it did before. He takes a long sip of his beer and is doing something on his phone.

'Perfect! So go and talk to him.' Frank leans into the table in an attempt to be more subtle but forgets to lower his voice.

'What would I say?' Part of me is desperate to talk to him and find out why he dislikes me so much. I want to know what his interest is in the house too, and why he looked so sad at the auction, but I am scared of approaching him. 'I don't think I can bear it if he is rude to me again. A girl can only take so much humiliation,' I whisper to Frank.

'You must be mistaken, love,' Frank leans even closer into the table but, if it is possible, his voice gets even louder. 'Just go and introduce yourself, tell him you saw him at the auction and want to say hi.' He makes it sound so simple.

'I don't know…' I feel insanely nervous. There's no way that I can eat my food now so I gulp my wine.

'You might as well. He must have heard every word that dad's said already, he knows that we're talking about him.' Jen is probably right.

'What do you mean?' Frank is offended. And still loud. 'I was being quiet!'

'Quiet in your ears, Dad. No one else's.' Jen rubs his arm fondly to show no harm is done. Not to her, anyway.

Pauline pats me on the back. 'They're right, go on, darling, what have you got to lose? If he isn't nice, and I'm sure he will be, then you will probably never have to see him again, you can come back to us and we'll get another bottle of wine.'

I smile gratefully at Pauline for her support and her genuine belief that a nice glass of wine can solve most problems. I take a deep breath.

'*OK!*' I say dramatically, as if this is some kind of life changing decision, 'I'll do it! 'Do I look OK?' I ask Jen quickly.

'Perfect!' She gives me a thumbs up, 'Go for it!'

I compose myself and stand up, bashing my knee on the edge of the table as I do so and knocking my glass of water over. It spills all over my chair and, as I try to catch it, I knock my cutlery to the ground with a clang and clatter that could be heard from the other side of the square. I curse my clumsiness. Why is it not possible for me to do anything in a serene or dignified manner? I close my eyes and stand very still, hoping that handsome man hasn't just heard the huge kerfuffle that I have caused right next to his table. When I open them, Jen is looking at me with half pity and half hilarity and Frank is clearly trying to hide his laughter, which I can see by the way his belly is wobbling and he is resolutely staring at it. Pauline shoots them both a warning look. She quickly hands me my still standing wine glass and a napkin to wipe the front of my dress. 'No turning back now, dear,' and she ushers me away from the mess at the table.

Chapter 19

I don't know how much the handsome man is aware of what has just happened behind him but he doesn't seem surprised to see me standing in front of him. He raises his head and looks me in the eye. I don't see hatred, which is a plus, though I can't say that he looks pleased to see me either. Regardless, I stick out my hand and introduce myself.

'Hi.' I try to sound confident. 'I'm Sophie. I saw you at the auction for the old Russo house; I thought I should introduce myself.'

He still doesn't smile; he looks deflated, despondent perhaps.

'I know who you are.' His accent is annoyingly, incredibly sexy and I can feel myself starting to blush. Damn cheeks giving me away again! I realise what he has just said. How can he know who I am? I lower my hand, which he hasn't taken, and nervously smooth out the front of my dress.

'You are from Mediterranean Dreams.' He still sounds sexy but there is a hint of distaste in his voice.

'Mediterranean Dreams?' I repeat, confused. Why on earth would he think that? He ignores me.

'Congratulations on winning the house.' He turns back to his phone, presumably to indicate that our conversation is over.

'Why do you think I'm from Mediterranean Dreams?' I blurt out, ignoring his obvious attempt to get rid of me.

'I saw it on your bag.' He keeps his eyes on his phone as he speaks. 'I saw you outside the house and then again at the auction. I was told that you would be bidding for the house. I hoped that you wouldn't get it but you did. I think there is little else to say.' His English is fine but he still isn't making any sense.

'I'm not from Mediterranean Dreams, I'm not from anywhere. Except Clapham I guess, if you want to put a name on it,' and as I try to tell him it twigs. I took my hand luggage with me to the house to carry the water the first time I saw him, and then I had it with me again when we went to the auction. I haven't removed the tags from the weekend that Andrew and I went on with Mediterranean Dreams last year. He must have seen the stickers and assumed that I work for them. It makes sense I suppose. After all, Mediterranean Dreams did bid for the house. He must think that I want to turn it into some kind of modern monstrosity, like the place that Jen stayed in. No wonder he doesn't like me, though I'm not sure I would warrant his hatred even if I was who he thinks I am. I don't owe him an explanation but I have an overwhelming desire to defend myself.

'Mediterranean Dreams were at the auction, but they didn't win it,' I tell him. 'I did. I am staying with a friend here and we fell in love with the house. We won the house at the auction. We want to restore it.'

Handsome man finally puts his phone on the table and looks up to face me again, he is clearly confused but his eyes are definitely softer than just a minute ago. 'Is that why you have been giving me such awful looks?' I ask. 'Because you think I want to turn the house into a modern chain hotel?'

For the first time since I have seen handsome man he looks abashed, and I can see the hint of an apologetic smile on his mouth.

'I'm sorry, I saw your case and I just assumed. Obviously I jumped to the wrong conclusion.' He does look genuinely sorry but I am indignant now.

'Well, you know what assuming does, don't you?' He raises his eyebrows, willing me to tell him. 'It makes an ass out of you and me!' I know I am being childish and churlish and as I say the words I hate myself for it but I still can't stop myself. Luckily he laughs out loud and gets up from his seat. Three pairs of eyes are staring at us from behind him and I try not to look at them.

He puts out his hand. 'I am very sorry. I made a mistake. Please forgive me. I'm Luca,' he smiles. A proper, big, dazzling smile, and I am taken aback by his beauty. So much so that I can't think of anything else to say. I take his hand and nod my head in acceptance of his apology.

'Would you like to sit down, Sophie?' he asks, and my stomach flips at the sound of my name coming from his mouth. I really have to get a grip.

'Sure.' I try to sound casual. I sit down and miraculously I manage to avoid knocking the table as I do so. Luca beckons to Paulo, who comes over to the table. 'I'm having another drink, would you like one?' he asks me.

'White wine would be lovely,' I say trying to compose myself. He orders a bottle and sits back in his chair while we wait for it to arrive.

'So, how did you come across the house?' he asks, and I can see that he is genuinely interested so I tell him the whole story, when I first saw it, how I fell in love with it and how I learnt about its history and want to make it a happy place again. Then I tell him about Jen and her parents and our ideas. I stop short of telling him anything about my life before Italy; he doesn't need to know about that. He listens intently and I try to read the expressions on his face as I talk. He still looks sad but his demeanour is relaxed and I can sense that he is relieved. He is certainly not as uptight as he has been every other time I've seen him. By the time I finish talking the wine has arrived and I am grateful to drink it. My mouth is dry from the talking and I need something to do with my hands. I take a large sip from the glass that he hands me.

'What about you?' I ask. 'What is your interest in the house?' He looks at his glass, avoiding my gaze again and focuses on the wine as he swirls it around slowly. For a while I'm not sure if he is going to answer or not. 'I don't mean to pry,' I say carefully after a few seconds have passed. 'You don't have to tell me anything if you don't want to.'

'It's OK,' he looks up. 'The house was in my family once. I was hoping to get it back.' He looks so sad that I want to stroke his face.

'Who is your family?' I ask tentatively.

'It doesn't really matter now,' he says, not unkindly. 'You have the house. I just hope that you look after it.'

He smiles but it is full of sadness. I can't help myself. I am desperate to know who his family is so I push him to elaborate.

'I thought the house belonged to the Russo family?' Luca takes a deep breath and something, pain or anguish maybe, flashes across his face.

'I'm Luca Russo.'

'Luca Russo?' I repeat. 'I thought the house still belonged to your family, before the auction?'

'It's a long story, I'm sure you don't want to hear it all.' I can sense that Luca doesn't want to talk about it but I really want to hear about it.

'Oh, I do,' I push. 'If you don't mind telling it, that is?'

Luca thinks about it for a while then he fills our glasses up and starts to talk.

'My parents are Rialto and Lucia Russo; you said that you heard the story, so you must know what that means. My mother and father lived together in the house until he died and the rest of the Russo family disowned my mother, who was pregnant with me at the time. She was thrown out of the house before I was born but she used to take me to it all of the time. She told me stories about my father, about the house, about how happy they were there. Sometimes we would walk around to the back garden and sit on the edge of the pool. She would

178

tell me how my father had dreamed of teaching me to swim in it. How he was filling the library with books he wanted to read to me. Everytime we went to the house I promised my mother that one day I would buy it back for us. For Dad's memory.'

His eyes glaze over and he stops short. Perhaps he feels like he has said too much. My eyes are welling up too, and suddenly I feel like a fraud. Like I have taken the house from its rightful owner.

'I'm sorry,' I whisper.

'Anyway,' Luca continues, 'My mother died last year, she had cancer.' He moves on quickly and I can see the pain etched on his face as he talks about it. 'When the Russo family decided to sell the house not long after, I thought that it would be my chance to fulfil that promise. To honour my mother's memory.'

The sadness in his eyes is unbearable and I feel my own swimming with tears. I take another sip of wine and try to swallow the hard lump in my throat.

'So that is why I hated you so much. I thought that you wanted to turn my mother's beautiful home, her memories, my memories, into a characterless, box hotel. I am sorry for that.'

'Please, don't apologise. I had no idea.' Part of me wishes that he had won the auction now. I feel terrible denying him of his life's ambition, of his promise to his dying mother.

'Why would you know? We haven't lived around here for years. Mum and I moved to Florence when I set up business there. When she got sick we came back less and less. It's only because my Aunt Sylvie still lives here and because of the line of work that I'm in that I knew about the house coming onto the market.'

'What do you do?' I ask him.

'I buy art and antiques for hotels and private collectors,' he explains. 'News of a property like this coming up for sale spreads in those circles and my aunt had got wind of it through village talk too.'

I am lost for words. I want to give him a big hug. He looks so much like he needs a cuddle. The urge to reach across the table and take his hand is almost overwhelming. I place my hands firmly in my lap to stop myself.

Luca empties the rest of the wine bottle between our glasses and tries to lighten the mood. 'So you can see how relieved I am to know that the house has gone to you and not to Mediterranean Dreams. I can tell that you really do love the place. I'm glad that it has gone to someone who appreciates it. I'm not sure what I would have done with the place anyway, not now mum has gone.' I smile gratefully at him for trying to make me feel better.

'Who were you at the auction with?' I ask. I want to know everything about him.

'My Aunt Sylvie, my mother's sister. She's the only family that I have left now. She spent a lot of time at the house with my mum and dad when they were younger, she loved it too. She's a realist though. She knew that the bidding went too high for me in the end. I'm glad that she was there to stop me going beyond my limit.'

As I listen to him tell me about his aunt I have an idea. 'Do you have any photos of the house?' I ask him.

'There are a few. My mum had some and my aunt has some too. I've seen a few from the renovation of the house when mum and dad first moved in and a couple from just before dad died, when mum was pregnant with me. Why?'

'It's just an idea.' I am nervous. 'But I was wondering if there is any chance that your aunt might like to come to the house. I so badly want to do it justice, to restore it sympathetically, back to its former glory. I just don't really know where to start. We have the wallpaper and curtains plus a couple of bits of furniture, but the rest of the house has been stripped.' I wait for his reply.

'The family took everything of any worth after my dad died, the paintings, and the furniture. Most of it was sold. It broke my mother's heart.' He winces at the thought.

'I would love to know exactly how it used to look, what it felt like to live there,' I say softly. 'If your aunt could help that would be amazing. We would pay her, of course,' I add quickly. I don't want him to think that I am taking advantage of her.

'I'll talk to her, I'm sure she would love to help. It would be a nice distraction for her too, she lost her husband last year and then my mum soon after. It's been really tough on her.'

'That's so sad.' I feel for the elegant woman from the auction who I am yet to meet.

'This might be just what she needs.' Luca is clearly thinking about it. 'She loved the house just like mum did. They were always talking about it. They especially loved the artwork. The Russo family art collection is quite famous.'

'I didn't know,' I say, willing him to continue. 'Mum and Aunt Sylvie took me to see a few of the paintings that were bought from the house by local museums after dad's accident.'

I can see his mind taking him back, maybe to the trips with his mum, maybe to images of the artwork. He is lost in his thoughts and I don't want to interrupt. It is only a few seconds before he composes himself. He looks me straight in the eye.

'Let me talk to her,' he says again, and he smiles at me. The devastating smile that throws me into disarray again. Behind us I see Jen stand up. I catch her eye and gesture for her to come over.

'Luca, this is Jen, my friend and business partner. Jen, this is Luca. Luca Russo.'

'Nice to meet you.' Jen shakes Luca's hand and I see her face change as she processes the name.

'Likewise. Congratulations on the house.' Luca is courteous and more formal than he has been with me.

'Thank you.' I can tell Jen is desperate to ask more but is holding back. 'We're off,' — she looks at me — 'Are you coming?'

I don't want to leave but I can't come up with a valid reason to stay so I nod and push my chair back to stand up. Luca reaches into his jacket pocket and pulls a business card from his wallet.

'Here, my number's on this. I'll talk to my aunt in the morning. Give me a call tomorrow and I'll let you know what she says'.

'Great! Thank you so much!' I reach for the card. 'It was lovely to meet you, Luca.' I will the colour in my cheeks not to rise as I look at him.

'You too, Sophie.'

He takes a wad of cash from his wallet and leaves it on the table before saying his goodbyes and walking away from us across the square. I watch him leave as Jen, Pauline and Frank gather around, impatient for all of the information. I tell them everything on the walk home.

'Poor boy, such a sad story. He seems like such a lovely chap.' Pauline is clearly emotional. Frank doesn't comment on the back-story but he likes the idea of getting Aunt Sylvie involved in the renovation work. We all hope that we will see Luca again. Me more than all of them.

Chapter 20

The next day Jen and I are up early. We eat boiled eggs and make a list of things to do as a priority. First on the list is to ring around builders, plumbers and electricians to get complete quotes on the work that needs doing in the bedrooms, bathrooms and kitchen. Then we need to get back in touch with the landscaping and pool guys that we have already met through Sara's dad.

The next big thing on the list is to make another list! We needed to plan exactly what other renovations are needed to change the house into our hotel and then finally, we can think about furnishing and decorating. There is so much to do it is more than a little overwhelming. I can see Jen biting her lip.

'Are you OK?'

She nods. 'Just taking it all in, there is so much to do!'

'Don't worry.' I hope I sound more confident than I feel. 'Once we start actually doing things it will be fine, everything looks worse on paper!' I pull out the timeline annex from the business plan that sets out what we want to do by when and hand it to her. 'We have a good plan, I'll update it with all of this.' I pick up the lists and notes that we have made since the day before. 'It's realistic, I'm sure it is, we just need to make a start on it. Tomorrow we can call everyone and get the ball rolling and then you will feel better about everything. In the meantime we should put some names to all of this, you know, divide up the jobs between us so that we can get started on things. What do you think?'

'Good idea.' Jen brightens. 'I'll have a shower then we can get to it. What are you going to do about Luca?' she asks casually, but I know that she is eager to know if I'm going to call him.

'I'm not sure.' I try to sound equally casual. I have been looking at my watch all morning wondering when would be an appropriate time to call, not too early so as to harass him, but not so late that he thinks I don't want his help. 'I'll probably give him a call once I've had a shower, see if his aunt is interested in coming over to the house again.'

'Good idea.' Jen tries to hide a smile that we both know is there. For some reason I am insanely nervous about calling Luca, which doesn't make sense because he gave me his number, he asked me to call and I said that I would. It is only about work, after all. While Jen is in the shower I sit on my bed and look at my phone. What should I say to him?

Just as I am trying to find the words, my phone flashes. Andrew is calling. I watch it guiltily and let it ring off. When the flashing has stopped I pick it up and fire off a quick text:

'Hi! So sorry, in a meeting and can't answer my phone! Hope you OK, speak soon! S x'

185

Suddenly the call to Luca feels like an easy one. Without thinking about it any further I pick up his business card, it is a thick cream with black and gold writing embossed on it. Impressive. 'Luca Russo. Arts and Antiques Specialist.'

I dial the number and he answers after just a couple of rings. 'Luca Russo.'

'Hi,' I stumble, like I always do when I'm nervous. Thank God he can't see me blushing this time. 'It's Sophie, we met yesterday.'

'Sophie, hi!' He sounds surprisingly cheerful.

'I just wondered if you have managed to speak to your aunt?' I ask. 'I thought perhaps you both might like to come over to the house today?' I hold my breath while I wait for him to answer.

'We would love to.' I breathe out as quietly as I can and try to keep my voice steady, despite the huge smile that has taken over my face.

'Fantastic, it will be so great to get your help.' I try to sound business-like. I hear him laugh lightly at the end of the phone.

'How about two?' he asks.

'Great, see you there.'

I hang up the phone before I have a chance to say anything silly. I can hear Jen coming out of the bathroom and I grab my towel.

'We're meeting Luca and his aunt at two,' I tell her as we pass on the small landing.

'Oh, great! Wash your hair!' she calls after me as I go into the bathroom and close the door behind me. I pick up her sponge, open the door again and throw it at her back.

'It's a business meeting!' I laugh as she shrieks and runs into her bedroom, quickly shutting her door so that the sponge lands on it leaving a big, wet mark. I chuckle to myself and jump into the hot shower that is still running.

By the time I have washed and dried my hair, got dressed in my pretty floral summer dress and put on a bit of make-up, Jen is downstairs working on our plans and to do lists. 'You look nice.'

'Thanks.' I ignore the obvious undertone. 'How are you getting on?'

'Good, making progress. Can you grab me a juice from the fridge, please? I'll talk you through what I've done before we go.' We work through the plans until it is time to meet Luca and his Aunt Sylvie, then we walk over to the house, excited to see it, and them, again. As we make our way up the hill and over the hump, I can see them already standing outside the large iron gate. They are both looking through it at the house and talking to each other so they haven't seen us coming. Luca is wearing a pale-yellow polo shirt with the same navy chino shorts that he was wearing yesterday. He looks absurdly handsome standing with one hand in his pocket and the other pointing at something beyond the gate. He is more relaxed than I have seen him, his stance and his face are less tense, even from this distance. My mother would call him 'dapper'. She likes a man who dresses well and takes care of himself.

Luca's aunt is wearing a pretty white, knee-length summer dress with navy flowers around the hem and a navy sash around the waist, which is tied in a small bow at the back. I recognise her face from the auction, but up close I can see that it is soft and pretty. She has bright white hair pulled back into a neat, low, pony tail and simple diamond studs in her ears. She is holding a smart navy, patent handbag on her arm, which matches the sash on her dress and the navy pumps on her feet. She is immaculate. I would have felt intimidated if she didn't have such a warm smile.

They turn towards us when they hear us approach. Luca does the introductions and Aunt Sylvie greets us as if we are old friends. She takes both my hands in hers and thanks me for letting her come back to the house.

'Please, don't thank me,' I say, embarrassed. 'You are doing me such a favour, I 'm so thrilled that you are here.'

She squeezes my hands. 'Let's go inside, shall we? I've been dying to see the place again, it's been so long.'

'Of course, let's.' Jen steps forward to push open the unlocked gate and hold it open for us to walk through. Luca puts his arm out for Sylvie to hold and she links hers through it as I let them walk ahead of me.

'This must have been so beautiful,' I gesture to the grand, circular drive way and the huge fountain at the centre of it as we pause to take in the grounds at the front of the house.

'It was,' Sylvie smiles. She looks around, taking everything in. Her eyes are full of nostalgia. I can't tell if she is thinking back to happy times or sad. There is so much emotion on her face that I want to give her some privacy, but when she speaks her voice is steady, still full of warmth and a hint of pride. 'It was such a grand house, you know, the best house for miles around. Everyone loved coming here. Rialto really knew how to entertain, and my sister was such a wonderful host. This was the place that everyone wanted to be!'

We reach the front door and I unlock it. When we step inside I see her grip tighten on Luca's arm. She says something quietly in Italian. Luca places his hand on top of hers. I don't want to intrude on what feels like a private moment, so I walk up the entrance hall to open the doors to the rooms either side and suggest that Jen goes through to open the back doors and let some air in. When I turn back I can see that Sylvie's eyes are thick with moisture. She is standing still in the entrance hall looking around. Luca speaks to her again in Italian and she smiles at him.

'No, child, I'm fine. I am. Just so many memories.' She rallies and rubs his arm then looks up at his tall frame. 'Come on, child, let me show you around your house.' I know she doesn't mean it to, but the phrase makes me feel uncomfortable, like I am an outsider in my own house, but as she walks past me she takes my hand and smiles warmly. 'I could tell you so many stories about this place.' There is a glint in her eye.

'Oh, please do!' I let her lead me into the morning room.

It is another long, hot afternoon so we open the doors onto the back patio to let the air circulate.

'It feels so empty in here.' Sylvie looks around her. 'When Lucia and Rialto were here it was always so full of life. There was a large record player in the corner over there.' She points to the far end of the room adjacent to the library. 'It was state of the art in its day, not like the fancy gadgets you all have now of course, but it sounded wonderful to us. Rialto loved music;

he was always bringing home something new for us to listen to. He would whirl Lucia around this room like she was floating on air. They were wonderful dancers.' Her voice is wistful; the obvious joy in her memories is tinged with a painful sadness in her eyes. Luca is standing very still by the window watching his aunt and listening intently to what she has to say. We walk around the house with Sylvie as if we are on a guided tour.

'We would sit for hours playing Bridge in here.' She walks into the library. 'On a Sunday afternoon Raymond and I...' she stops and looks at us. 'Raymond is my husband.' She pauses. 'I apologise. He *was* my husband. I don't think I will ever get used to that,' she sighs, her breath heavy with sadness. 'He will always be my husband in here.' She taps her heart gently with her hand and her eyes mist again but she still smiles. 'We would play cards with my sister and Rialto every Sunday afternoon. Sometimes Rialto's brother would come with whatever girlfriend he was seeing at the time,' — she laughs at the memory — 'We would play all evening, with the record player in the background. The girls would drink sherry and the boys whisky. They were good times.'

'So, Rialto's brother liked your sister?' I ask surprised. 'I thought that his family disapproved of Lucia.'

'Oh, they did,' Sylvie nods. 'Very much so. But Roberto was different from the rest of the family. He was the youngest brother and he loved Rialto very much. He looked up to him and he was very fond of Lucia. Actually I always thought he had a bit of a thing for her. He was the wild child of the family, never did what he was told. The only one that he listened to was Rialto. He was devastated when he was killed. I think it affected him the most.'

She takes a deep breath; the memories are etched on her face. Luca is watching her closely and the sadness is mirrored in his face too. It is hard to watch but fascinating to listen to. 'After your father died,' — she turns to Luca as if he should be the one to hear this — 'Roberto retreated back into the family. I know he would have wanted to help your mother desperately but he had watched his parents lose their beloved son and they needed him badly. He needed them too. Without Rialto he had no one else. I know that he must have felt terrible and I know that he would have tried to help Lucia, to stop his parents from throwing her out of the house, but they were stubborn people. They wouldn't have listened. He was powerless to help and very much caught up in his own grief. It is all very sad.'

'Are you OK, dear?' she asks Luca as he walks across the room and stares out of the window.

'I'm fine.' His voice is hoarse. 'I think I'll wait outside whilst you walk around with the girls, if that's OK, get some air.'

'Of course, child.' Sylvie's voice is kind and concerned. We watch Luca walk out of the room. 'It's very hard on him, you know,' she tells us. 'He misses his mother terribly. They were so close. This house was so much a part of his childhood, even though he never lived here. We would bring him here to tell him stories. I think this is where he feels closest to her. Being inside must be quite emotional for him.'

'Of course.' I hold back an overwhelming urge to go after Luca.

'Shall we go upstairs?' Sylvie asks. 'I'll show you where I used to sleep!'

'Oh, yes please, let's.' I am grateful for the change in tone. The three of us walk through the bedrooms and Sylvie tells us more stories about the people who had stayed in them and even some of the couples who had got together in them. Jen and I are entranced. It feels like we are walking through a movie of her life and we are completely taken in by her and her history. We must have been up there for quite a while because, just as we are taking in the view from the bathroom window, I hear Luca call up the stairs.

'Is everything OK up there?'

'Oh gosh,' Sylvie laughs. 'I think I have got quite carried away! We should go back downstairs. I must be boring you something silly!' She calls back to Luca: 'Sorry, darling, I've been chatting away, lost track of time, we are coming down now.'

'No hurry,' Luca laughs. 'Just checking you haven't got lost!' he laughs again and we hear him walk back in to the morning room.

On the way downstairs we are insistent that Sylvie hasn't bored us for a single second. 'I could listen to you all day,' Jen tells her. 'Such wonderful stories.'

'It's true, Sylvie,' I agree. 'I really feel like I know the place now, like I understand its personality. Not only have you been a captivating storyteller, you have helped us no end. I think that we might just be able to do the place justice now.' Sylvie goes pink with pleasure at the praise.

'I have some photographs,' she tells us. 'They are packed away in some of Lucia's boxes. I haven't been able to go through them yet but I think that I can face it now. Would you like to see them?'

'We would love it,' I gush. 'If you don't mind, that would help us so much.'

'It would be a pleasure, dear. I'll have a look tonight. It has been so nice being back here. I'm sure I sound like a very silly old lady to you, but somehow it has helped to fill a few holes. I was worried that I would find it too hard, but actually it has been very cathartic. I feel close to them all again. Is that silly?' For the first time she looks fragile.

'Not at all.' I put my hand on her arm. 'You are welcome here any time, Sylvie. In fact, if it wouldn't be too much of an imposition, I would absolutely love it if you would like to be involved with some of the decoration work. I will be doing a lot of the house on my own whilst Jen is still at college, and I would be so grateful for your help.'

Sylvie positively glows. 'I would just love that. I have been quite lonely these past months, what a wonderful gift that would be.'

'You are the gift! It would mean a lot to us. Plus I will get to hear more of your wonderful stories!' I laugh and so does Sylvie

'Deal!' She opens her arms wide so that Jen and I can give her a hug. Feeling buoyed by events, we all head out into the garden full of smiles and laughter.

'Well, you look happy.' Luca is clearly pleased to see his aunt looking so full of joy.

'The girls have asked me to help them with the house. I'm delighted,' Sylvie tells him.

'That's great.' Luca looks pleased. 'They couldn't have picked a better woman.' Sylvie smiles at her nephew and blushes.

'Shall we have some tea?' Jen asks. 'I bought some supplies in yesterday so I can probably rustle up a biscuit or two.'

'That would be lovely.' Sylvie rubs her hands together. 'I am a little peckish now.'

Luca pulls together the few bits of furniture left in and around the house so that we can all sit together outside. There are two iron patio chairs which have definitely seen better days, a small wooden chair from the morning room and an upended wooden box that Luca sits on. We drink the tea and arrange to meet at the house again in a couple of days' time to look at the photos and discuss ideas for furniture and decoration. I know that Sylvie is going to be no end of help. She knows specialists who can restore the curtains and the chandeliers, plus she remembers everything that was originally in the house and can describe it all perfectly. All in all it is a very successful afternoon. I feel much more confident about work starting the following day, and I feel closer to the house than ever. As we leave I thank Sylvie and hug her again. I catch Luca's eye over her shoulder and, just for a second, his gaze lingers on mine. He smiles and mouths the words 'thank you' to me. I want to say something back but he has already turned around to open his car door. Jen and I wave them off.

'Well that was a success.' Jen says what I am thinking: 'What an amazing lady.'

'Amazing,' I agree, and we head back to the cottage.

Chapter 21

Work starts in earnest the next day. The house is a hive of activity as builders, plumbers and electricians all come and go. Frank has done an amazing job persuading people to start working for us straight away, and Sara's dad has drafted in a team of his builders, who are already making headway upstairs. There is dust everywhere. I make a trip to the village to stock up on supplies for the workmen — though I'll probably keep the cream meringues for myself! I chat to Katarina, who offers to drop round a selection of sandwiches and cakes at lunchtimes during the week, which I think is an excellent idea. I'm pretty sure that she just wants an excuse to get away from the shop and have a nose around the house, but I am grateful nonetheless and accept her offer. It will save me making the trip into the village every day and, with the amount going on at the house, there isn't going to be a minute to waste.

By mid-afternoon the house looks exactly the same on the outside but is (I hope) an organised mess on the inside! The floors are covered in groundsheets and the groundsheets are covered in dust and mess. Prepping the house, the builders and the tradesmen is exhausting work, and the day comes and goes in a blur, which sets the tone for the rest of the week. Walls are knocked down and rebuilt, a steady stream of people come and go with an array of machinery and tools. At times I wish I have another body, or a few actually, as I run from one room to another answering questions and asking questions in an interesting mix of broken English (the workmen) and very broken Italian (me, with the help of a guidebook and a key phrase sheet that Frank has helpfully written for me).

It is exhausting but I am elated at the progress that is being made in such a short time. I pitch in where I can and every evening ends the same way, with me aching from body to bone, exhausted but excited. I am still amazed that it is all happening but there is no mistaking the chaos around me. In the afternoon on the last day of our first week of work on the house, I stand in the morning room and try to assess what still needs to be done before I can go home and get a couple of days' much-needed rest over the weekend. I wipe my forehead, which is sweating from the combination of hard work and the hot afternoon sun that is streaming through the windows, now bare without their curtains. As I wipe my now wet hand down the front of the old t-shirt I am wearing over my cut-off denim shorts, Pauline and Frank come through the back doors.

'Right, love, we're done for the day,' Frank tells me. 'Pauline and I are going to dinner with some young chap called Jake. Do you know what we should expect?' He smiles as he asks me the question.

'Don't put Sophie in a position, Frank!' Pauline playfully taps him on the arm. 'I'm sure Jake is wonderful, I can't wait to meet him!' She raises her shoulders and eyebrows at the same time in excited anticipation.

'Well, you have nothing to worry about!' I look at Frank. 'Jake is really great. You'll love him.'

'Jake is great, eh?' Frank laughs at the accidental half-rhyme. 'Well, we'll see. There is little else that can be done here today, love. The builders are packing up but they will be back again early on Monday morning. You should head home and get some rest. It's been a good week.'

'Thanks, Frank,' I say, grateful for the confirmation of good progress and the excuse to go home and put my feet up with a glass of wine. Pauline and Frank leave but I stay behind for a little while longer, to collect and wash up the empty mugs and glasses left lying around by the builders and to ensure that all of the windows and doors are locked. As I pull the front door closed and put the key in the large lock to secure it, I hear the noise of a car pulling into the driveway. I hope I haven't forgotten something, I'm not expecting anyone. I turn to see who has arrived, racking my brain to remember a delivery I might have missed but I am pleasantly surprised to see Luca pulling up in a large black BMW. His engine is still running but he lowers the window and calls to me:

'Sophie, hi! Are you finished for the day?'

'Hi! I am, thank goodness! Just locking up.'

'Are you too exhausted for dinner?' he asks. 'Just want to say thank you for everything with Sylvie?'

'That would be lovely, though I should be doing the thanking, not you!' I am very glad that I am still a fair distance away from the car so that he can't see my damn cheeks turning pink. Suddenly I remember what a state I must look. 'Do you want to go now, though? I really need to change, I'm full of dust and dirt!'

'No problem.' Luca leans over and opens the passenger door from the inside. 'Jump in, I'll run you home. I can wait while you get changed.'

'Great, thanks.' I am not at all pleased at the prospect of sitting so close to Luca when I am looking, and quite possibly smelling, so far from my best, but I don't have much choice now, so I get in the car and open my window in the hope that any untoward smells might waft outside before they waft under Luca's nose.

'How are you?' he asks as I get in.

'Good, thanks.' I stare straight ahead so that he doesn't have a chance to look at my make-up-free face close up. 'This is a nice surprise,' I add and Luca smiles.

'Well I was passing, heading back to Sylvie's actually, but she has her bridge night tonight and I saw you leaving so thought I would chance my luck!' I am delighted that he wants to take me for dinner and smile inwardly at the thought that he thinks seeing me is lucky, but irrationally I am slightly put out that it's a spur of the moment thing and not a planned visit because he wanted to see me. But why on earth would he have done that, he barely even knows me, after all. We reach the cottage quickly and Luca pulls up outside.

'Would you like to come in and have a drink while I get ready?' I ask, not wanting to leave him sitting outside. 'I won't be long, I promise!'

'Lovely, thanks. Take your time.' Luca opens his car door and walks around to my side. As I open the door he grabs it at the top and pulls it back. 'Allow me.' He looks right at my face now and smiles. The combination of his smile and accent is pretty devastating.

'Thanks,' I mumble and look away from him quickly. I turn and walk past him into the cottage, keeping my eyes firmly on the ground. Inside Jen is downstairs looking gorgeous in cream trousers and a mint-green, silk top, clearly ready for the date with Jake and her parents.

'Hi!' she greets me happily, then spots Luca behind me. 'Hi, Luca.' I can hear the surprise in her voice. 'How are you?'

'Hi, Jen, I'm great thanks. You look nice.' Jen blushes, which is a rarity.

'Thank you! I have a date,' she explains, as if she wouldn't be looking nice otherwise. 'With my parents and my boyfriend!' she grimaces but we both know that she has nothing to worry about.

'Good luck with that!' Luca grins.

'Thanks! Can I get you a drink?' she offers.

'Lovely, thanks. Whatever you have is great.'

'I'll get it.' I leave them in the sitting room and go into the kitchen where I take a beer from the fridge and pour it into a glass before taking it back out to him. 'Right, then,' I say, handing it to him, 'I'll just nip upstairs and get ready. Make yourself at home.'

I can tell that Jen is desperate to find out why and how Luca is here but, before I have a chance to get her upstairs on an urgent clothes-picking task, a car beeps outside.

'That must be my parents.' She grabs her bag and heads for the door. 'Wish me luck!'

'You don't need it!' I shout after her. 'Have fun!'

'Thanks. You too!' She shoots me a quizzical grin that makes it clear she wants to know everything as soon as she gets home and closes the door behind her.

I shower as quickly as I possibly can. It is typical that this is the first time in ages that I get to go out with a gorgeous man and I have about five minutes to get ready! As I wash my hair I try and think of some conversation savers. I always like to have a few topics of conversation prepared to bring up in case of an awkward silence but my mind is so consumed by everything going on at the house, that I struggle to come up with anything that doesn't involve local tradesmen and building materials!

Out of the shower I put on my minimum make-up requirements: tinted moisturiser, blusher, mascara and some lip gloss. I don't want Luca to think that I need hours to get ready, much better for him to think that I'm a natural beauty and only need a few minutes to prepare for a spur-of-the-moment dinner with a gorgeous man! I work super quickly and, as I dry my hair, I kick open my wardrobe door and peruse the contents to find something to wear. Running out of time (in my head anyway) I decide to wear the coral dress that I wore for the dinner party. It is the newest and prettiest thing that I have and he hasn't seen it before. Damn it! He has seen it before! I flash back to seeing Luca outside the house as I dragged the case of water up the hill in my dress from the night before and a pair of flip flops! Why hadn't I just pulled on some shorts for goodness sake? I rifle through the hangers but nothing looks right so I wrap a towel around myself and dash

201

across to Jen's room. She was clearly having outfit dilemmas too, as most of her wardrobe is strewn across her bed. On the top of the pile of clothes is a simple white shift dress with a scooped back. I slip it over my head. It is longer on me than it is on Jen and a little snugger but it is simple and elegant and it looks lovely against my tanned skin. I quickly rub some moisturiser into my legs and spray perfume on my wrists and neck, then all over me, before I grab my bag and go back downstairs. I check my watch. Twenty-five minutes. I'm pleased: less than half an hour is not bad at all.

'You look great.'

I'm sure Luca is just being courteous but I thank him anyway, relieved that I can look at his face now that mine is not covered in dust and sweat. I notice that his glass is almost empty. 'Would you like another glass or shall we go?' I ask him.

'Let's go.' He hands me the glass anyway and I put it in the kitchen. 'There's a nice little trattoria in the next village if that's OK?' he calls after me. We step outside and I close the door behind us.

Chapter 22

The trattoria is a quaint place with traditional, red and white checked tablecloths and small oil lamps in the middle of each table. There are a few tables outside, along with a large blackboard that has the menu written on it by hand. Two other couples are sitting outside and a large family occupies most of the room inside. Luca speaks smoothly in Italian to the middle-aged man who comes out to greet us and who then ushers us to one of the remaining tables at the front. We sit down and he speaks again to Luca, then nods and smiles at us both before going back inside.

'Would you like wine?' Luca asks me.

'Yes please, I'd love a glass of red.'

Luca orders two glasses of red wine from the young waitress and we read the menu on the blackboard in silence while we wait for the drinks.

'It all sounds so good.' I break the silence when it starts to get uncomfortable. It has probably only been a few seconds but I have never been good at silences and I am beginning to wish that I had concentrated more on those conversation savers. 'I'm hungry!' I add.

'Good, the food is nice here, you'll like it. What are you having?'

Not sure if he is having a starter or not, and too embarrassed to ask, I tell him I would like the Spaghetti Vongole.

'Good choice.' He nods his approval and, when the waitress comes back with our wine, he orders my spaghetti and something for himself, which I think is the lamb. 'I've ordered some bread and oil too,' he tells me when the waitress has gone off with our order. 'You need energy with so much work going on in the house!'

'Thank you.'

I am touched and pleased because I really am ravenous! Thankfully we chat easily as we tear the bread and use it to mop up the oil and balsamic vinegar in a small terracotta dish in front of us. Luca tells me about some of his favourite restaurants in the area and asks about Jen, where she is studying and what type of food she plans on making in the hotel.

'I'm not sure really, we haven't discussed menu details yet.' I tell him. 'I know that she wants to offer cookery weekends though, and she wants food to be a big feature so I'm sure she has been putting a lot of thought into it.' I make a mental note to talk to Jen about the food and menus for the hotel.

'If she wants to do some research she should go to La Sirensa,' Luca is clearly a foodie, which I love. 'It's in the hills about an hour north from here and in my humble opinion it is the best food in Italy.'

'Wow! That is some claim!' I laugh.

'It is but trust me, it's true.' He laughs too. 'I will take you there if you like, then you can taste it for yourself.'

'I would love that!' The combination of wine and butterflies in my stomach is making me feel giddy. The food arrives just in time and I dig straight in. It really is good, though I am starting to regret ordering the spaghetti. I forgot how difficult it can be to eat and I struggle to look poised and elegant as I flip and scoop the errant bits hanging off my fork into my mouth.

'So what did you do in England?' Luca seems genuinely interested, it doesn't sound like a conversation saver but then men probably don't even think about things like that anyway.

'It's a bit of a long story,' I warn him but, with his encouragement, I tell him about giving up my job at Morgan Stanley and working at Stationery Is Us until I came to Italy and found the Russo house, which is now my house.

'So the house is your purpose, your dream.'

I'm not sure if he is asking a question or making a statement and I feel uncomfortable telling him that I think the house is part of my path in life when it has been so much a part of his. I tread carefully. 'I think it is. I'm sure it is. All I really know is that I have never felt so alive. Or so happy. It just feels right. I still can't actually believe that this is all happening to me, I can't believe my luck.'

To my relief Luca smiles, the dazzling smile, and my stomach flips.

'I think it's amazing, I admire your courage and ambition.' He pauses and looks at me. I beam inwardly and blush outwardly, for once though I don't care, the sun has set and the evening light is low so my cheeks can do what they like so long as Luca is saying nice things to me. 'And I think you're right,' he goes on. 'I think that the house is meant for you. I can see how much it means to you and what a great job you are doing with it.'

I am so pleased and relieved that I think I might cry. I sip my wine and try to compose myself. 'Thank you. That means a lot.'

He raises his glass. 'To the house.' I clink mine to it and feel absurdly happy.

'What about you?' I ask him. 'How did you get into arts and antiques?'

'I don't remember ever not loving them,' he says. 'Art was such a big part of my life when I was a child. Whenever we had a spare day mum would take me to the galleries and museums in Florence. Sometimes we would travel further afield, to Pisa and Rome. It was a shared passion. She took me to see some of the paintings that once hung in the house and I loved them because she loved them. There were some amazing pieces. To have to part with them after living with them every day must have been torture for her.' I can see the sadness that I have seen so many times already in his face again but it doesn't stay for long. 'It was a natural progression to go into the business. I just love being around beautiful things. I find peace in them.'

'How wonderful to love what you do so much. I can't tell you how much I would envy you if my life hadn't changed so dramatically in the last few weeks!'

It is a revelation to me that I don't envy him. It is a nice feeling to be happy for someone else without wanting to be like them. I think being happy makes me a nicer person. I smile to myself at the thought.

'I can take you to see some of the local specialists that I know if you would like, help you find some new pieces for the house,' Luca offers.

'That would be amazing, thank you!' I am very aware that this is the second time tonight that Luca has suggested that we see each other again, albeit on a professional level this time and I try desperately not to give away how thrilled I am at the prospect.

'Would you like dessert?' Luca changes the subject. I am full now with bread and pasta but I don't want to go home yet.

I shake my head. 'I couldn't possibly, but I would love a cappuccino if you have the time.'

'All the time in the world.' He beckons to the waitress and orders a cappuccino and a black coffee. I settle back in my chair, pleased that I get to enjoy his company a little longer.

'When do you expect to have all of the work done on the house?' Luca asks, returning to our favourite topic.

'Hopefully by the end of August, at least that's when the main body of building work and decorating should be finished,' I tell him. 'I'll need to do some furnishing and stocking afterwards but the plan is to be open for business by the beginning of September. I need to start work on the cottage in the grounds soon too,' I add as an after-thought, but more to myself than to Luca. 'The sooner I can move in there the sooner I can be on site all of the time and really make it my home.'

'Is it a big job?' he asks.

'Not really. Mainly cleaning and painting, a bit of modernising. I just need to find the time amongst everything else.'

'Well, I'd be happy to help,' Luca offers — that's three! 'I've plenty of time on my hands, August is my quietest month by far and I am planning on being around to spend more time with Sylvie whilst I can, and I'm pretty handy with a paint brush!'

'That would be amazing, thank you so much!'

This dinner is getting better by the minute!

'Sure.' He sounds casual. I must not read too much into this. 'So are you going to have a launch party? When everything's ready?' he asks me.

I haven't thought about a launch party but now that he mentions it I can't believe that I haven't! I'm usually the first to plan a party. 'I don't know!' I admit. 'I mean, of course, yes, we will have to do something but I haven't planned anything yet. Is that terrible? It's all been a bit of a whirlwind!'

'I wouldn't worry,' he leans back in his chair. 'But it's a good time to start thinking about it. September is a wonderful month here, not too hot but still warm, and the countryside is beautiful, it would be a great time to launch before the winter sets in.'

'You are so right.' I'm embarrassed that I haven't thought of it already. 'It's next on my list!' I laugh and I add it to the ever-expanding list in my head of things to talk to Jen about. 'I'm so glad I came tonight, you have been such a help!'

For a split second I think Luca looks put out and I am just about to explain that I am not only pleased I came because of his offers of help, but before I speak he smiles again. I watch as the corner of his eyes wrinkle. He is smiling with his eyes. I am sure that I don't need to tell him that I am pleased I came because I like him, because I like his company. I really do, but I don't think I need to say it just now.

We finish our coffees and Luca insists on paying the bill. Then we drive home through the country lanes. In the dark I can't recognise one road from the next but it doesn't take long. Luca pulls up outside the cottage, and again he gets out of the car to open my door for me. I can't say I'm not used to this. Andrew has done it for me many a time but somehow with Luca it feels more real. Authentic somehow, as if he was brought up to do it and would do it for any woman as a matter of course, whereas I'm pretty sure that Andrew just does it to make an impression.

I step out of the car.

'Thank you for a lovely evening.' I look at Luca's face briefly wondering if he is going to kiss me.

'Thank *you*.' He emphasises the 'you'. 'And thank you again for involving Sylvie with the house; it really does mean a lot to her.'

'Not at all, she will be an enormous help and a pleasure to have around. Can you tell her we will pick her up at one on Monday? We're going to Florence to look at furniture and she's coming to lend her expert eye.'

'Of course.'

He leans in and my stomach lurches as I think he is going to kiss me, I tip my head towards him ever so slightly but he turns his face and kisses me squarely on the cheek. Desperately hoping that he didn't realise my mistake, I quickly say goodbye and scuttle down the path to the cottage without looking back.

Jen isn't home yet and I am relieved not to have to re-live everything because I am really exhausted and a little mortified at the last turn of events. I take my make-up off half-heartedly and climb into bed. I prop my little window open to feel the gentle night breeze on my face. It feels wonderful to lie down under my soft sheets. I play my conversations with Luca over and over in my head until I fall into a deep and dreamless sleep.

Chapter 23

I wake up blissfully late and without an alarm clock. The cottage is quiet except for the birds, who are chirping sweetly outside by bedroom window. Jen is obviously enjoying a lie-in too. Downstairs I open the back doors and the kitchen windows and let the warm air and sweet smells flood through the cottage. I take a long, deep breath, close my eyes and throw my head back. Sometimes it feels really good to be alive, and today is one of those days. The only thing that could make me feel better right now is a bacon sandwich with ketchup and mayonnaise. I go to the fridge, my conversations with Luca last night are still running through my mind. I put some bacon in the frying pan and pop a couple of pieces of bread in the toaster. Immediately the smells waft around me and my stomach rumbles hungrily at them. The smell must have made its way upstairs too as I can hear Jen moving around and I put a couple of extra rashers in the pan. She comes down just as the toast pops.

'Morning! Bacon sandwich?' I ask her.

'Amazing!' she smiles gratefully.

'How did it go with Jake and your parents?' I ask her, but I can tell from her general air of happiness that it went well.

'Brilliant,' she confirms. 'They got on like a house on fire. We had a really lovely night.' I hand Jen her sandwich and we take them into the garden and sit on the patio, eating them hungrily. 'Oh my God!' Jen exclaims, wiping ketchup from the side of her mouth.

'What's wrong?' I look around panicked by her tone.

'I can't believe I have been up for nearly ten minutes and I haven't asked you about Luca yet! I must still be half asleep!'

I laugh, relieved that it is nothing more serious, and take another bite of my sandwich.

'Sooo.' She pushes against my arm. 'What happened? I didn't even know that you were going to see him last night, I can't believe you didn't tell me!' She tries to grab my plate with the last quarter of sandwich on it. 'No more food until I hear everything!' she laughs.

'OK, OK!' I laugh too. 'I didn't know either, he was passing the house and pulled in when he saw me, to thank me for involving Sylvie, then he asked me to dinner.'

'That's nice! So how was dinner? Did anything happen?' Jen gets straight to the point!

I cringe at the memory of the missed kiss. 'No, of course not, it was just a thank you dinner, that's all! It was a great night though and he has offered to help us find some art and decoration pieces for the hotel. Oh, and paint the cottage too!'

'How lovely of him!' Jen is impressed. 'He must like you! Are you going out again?'

'I don't know,' I say truthfully. 'But he did say that he would take me to some fancy restaurant that he knows up in the hills, so maybe.'

'Umm, I'd say that's pretty definite!' I can tell Jen is excited for me but the memory of our goodbye is still fresh in my mind and I can't bring myself to believe that there will be a second date. Or even that we have had a first date. It was just a thank you dinner after all!

'We'll see.' I make light of it all. 'Luca did mention something important though, I think we should talk about it.'

'What?' Jen stuffs the last piece of sandwich in her mouth and looks at me.

'He asked if we are having a launch party for the hotel, when the work is finished.'

'I hadn't thought of that!' Jen exclaims.

'Exactly!' my tone matches hers.

'Of course we need a launch party. How have we overlooked something so important?' She throws her hands up.

'That's what I said! But to be fair the last couple of weeks have been a bit crazy and the work has only really got going in the last week. There can't be a launch party without a hotel to launch!'

'True,' Jen agrees. 'It has all happened super fast but we do need to start thinking about it now. We will need time to plan it and to get invites out, so the sooner we get on to it the better.'

I agree with her and I suggest going to the village for lunch later where we can start to make some plans. 'We can talk to Paulo and Katarina too, they might be able to help us with the catering and supplies.'

'Good idea,' Jen nods. 'My class graduates at the end of August. I could talk to a couple of my classmates and see if they want to help with the catering too.

'Great idea.' I am enthusiastic and Jen is clearly pleased. Feeling full and looking forward to planning the party, we treat ourselves to a lazy morning in the cottage throwing around ideas before we get dressed and walk into the village.

The afternoon is as long and lazy as the morning but it is productive too. Katarina and Paulo are pleased to see us and they sit with us intermittently throughout the afternoon. We chat comfortably and update them on developments with the house and some of our plans for the launch party. Katarina is very excited at the prospect of a party and offers to help with the decorations and serving the food. She tells us that she has a couple of friends who could help serve too and offers to ask them as soon as we agree on a date. Paulo is lovely too. He offers his help with food and drink supplies once we decide on a menu. He also tells us about a vineyard that his uncle owns in Umbria and suggests that we might like to go and taste his wines to see if he would be a suitable supplier to the hotel. I am thrilled. Not only am I desperate to go wine tasting and to check out some local vineyards, but we also need to start sourcing suppliers for when the hotel is up and running and it is nice to have some trusted recommendations.

By the end of the day we have achieved quite a lot. We have drawn up a guest list, which includes asking Fi to spread the invite across as many of her journo friends as possible; we have decided on a traditional Italian menu that Jen will create. We want a buffet but nothing run of the mill, an impressive

214

spread that looks incredible and tastes incredible too, plus lots of canapés. And we agree a date: Saturday 13th September. The launch of our new life. Four weeks today!

Chapter 24

After a quiet Sunday spent catching up on paperwork for the house and finalising plans for the launch party, which leaves Jen and me with yet another huge 'to do' list, I do at least feel rested and prepared for the busy week ahead.

Actually I am quite pleased with my share of the list. Jen has taken on all of the catering responsibilities and we have already sorted out the invites, which we designed and emailed out last night, so I am left with some of the more fun tasks, like sourcing the flowers, chair covers and drapes, fairy lights and candles etc. I want to get huge lanterns holding giant church candles to flank the driveway and the swimming pool, as well floating candles for inside the pool and fairy lights in the trees and the trellising around the house. Top of my list is to talk to Sylvie about a local garden centre where we can stock up on candles and lights as well as vases and, of course, the flowers.

Jen is at college in the morning but we have agreed to meet at the house after lunch so that we can pick Sylvie up for our trip to Florence. Our task for the afternoon is to pick out tiles and taps for the bathrooms, as well as furniture for the dining room and reception, which is going to be set up in the formal room to the right of the main entrance hall. I don't know where to start with it all really. Although I like to think that I am good at interior design and decorating and I certainly love to do it, experience has taught me otherwise. I am grateful that Sylvie and Pauline are coming to make sure that I don't mess it up. I shower and pull on my jeans and a white cotton shirt.

When I reach the house, Jen is already inside with Frank, talking to the builders about the last en-suite that needs fitting upstairs. She waves to me and raises a finger to indicate that she will be finished in a minute. I wait outside, not wanting to get drawn into the work going on inside in case I never get away! There is lots of activity outside as well, the landscape gardeners are laying lawn around the circular driveway and digging out flowerbeds around the fountain, which is being power cleaned by someone else and prepared for the new lighting to be installed around the rims of each layer.

When Jen has finished with the builders, she and Pauline come out and give me a running commentary on the progress as we drive to Aunt Sylvie's. The work is coming on well and I am encouraged by their news. Sylvie is ready and waiting at the gate outside her small cottage when we arrive.

If I had been hoping to see Luca, which I was, I would have been disappointed, which I am. There is no sign of him. Sylvie looks radiant in white capri pants and a yellow, boat-neck t-shirt trimmed with yellow and white flowers. The bright colour brings out the colour in face. She is obviously pleased to see us, waving widely as we approach.

'Hello, ladies!' she smiles at us all as Pauline opens the car door for her and helps her inside. 'I am so looking forward to our shopping trip!'

'So are we! Thanks again for coming.' I give her a little squeeze as she moves in next to me on the back seat. I desperately want to ask where Luca is, but I don't want to look too keen so I resist the temptation.

We have a very successful afternoon. After spending several hours in a very large trade and furniture suppliers just outside Florence, we have ticked off nearly all of the big things on our list and more besides. We order tables and chairs for the dining room; armchairs, coffee tables and card tables for the library; a beautiful curved, walnut reception desk flanked with drawers on either side; bedside tables, chests of drawers and wardrobes in hand-carved, solid wood for each of the rooms upstairs; and several large sofas for the morning room in primrose-yellow to match the curtains. We also choose some beautiful, rattan sun beds and outdoor furniture with white and pistachio striped upholstery for the patio and gardens. With most of the big things taken care of, we spend nearly two hours in the linen warehouse. We take our time choosing bed linens in soft pistachio-greens, rich, creamy truffle-browns and cool sky-blues. We order the thickest, fluffiest towels and robes in pure white and also white table linens with the same pistachio trims and runners.

By the time we have finished we are absolutely shattered but extremely pleased with our choices and high on the satisfaction of a great day's work. It is wonderful to finally be able to visualise the details.

To celebrate, Sylvie directs us to her favourite pizzeria. We sit outside in the warm evening air and order a bottle of Prosecco to go with our food. We sit for a long time and chat happily about the house and about the launch party. Sylvie regales us with more stories of the parties and the people that used to pass through the house when Luca's mother lived there with Rialto. The evening passes quickly and the Prosecco goes down easily. We treat ourselves to ice cream and relish in the decadence of each others' company as well as the wonderful food and drink.

It is a gorgeous evening in every sense. I don't want it to end, but as the best evenings always do, it passes so fast that without even realising it the stars have come out above us and the dark has settled around us. My watch says eleven fifteen p.m. by the time that we finally relent and ask for the bill, then stroll back to the car full of food and all of the best things in life. Pauline drives us home and despite our long day we chat and giggle all the way.

When we pull up outside Sylvie's place, Luca opens the front door and comes out to the car. Pauline winds down her window and Luca opens the back door to help Sylvie out. 'Hi, girls.'

I have forgotten how sexy his voice is. My stomach flips at the sound of it. 'I don't think I need to ask if you had a nice day.' Luca grins as Sylvie leans heavily on his arm to get out of the car.

'It was wonderful.' Sylvie straightens herself and then wobbles and grips Luca's arm again. 'I think these girls are a bad influence on me!' she giggles. 'I must be tipsy!'

She looks back into the car and winks at us. We laugh and all shout our thanks again and wish her a goodnight. Luca laughs tenderly at her too and, once she is steady on her feet, he links her arm firmly around his and leans into the open window. 'Thanks for taking care of her and bringing her home.' He sounds more like a parent than a nephew. I catch his eye and he smiles at me, his eyes wrinkle again and the cuteness is too much to bear.

'Of course!' I try hard not to sound drunk. Or swooning. Before I can think of anything else to say to delay him going inside, he taps the car roof and wishes us all a good night. He walks Sylvie down the path and back to her cottage.

We wait for them to go inside and, before he closes the door, Luca turns to wave us off. '*I'm free tomorrow if you would like some help in the cottage?*' he shouts down the path.

'*That would be wonderful!*' I shout back.

'*See you in the morning, then.*' He smiles and closes the door. Pauline turns the engine on and we drive away. I sink back into my seat and close my eyes. I think I must be radiating happiness right now.

Chapter 25

Tuesday morning arrives with a headache and a wooziness, which makes it difficult to determine if the churning in my stomach is a result of the previous evening or anticipation for the day ahead. I shower and wash my hair, even though I wouldn't normally bother for a day working in the house. I pull on my denim shorts and a white vest top then put some make-up on. I try not to make it too obvious that I have made any special kind of effort.

Jen and I walk to the house together as she isn't at college until the afternoon. Luca is already outside when we get there, though I think he has just arrived.

He smiles as we approach and hands me a large bottle of water and a small box of paracetamol. 'I thought you might need these.' He smiles and looks down at his feet where a large bucket is filled with sponges, cloths and various cleaning sprays. 'And Aunt Sylvie thought we might need these,' he laughs. 'She offered to help but I think she is a little delicate this morning so I sent her back to bed!'

'Thanks!' I take the bottle and the tablets from him, 'All gratefully received!'

'Poor Sylvie.' Jen takes the paracetamol off me and pops two out for herself. 'I hope she doesn't feel too bad?'

'She'll be fine.' Luca picks up the bucket and starts to walk around the side of the house towards the cottage. 'She hasn't stopped telling me what a wonderful time she had and how lovely you girls are, she is quite taken with you all.'

Jen and I smile at the compliment. 'Well the feeling is definitely mutual.'

Inside the cottage it is dark and I can smell damp. We walk around the downstairs and open the wooden shutters and windows to let light and air in. As I push open the first set of shutters a huge plume of dust covers me from top to bottom and hangs in the sunlit air around me.

'Wow!' I cough and wipe my face. 'This place is going to take some serious cleaning! I hope you're up to the task!'

Jen and Luca laugh at me, still standing in a mass of swirling dust.

'We better get started.' Luca chucks me a sponge and opens the kitchen shutters a little more carefully than me, managing to avoid my fate.

The cottage has tiled floors throughout. Downstairs is really just two rooms. There is a compact kitchen, which has a gas stove, a wood burning oven and a simple wooden table with four chairs; and another through-room, which has two sofas, covered in large sheets, a fireplace and double doors at the far end that lead out onto a small private garden, which is fenced off from the wider grounds that surround it. The walls must once have been white but they are now stained and grey. There is a space on the wall above the fireplace where a painting must once have hung. Luca's eyes rest upon the space, but he doesn't say anything and I don't want him to know that I have noticed so neither do I.

Upstairs there is a bathroom and two small bedrooms, each of which has large double windows, one over-looking the pool to the front of the house, the other the Tuscan countryside to the back. Each room also has an old-fashioned, dark-wood wardrobe and a small chest of drawers, still in relatively good condition. I open the wardrobe door in the room that I have already decided will be my bedroom (the one that overlooks the pool and my beautiful house). It is empty except for a full-length mirror on the inside door and a couple of wire hangers on the top rail. It dawns on me that I will have trouble filling the wardrobe with the limited clothes that I brought with me for my fortnight's holiday. I make a mental note to talk to my parents tonight about getting the rest of my things sent over.

Downstairs, Jen plugs in her iPod speakers and iPod, then turns her Ed Sheeran album up to full volume so that we can all hear the music. I go back down and we decide to divide and conquer. Jen takes the bedrooms, I take the kitchen and Luca starts in the living room. We dust, wipe, scrub, sweep and mop till our hands hurt.

By lunchtime we have made brilliant progress and the place is already starting to look and smell a lot better. We stroll over to the main house to meet Katarina with the lunch delivery and sit on the lawn beside the main patio area, eating freshly made goats' cheese and sun-blushed tomato ciabattas and hot, flaky cheese straws dipped in a red pesto paste. Katarina sits with us and we all chat easily about everything and anything for half an hour. Once we have finished eating and Katarina has gone back to the patisserie, the three of us lay back for a while, basking in the sun and enjoying each other's company until we can't justify ourselves the time any longer.

The afternoon is searingly hot and it is hard, sweaty work clearing and cleaning out the rooms. By the end of the day we are all absolutely shattered.

'I think we all deserve a beer.' Luca wipes his brow with a clean cloth and looks around admiring our handy work. 'The place looks great! A lick of paint and you can move in.'

'I think you're right!' I agree.

'Of course I am!' he smiles and I laugh at him and thank him again for his help

'I really am so grateful.'

'Don't be! I've actually had fun. I'll help you paint tomorrow if you like? There is a stack of white paint in the storage. It shouldn't take too long if we work together. You might even be in by the weekend.'

'That would be amazing.' I tell Jen what Luca said as she walks into the room laden down with a broom, mop and bucket.

'Fantastic! What a day though, I can't believe you want to do it all over again tomorrow! Thanks so much, Luca, it would all take so much longer without you.' Luca waves away her thanks.

'So, how about that beer then?'

'Sure, but only if you let me buy,' I say.

'Deal,' Luca agrees. 'But just so you know, I won't allow that next time.' He grins and my heart skips a beat at the thought of a next time.

'Are you coming?' I ask Jen.

'Just for one, I have to get home.'

I'm pretty sure that Jen doesn't have to get back home any time soon but I don't say anything.

We leave the cottage and Jen locks up behind us then walks deliberately slowly back to the main house, letting Luca and me walk ahead.

We chat absent mindedly as we make our way down the side to the front and are all caught out by a huge crash and a shattering of glass. It all happens so quickly. As I hear the noise, Luca scoops me quickly and firmly to the side of the path against the wall. He holds one arm out in front of me and the other out towards Jen behind us to stop her walking any further forward.

'What the hell was that?' I gasp, winded by the impact.

Luca looks up at the trellis above our head and back down to the floor in front of us.

'One of the lanterns has fallen.' He looks back to us. 'Are you OK?'

'I'm fine' I say, suddenly very aware of how close his body is to mine. I can feel the heat coming off him and see the beads of sweat on his forehead.

'Jen?' he asks and she nods to indicate that she is fine too. Luca walks over to where the lantern lies shattered on the floor and inspects the trellising above it. 'These vines are old.' He touches them. 'The lanterns have been here for years, they aren't properly attached, this is probably not the only one that's loose. You're going to have to take them all down. We're lucky, this could have killed us!'

He is right and I'm shaken at the thought.

'Definitely.' I look at Jen who agrees.

'It's a shame though,' she says. 'They are so beautiful, but of course we don't have a choice. They are candlelit anyway.' I haven't actually noticed this but it would explain why they are never on! 'So they are probably a health and safety hazard even if they don't fall on the people walking beneath them. We can buy some electric lanterns and replace them, get them hung up properly in time for the launch.'

Luca looks at us both. 'Right then, I'll take them down first thing in the morning and put them in storage until you decide what you want to do with them.'

'Thank you.' I'm grateful that he is here and I go inside to get a broom and sweep up the mess from the shattered lantern.

Once it is all cleared we set off again into the village for that beer. Jen stays for one, as she said she would, and then makes her excuses and leaves. Luca and I order a second beer and drink it slowly. I enjoy the respite from the burning heat as the sun goes down behind the village square. We chat comfortably and discuss plans for finishing the cottage and finding new lanterns. As we near the end of our second drink I'm about to suggest that we order a third and perhaps something to eat when I see Sylvie walking across the square. I wave at her and she makes her way over to us.

'Hello, you two,' she smiles widely, clearly pleased to see us. 'How did you get on today?'

'Great, Luca was such a help,' I tell her.

She smiles indulgently at her nephew. 'Oh, he always is.' She pats his shoulder in a motherly way.

'Would you like to join us for a drink?' I ask her.

'I would love to, dear, but I really must get back. I have meat in the oven; I only popped out to get a couple of things for Luca's dinner.'

'You shouldn't have done that,' Luca chastises her gently. 'You know I don't expect you to cook for me.'

'I know you don't, dear, but I like to. I don't have anyone to cook for any more and I enjoy it, you know I do. You don't stay with me very often, let me spoil you.' Luca smiles fondly at his Aunt.

'Well,' – I finish my beer – 'I will let you two get home and I should get back myself, Jen will have my dinner waiting!' I fib in case Luca feels bad about leaving. I don't know if he realises but he smiles and I can see gratitude in his eyes as they crinkle. My hand is rested on the table and very briefly he places one of his hands over it.

'See you in the morning.' He takes his hand away and I watch them walk across the square together before heading home in the other direction. I can feel the warmth from where his hand touched mine and I smile stupidly to myself, full of the joy of possibilities.

The four of us (Jen, Jake, Luca and I) meet early again the next morning. Luca and Jake get to work straight away, taking down the rest of the lanterns at the side of the house and putting them in our storage sheds before, we all crack on with painting the cottage. It is another stifling day. All of the doors and windows are wide open. Jen's iPod is playing *The Best Of The 80s* and we are all in good spirits despite the heavy heat. Luca and Jake seem to be getting on well as they paint the kitchen and hallway together. Jen and I work in the sitting room, singing along happily to her playlist. We are so caught up in the music and the painting that we have almost forgotten that the boys are in the next room. As Cyndi Lauper takes us back to our teens, we dance around the room together using our brushes as microphones and sing at the tops of our voices. We are so distracted, in full chorus, belting out *Girls Just Wanna Have Fun* with our backs to each other, moving our bums side to side in unison, that we don't notice the sniggers coming from Jake and Luca until they have turned into loud laughter. Clearly busted but too happy to be mortified, we collapse in a heap of giggles, much to the amusement and bemusement of Jake and Luca. Once they have helped us to our feet we get back to work and every now and again we even hear them singing along with us. Alas we don't ever catch them bum wiggling each other!

Despite our antics, by two p.m. we have already finished the painting downstairs. We are pretty chuffed with ourselves and go over to the main house to see if there is any of Katarina's lunch delivery left. We eat the remainder of the lamb and potato pasties quickly as Jake and Jen need to leave for their afternoon at college. Luca and I stay and after lunch we start work on the upstairs.

'Should we take a room each?' I ask as we set the paint down on the dust sheets at the top of the stairs.

'How about I cut in and you fill,' Luca suggests. 'Then I get to have your company at the same time.'

'Great,' I blush.

'Perhaps you can do that little dance for me again too?' he laughs, so I flick my paint brush at him, splattering his shirt (which is already pretty covered in paint, to be fair). 'Hey!' he laughs again, and turns away from my brush covering his face. 'Do you really want to start that?' There is mischief in his eyes. Getting dirty with Luca doesn't seem like such a bad idea to me but I am pretty sure that I will be the one who comes out worse if we go head to head in the paint flicking stakes, so I hold my hands up in surrender.

'OK OK! Let's paint!' We flick the iPod back on and to the sounds of U2 we paint happily for the rest of the afternoon.

As the air cools slightly and the brightness of the blue sky starts to mellow, we are finally finished. My arms are aching from my fingers to my shoulders and my back is killing me but it is worth it. I am thrilled with the result. I put by brush down, arch my back and stretch my arms above my head.

'That was hard work!' I hear my back click with the stretch. Luca looks at me and I see his eyes briefly stray to my bare stomach, as the stretch makes my t-shirt ride up. He moves them quickly back to my face.

'You did great, the place looks lovely. You'll be able to move in by the weekend.'

'I can't wait! And *we* did great,' I correct him. 'Thank you again.' Luca doesn't say anything, he just flashes one of his sexy smiles at me and gathers up the paint pots and brushes to take downstairs and wash out in the kitchen. 'So what are your plans for the rest of the week?' I ask, trying to sound casual.

'I have to go to Florence tomorrow, I need to pick up a couple of things that have come in for work. Then I'm off to Naples for a long weekend to see some friends.'

I feel a wave of disappointment that he won't be around, which is ridiculous as it's not like we have any plans to see each other. Since our first dinner he hasn't even mentioned going out again but, irrational or not, I don't like the idea of him going away.

'Oh, lovely.' I try to sound cheerful. 'When are you back?' I know it isn't any of my business but I can't help myself. He doesn't seem to mind.

'Tuesday morning probably.' He fills the last paint tray and leaves it to soak in the sink. 'I'll see how I feel after the weekend. How about you? What's next with this place?' he asks.

'Oh, lots! The plumbers are coming tomorrow to install a filter system for the water in here. The landscape gardeners are starting work around the pool and in the gardens around the back too. I need to make another trip to Florence and your aunt is taking me to a garden centre on Friday to get flowers and plants.'

'That's good, she'll probably take you to the place I was going to suggest to you for the new lanterns, I'll check with her tonight. You will have to see if the builders can find a way to hang them securely for you.' I make another mental note to do that. Even though the building and decorating is coming on wonderfully there is still so much to do. I should really update all of the paperwork and keep on top of the little things that Jen and I are responsible for.

'Are you OK?' Luca interrupts my train of thought.

'I'm fine, just thinking about how much there is to do. I've been a little slack on the paperwork the last couple of days so I've a million things going through my mind! I'll update everything tonight,' I tell myself more than Luca.

'Well, I should probably leave you to it then. I have to get back and make some calls for my trip tomorrow.'

'Oh, right, sure.' I hope the disappointment in my voice is not too obvious. 'Well, thank you again. So much. I'll have to make it up to you!'

'No need, this is my thank you, remember. Besides, I've enjoyed myself.' I feel awkward now, I don't know whether to suggest we speak to or see each other when he is back from Naples. I have no idea if he wants to see me again or if this was really just a way of paying me back for involving Sylvie. Luca doesn't give me a chance to say anything anyway, he picks up his bag. 'Good luck moving in over the weekend. Let me know if you need any help next week.' He heads out of the door without so much as a kiss on the cheek and shouts goodbye over his shoulder. I am alone in the cottage for the first time since I opened its doors just two days ago. I watch Luca walk away with barely a backwards glance and a wave of tiredness washes over me. I am done for the day. I collect my paperwork from the big house and take it back to Jen's cottage to work on before an early bath and bed.

The rest of the week and weekend pass in a blur. Work has started in earnest outside of the house. The fountains, statues and the pool are power cleaned, the tiling on the patios is fixed, lawns are laid and flowers are planted. Sylvie and I spend Friday morning at the garden centre and pick out the most beautiful flowers for the borders. We choose vivid red and pure white geraniums to border the fountain in the main driveway and a beautiful mix of flowers in softer colours for the gardens, including white and pink roses, violets and lilac, jasmine and crocuses. We order more white roses and giant balls of hydrangeas in cornflower blue for the launch party too. We manage to find some electric lanterns that still look authentic and find some really pretty solar powered fairy lights to string into the trees and trellises. Over the weekend Jen and I move the few bits that I have with me into the cottage on the grounds and make an emergency trip to Florence to pick up a kettle, toaster and various other things of importance, like a bed, which takes us all of Sunday morning to assemble.

By Sunday night I am ready to move in. Jen and I hang up my few clothes, put new bed linen on and fill the fridge with some basic supplies. By the time we have finished, the place is starting to feel like home. It still needs an injection of personality but that will come with time. It is clean and well equipped. And it is mine!

I say goodnight to Jen after a take away pizza and a bottle of wine on the sitting room floor. I hug her hard at the front door. 'This feels strange,' I say, 'To be living in different places.'

'I know,' Jen agrees. 'It won't be for long though, I'll be in here as soon as the lease is up on the cottage. Are you sure you will be OK on your own? You don't have to move in yet.'

'I know, I'll be fine,' I reassure her. 'I'm excited to be here, I just can't wait for you to be here too!'

Jen hugs me again. 'I still can't believe we're doing this!'

I give her a last little squeeze. 'Drive safely.'

It is liberating to be on my own in my own place. I go upstairs and open my bedroom window then I sit on my bed and look out over my beautiful house. I lose myself in my thoughts and the beauty of my surroundings until the empty pool space merges with the sky that hangs low around it and the stars start to emerge in the darkening blanket above it. I luxuriate in the peace and let my thoughts drift to Luca. I wonder where he is right now and what he is doing. Hopefully he will be back in a day or two and I can find an excuse to see him again.

Chapter 26

The first morning on my own in the cottage is not as peaceful as the evening before it. The builders are at the main house by six thirty a.m. and the noise starts as soon as they do. I get up and pull on my denim shorts and a vest, which has become my default work outfit, and head outside to see what is going on.

There are two men with very loud machines walking along the bed of the pool. I wave to say 'hello' as I pass them and they wave back, still cheerful at this early hour. I sit at the small desk I have set up in the library with my laptop and the pile of paperwork that grows taller everyday with invoices, receipts, warranties and an array of other official looking documents. I cast my eyes over the work-plan.

Of course! The pool is being filled today. How exciting! I spend the morning sorting the teetering pile of papers and in the afternoon Jen and I clear out some space in the cellar to make way for the drinks that are arriving this afternoon for the launch party. When Jen leaves at six p.m. there are still men working on the pool outside so I wait in my makeshift office and catch up on emails, work and personal.

It is nearly eight p.m. by the time the pool guy knocks on the library door to tell me that the job is finally done. I close my laptop and follow him outside. I am excited to see it, even a little bit nervous, as I walk alongside the newly-laid lawns which are being drenched by sprinklers. The intense heat of the day has subsided and it is a still, balmy evening. As we reach the pool I look out in anticipation and I am not disappointed. It is divine. Like a dying plant quenched and brought back to life in all its colourful splendour, the pool has been restored to its former glory. It looks bigger with the water in it. The surface is set like glass and is lit by solar panels that have been installed along each of its now clean, white stone sides and on the front edges of the wide stone steps that slope gently down into the water. The water is like liquid mercury in the dusk light, it is romantic and beautiful. My eyes well up, it's a milestone. The pool is symbolic of the rest of the house and now that it is restored to its former glory I realise how close we are to achieving our dream. A cough from beside me reminds me that the pool man is still standing next to me, probably waiting for me to say something. I sniff and wipe my eyes, embarrassed.

'Grazi, grazi, questo e bello,' I tell him in my terrible Italian accent. He looks happy and bids me goodnight in Italian. I stand alone at the edge of the pool and enjoy its beauty. I take a quick picture on my phone and send it to Jen:

'First milestone! It's beautiful! Can't wait for you to see it!'

I wish Jen was with me. This is her moment too and I want to share it with someone. I wonder if Luca is back from Naples yet, perhaps I will text him tomorrow and invite him over to see the pool. Aunt Sylvie should see it too. I go back to my cottage and after a quick shower get into bed and fall fast asleep.

In the morning I wake up earlier than usual, excited like a child at Christmas. I sit up in bed and pull the curtain back to look at my beautiful pool, basking in all its glory in the bright morning sunshine. It looks even better than it did last night. It is a vivid turquoise and as still as the air around it. The heat in my room makes it even more enticing; I get up and go quickly outside to dip my feet in it. I stand at the water's edge and poke my toe into it. It feels cold but despite the early hour the sun is hot and I have an overwhelming desire to dive into its serene stillness. I look at my watch: five forty-five a.m. I probably have an hour or so before anyone will arrive at the house. Feeling brave and naughty in equal part, I drop my dressing gown to the ground. I have always wanted to swim naked. I went topless once in my early 20s in a pool in Tenerife because most of the other girls were but I felt so self-conscious that I got out after a couple of minutes and didn't do it again. Now it feels like such a decadent thing to do, I can't help myself! I look around even though I know I'm the only person here. I walk slowly down the deep, wide steps into the cold water. I gasp and jump as it hits my bare stomach. Goose bumps come up on my arms and I watch the little hairs, blonde from so much time in the sun, stand on end. Slowly I put my arms in front of me and smoothly submerge my body into the water. It feels amazing on my skin and an incredible sense of freedom surges through me. It is heaven and in this moment I am truly happy. I can't remember the last time I felt so happy, although joyfully I realise that it probably wasn't that long ago. It is trance-like moving alone through the water in the still of the early morning. I close my eyes and swim slowly from one end to the other. With each stroke my face lowers into the water and the cold hits me again. I wonder at the incredible pleasure I feel from such a simple thing. As I feel myself near the end of the pool I stretch out my arms and touch the hard stone edge with my fingertips. I open my eyes and pull myself into the pool wall then dip my head backwards to smooth my hair in the water behind me. As I lean back and put my face to the sky I close my eyes again and feel the brightness of the sun on my face. I linger in the position and am surprised when the warmth on my face disappears and the brightness dims. I didn't see any clouds in the sky this morning. A sinking feeling comes over me but my feet are still firmly planted on the bottom of the pool. I keep my eyes shut, hardly bearing to open them and stand deadly still, afraid to move. Please let there be cloud. I pray inwardly that I am still on my own and pull my naked body closer to the pool wall, then I open my eyes, just a crack, and look to where the bright sunshine had been above me only a few seconds ago.

'Good Morning.' Luca's flawless face is smiling down at me.

Damn! Damn, damn, damn, damn, damn! I groan at his smirking face. If I was any closer to the edge of the wall I would be inside it. Damn Luca and his gorgeous face, why couldn't he just have been a cloud? The water is still cold but my body is burning from top to toe, my cheeks are practically in flames. I have no idea how long he has been standing there but I hope vehemently that he has just this second arrived. This is so typical, I do one crazy thing in my whole life (well that is not strictly true but this is definitely something that I wouldn't usually do), anyway, one moment of madness and I get totally busted.

'What are you doing here?' I splutter and refuse to meet his eye.

'I was on my way home from Naples,' I can hear the amusement in his voice, he is clearly trying very hard to contain his laughter. 'I wanted to stop by and drop this is in on my way, a little house warming gift I picked up for you.'

Curiosity gets the better of me so, still pulled as tightly as possible to the edge, I raise my head to look at him and he nods towards a large square parcel wrapped in brown paper that is leant against one of the poolside chairs. Great. He has come bearing gifts and I am naked in the pool. I am too embarrassed to be grateful.

'But it's so early!' I sound indignant.

'I was just passing, I left Naples early to avoid the morning traffic, I thought I would try my luck. I'm glad I did now!' Unable to hold his laughter in any more he lets it all out. It is beautiful to see him laugh but I am still furious, at myself mostly but I direct it at him. Where is the chivalry? A proper gentleman would surely never let on if he saw a woman swimming naked in a swimming pool. He is clearly enjoying my predicament but his laughing face is just so gorgeous that

I can't possibly stay mad. I give in and laugh too, splashing him gently with the water.

'Don't laugh at me!' I chastise him through my own laughter.'

'Sorry!' his apology is not sincere, he doesn't sound sorry at all. He looks at his watch. 'It's six thirty a.m. I thought you might be up with the builders.' He looks around. 'But clearly they are missing the show!' he laughs again. Damn him and his sexy laugh.

'Six thirty! Christ! They will be here any minute. I have to get out.'

'Sure,' he reaches down to me. 'Would you like a hand?' The gleam in his eye and the smirk on his face makes it very clear that he knows I am naked, just in case there was any doubt left in my mind. I get that sinking feeling in my stomach again and I glance quickly around to see my robe lying on the floor at the opposite end of the pool. He follows my gaze. 'Would you like me to get your robe?' he asks, regaining his composure and finally deciding to behave like a gentleman.

'Yes please.' I am too embarrassed to think of anything witty. Just for a second I wonder what Luca would do if I just swam back down the pool and got out to get my robe myself but I know I won't do it, not in a million years. I watch as Luca walks around the pool, collects my robe and brings it back to me. He holds it out to me. I go to take it and then realise that I can't take it off him without either getting it wet or getting out of the pool first. I'm pretty sure that he realises it too!

'Umm, could you just put it on the ground, please?' I'm dying inside.

'Sure.' He places it on the floor next to me. 'Would you like a hand now?' He reaches out to me again. The bastard. He is teasing me and he's clearly enjoying it. I contemplate grabbing his outstretched hand and pulling him into the pool with me. That would serve him right! Perhaps he can read my thoughts because he laughs and relents. 'OK, OK,' he holds his hands up in mock surrender, 'I'll turn around.'

As soon as he is facing the other way I pull myself quickly out of the pool. I am pleased he can't see me as I heave my wet body out and throw one of my legs up onto the side before I stand up. Not my most elegant look! I keep my eyes on him as I tie my robe tightly around my waist, not entirely trusting him not to turn around. As soon as I'm decent I compose myself and walk ahead of Luca to the chair where his gift is waiting. Trying to ignore the fact that he has just seen me naked and that I am obviously still naked under my robe, I sit down and scoop my wet hair into a knot at the nape of my neck. He always looks suave and sophisticated… and clothed. I'm painfully aware that yesterday's mascara is probably smudged under my eyes and that it is also the only make up on my face at the moment. I keep my eyes low so that he can't see my face too closely and thank him for the gift.

'It's just a little something. I thought it might look good in the space above your sofa.'

'That's really kind of you.' I finger the corner of the brown paper so as not to meet his gaze. The humour has gone from the moment and I think that he can sense my discomfort because his tone changes back to its usual more businesslike self.

'Well, I should get on; I really just wanted to drop it off whilst passing. Sylvie is expecting me back for breakfast. Don't get up,' he adds as I adjust my robe to stand up, 'I'll see myself out. You should probably get back into the cottage before anyone else arrives.'

I see the smirk return to his face just before he turns and walks away. I am almost delirious with embarrassment. I walk quickly back to the cottage with the gift, still not sure whether to laugh or cry. In the cottage I put the present on the floor and rip the brown paper off it. I catch my breath as I see the most exquisite framed picture of the big house. It looks like an original painting of it, set amongst the rolling hills at sunset. The colours are exquisite and it captures the essence of the house. The romance, the warmth, the history. There is a signature in the corner but I can't work out the name. The date is easy enough to read though: 1968. I work the years back in my head. His mother would have lived in the house at that time. I am glad that Luca isn't here to see me open it because I don't think that I would be able to express just how much I love it. I place it on the sofa and cover it with the brown paper to protect it, then go upstairs to get ready. I'll text Luca later to say thank you when I have worked out exactly what I want to say. Thinking of the picture as I get dressed reminds me that we still haven't chosen any artwork for the main house and it gives me an idea. I jot down a note to myself to call Michael, Jen's friend Sara's husband, who I met at the dinner party a few weeks ago and who I hope might be able to help me.

The day passes in a blur again. People come and go all the time, invoices need paying, deliveries need signing for and instructions need giving. I don't have a chance to think about what I will text Luca until I'm finally back in bed that night. I sit with my window open enjoying the breeze in my room and look at my phone. After several deleted drafts I settle on:

'Luca. Thank you so much for the beautiful picture. It is the most perfect gift I could imagine. I really love it.'

Short enough not to be gushing, but I hope heartfelt enough to show him how really grateful I am. I click send and turn off my bedside lamp, looking forward to going to sleep. Just as I am drifting off my phone flashes and beeps. I reach for the green light in the dark room and open the message:

'Glad you like it. It was good to see you this morning. Everything at the house is looking great.'

I read the message and groan at the memory of our meeting this morning. I stuff my face into my pillow at the embarrassment. Whilst I am still face down in the bed linen my phone beeps again. I pick it up and read it:

'Are you free for dinner tomorrow night? I'd like you to try the best food in Italy!'

I throw my head back down into the pillow but this time to muffle the excited scream that I let out. My tiredness has suddenly and completely disappeared and I want to get out of bed and dance around the room. I settle instead for punching the air above my head with both arms over and over. If Luca could see me now I'm sure that he would withdraw the offer on account of my lunacy. I compose myself and reply:

'Dinner would be lovely.'

Too excited to sleep I sit up and wait for a reply. After just a few seconds I put my phone on the bedside table because obviously if I put it down and don't look at it, it has a much greater chance of beeping! A few more seconds go by and I turn out the light. Just as I do the light on the phone flashes again and it bleeps loudly. I squeeze my eyes in delight and open the message. I could not have felt more disappointed or surprised to see Andrew's name staring back at me:

'Hi Soph, just wondered if you got my voicemail about coming over to see you with your parents. They have invited me to come with them next week. Am so excited to see you! I've sent you an email. Give me a call when you can. Lots of Love. A x

Oh my God! My stomach lurches to the other side of my room. My bloody parents! I know they love Andrew but really this is too much. I am just going to have to call them tomorrow and tell them to disinvite him. In my heart though I know that this is not going to happen and I am going to have to let him down all over again. I'm tired again now and I don't want Andrew to know that I'm awake so I resolve to speak to him the next day. I nestle back down under my sheet and just as I get settled again the phone beeps one more time. Desperately hoping for Luca and not Andrew, I open the message:

'Excellent, I'll pick you up at 7 for dinner at 8.'

I beam at the phone and quickly fire off a reply:

'Perfect.'

Then I put my phone on silent not wanting my happiness to be disturbed by anything else. I fall asleep planning my outfit (from Jen's wardrobe) for tomorrow night.

Chapter 27

Despite how busy I am, the next day is interminable. I can't wait to finish up in the house and get ready for dinner with Luca. I throw myself into as much as I can to stave the nerves off and to help pass the time. When it finally reaches four p.m. the builders, plumbers and electricians pack up their bags and leave for the day. I'm exhausted. I can't wait to get into a hot shower and let it beat some life into me. I have loads of time, Jen is coming over with some dresses for me to try on at six and Luca is due at seven.

Although I'm anxious for the time to go, I also don't want to get ready too early and be hanging around for Luca to arrive, so I sit down and open my laptop to check on the replies for the launch party and update the work plan. That should kill half an hour until the beautification process begins. The laptop pings to life and I login to my emails. So far we have received a steady stream of RSVPs from the invites we sent out last week. It's reassuring to know that we will at least have some guests at the launch party. Fi has confirmed that she will be coming with the travel editor from her magazine, which is amazing, she has also sent an invite to the editor of the travel specialist magazine at her publishing house but so far we haven't heard back from them. Jackson is coming too. He will be on a shoot in Rome the day before for the Sunday Times and will head over to us from there. My parents, Frank and Pauline, and Fi's parents are coming, as well as all of our local friends and their families. Luca offered to extend some invites to a few friends and business colleagues in Florence and we have had a couple of positive responses from them too. We have sent invites to all of the other newspapers and magazines that have travel sections, as well as various online review sites and travel guides but so far the responses have been limited. Hoping for some positive replies, I scroll through the copious amounts of junk mail until I see something that I recognise. There is an email from Condé Nast Traveller magazine, I click on it with one hand and cross my fingers on the other while it opens:

To: SophieDucall2@hotmail.com
From: Sheila@condeNastTraveller.co.uk
Dear Ms Duvall,
Thank you for the invitation to the launch party of your new hotel. Unfortunately we will not be able to send any of our contributing staff on this occasion. However, please feel free to send some of your promotional material to our editorial team. You can also contact our advertising team at advertising@CondeNastTraveller.co.uk to ensure that you can reach our wide readership and benefit from our considerable and competitive circulation numbers.
We wish you luck with your venture
Regards

Sheila Halpin
Editor

I close the email, deflated by their response. Traveller has always been one of my favourite magazines. When I was at Morgan Stanley I used to buy it every month. I had a collection of them on the shelf in my living room flat, the key destinations in each issue are written on the spines, so whenever I was researching a holiday I would just look along the shelf for the places I was interested in and see what they recommended. I scribble a note to myself to remind me to look into advertising and keep scrolling through the invites. There is a nice response from George, the bank manager, who will be attending with his wife, and also from Pauline and Frank's specialist travel agent, Sue Ryder, who will also be attending. The latter positive responses brighten my mood after the Traveller loss.

I skim my eyes over the rest of the emails and just as I reach the bottom of the page I see Andrew's name and feel the familiar tug in the pit of my stomach. Reluctantly I open it:

To: SophieDucall2@hotmail.co.uk
From: AndrewPorter@RichmondEstates
Hi Soph,
I've tried to call a couple of times but I imagine everything is a bit crazy with the house at the moment. I just want to confirm that I am coming over with your parents for the launch party. I can't wait to see you. I have missed you so much, not speaking to you every day has been difficult!

I know you are doing everything you can not to be a burden on me or to put too much pressure on me, and I am grateful for that, but I really think that we can make this work.

I love you, sweetheart. Can't wait to see you.

Andrew x

Damn! I really do need to call my parents about Andrew coming over with them. I should have done it first thing this morning but there is so much going on with the house that if I don't write myself a reminder I just forget whatever it is I have to do. I hope he hasn't booked his flights yet, poor Andrew. I really need to put a stop to this but I can't face composing a reply now. I need time to think about it and word it properly and I definitely don't want to be doing that just before Luca arrives!

I look at my watch. Christ! How has an hour passed? I need to get ready. I leave the laptop open on the coffee table so that I remember to reply to Andrew in the morning and skip up the stairs two at a time.

After a ridiculously long shower and the last of my bottle of Ralph Lauren Romance shower gel (the one I save for special occasions!) I am reinvigorated. It is another beautifully warm evening so I open the window in my bedroom as wide as it will go and pour myself a cold glass of white wine from the fridge to steady my nerves. I sit on my bedroom floor in front of my open wardrobe door with the long mirror. I get to work with my make-up, hair products, brushes and hairdryer spread around me on the floor. I have just finished drying my hair, which I do in sections (I don't think I have ever done that before) and I'm pleased with the result. It has settled nicely for once and is streaked with natural blonde highlights from the Tuscan sun, which makes it look bright and bouncy. I'm admiring it in the mirror when Jen arrives loaded down with dresses.

'Hi! You look gorgeous, your hair is lovely.' She squeezes past me with the pile of clothes.

'Thanks!' I take some of the dresses out of her arms and we go upstairs to my room.

I lay them all next to each other on my bed to assess them properly. There is the cream one that I wore last time I saw Luca and the blue one that Jen bought with me in Florence. There is also a simple but stunning black, strapless fit-and-flare dress and a beautiful, fitted red dress that is knee-length and has a scooped front and back. I grab Jen a glass of wine and she sits on the bed as I try them on. After a twirl in each of them we narrow it down to the black or red dress. I try them both on again. The black one is simple and elegant. It fits me nicely and is definitely the safe option. The red one is sexier. It sits close to my body and hugs my curves but I'm a bit self conscious in it. I'm not used to wearing tight clothes and red is a pretty daring colour for me.

'It has to be that one,' Jen is adamant. 'You look a total knockout in it, look at your figure; I would kill for curves like that!'

I turn to look at my back (my bum) in the mirror, still not convinced, there are certainly a few more curves than when I arrived here.

Jen senses my hesitation. 'Soph, you look amazing, your waist is tiny, and you go in and out in all the right places. Luca won't be able to take his eyes off you!'

I trust Jen's opinion, I know she wouldn't let me go out if it didn't look good so I ignore my niggling self doubt and slip on a pair of black killer heels to go with it.

'Perfect, there is no way he will resist you in that,' Jen winks at me.

'Here's hoping!' I laugh.

I haven't been this excited about a date since, well, I don't think I have ever been this excited about a date! Perhaps when I was fifteen and Tommy Harper from the year above asked me to the sixth form ball, that was a pretty big deal, but since then I've never even really even had a proper 'first date' except with Andrew. Which was lovely but there was no spark, he was always more into me than I was into him, which takes away from the excitement I think. It was lovely not to play games with Andrew but I have missed the butterflies and I definitely get them with Luca. It's like I have no control over my body when I see him, it either shakes, blushes, or rolls around inside. Just thinking about it makes me feel funny all over again.

I take a gulp of my wine and Jen and I go downstairs to wait for Luca to arrive. We don't have to wait long as out of the window I can see him walking up the driveway.

'He's here! Eek!'

Jen smiles at me and squeezes my shoulders reassuringly. 'You look beautiful, relax, he will love you just as much as I do!'

I put my hands over hers. 'You're the best.' I rub them quickly and then open the door.

As predicted, Luca looks incredible. In perfectly fitted jeans, a crisp white shirt with an open neck and a light-beige jacket, he is all blond hair, white teeth and cute, wrinkly eyes.

Also as predicted, I totally lose my cool as I let him in. I faff around looking for my bag and keys, wishing I had got them ready before, and talking ten to the dozen about God only knows what. Jen leads Luca into the sitting room to show him the painting that is now hanging above the sofa and to thank him for it.

'Calm down!' she mouths to me as she ushers him in.

I stand outside and take a few deep breaths. I'm starting to sweat, which will ruin my hair and make-up, so I give myself a firm talking to and pull myself together, then walk back into the room.

'Sorry about that, I'm ready now.' I stand in front of them and smile. 'Shall we go?'

'Sure.' Luca stands up. 'You look beautiful,' he says and he seems earnest. 'I love the dress.'

'I told you!' Jen mouths behind Luca's back and I smile at both of them. The three of us walk out past the main house under the newly-lit trellising. Luca's car is parked next to Jen's and when we reach them we say our goodbyes and drive off in separate directions.

Luca drives up into the hills. We talk about our days for a while and I ask how Sylvie is but the conversation is soon overtaken by the sheer beauty of our surroundings. As we drive higher we are surrounded by the most exquisite patchwork of soft and bright green hills. Their rise and fall is only broken by the straw yellow fields of grass, parched by the hot, Italian sun, which hangs like a huge, orange ball suspended in the sky, a perfect circle of light, melting the fields below into each other with its radiant warmth. The countryside is peppered with lines of vineyards standing side by side in the distance and the odd farmhouse isolated in the tranquillity.

The longer we drive, the lower the sun sinks. As it skims the top of the fields and hills below it bathes them in a soft glow and tinges their edges with orange flames that reach up from the ground. The sky above the sun is turning a rich indigo, it is streaked with blues and violets, like folds of velvet, and soft pinks and reds that promise delight in the morning. We drive for almost an hour before Luca pulls the car off the main road that continues to rise in tight circles above us. He heads down a dusty lane and stops at the end of it next to a small stone built house with large, dark wooden doors. It doesn't look too much from outside but it gets better. He opens my door and takes my hand to help me out then keeps a hold of it as he leads me to the back of the house. When we turn the corner we are met by a sea of white fairy lights twinkling enticingly above our heads, they are strung around and across a small square of cypress trees that flank about fifteen tables set up in the middle beneath them, all individually lit by lanterns set at the centre of crisp white linen overlaid with white organza that drapes romantically to the floor. It is magical, truly breath taking.

'This is amazing,' I feel absurdly emotional at the unexpected beauty.

Luca is clearly pleased by my reaction and smiles widely as he takes me through a small wooden gate into the square between the trees.

'Luca, my Luca!' A large man with a friendly face that is dominated by a thick black moustache walks over to us and spreads his arms widely, embracing Luca as he meets him and slapping him hard on the back. He speaks to Luca in Italian and I don't quite catch the words but I can tell that there is genuine warmth and affection in the greeting. Luca speaks back briefly and with equal warmth then puts his hand on the small of my back and introduces me. The man is called Carlo and he takes both of my hands into his large, warm ones and kisses me on both cheeks.

'Bellissimo, bellissimo, my pleasure.' His welcome is infectious and I return the greeting.

He takes us to surely the most beautiful table outside; it is nestled in the corner, slightly away from the rest of the tables and set with a lantern in the middle as well as two small vases of pink roses flanked by tea lights. Carlo pulls out my chair for me and speaks to Luca again before blowing us both an exaggerated kiss and leaving us to our beautiful surroundings.

'Carlo is lovely! How do you know him?' I ask Luca.

'He's my godfather. He was my father's best friend,' Luca explains. 'When dad died before I was born my mother asked him. She knew that my father would have and she wanted to honour that. We're close, we always have been.'

'That's lovely,' I say. 'For both of you.'

Luca nods. 'He's been like a father to me. Mum and I came here all the time before she died.' I see the sadness creep into his face again and want so much to make it go away. Luca changes his tone and lightens the mood. 'We didn't only come here because he is my godfather of course! I told you before; it's the best food in Italy!'

'Well, if it is anything as wonderful as the setting, I'm in for a real treat,' I say honestly, and Luca grins that eye-crinkling grin that makes my stomach flip. I'm relieved to be sitting down because if I was standing there is a good chance that my knees would give way!

Carlo is back at the table a moment later with a bottle of Prosecco. 'My very best, bellissimo,' he smiles and pours me a glass before lodging the bottle in an ice-bucket behind the table. He gives Luca a bottle of sparkling water and hands us both a menu.

'Are you not having any?' I pick up my glass and look at the bubbles rushing to the top before taking a grateful sip, it is cold and creamy but with the sharpness of the fizz and I love it.

'I'll have some red with my food; I want to get you home safely!' Luca puts his serious face on.

'Of course,' I've only just got out of the car and already I have forgotten that he is driving, I have to get a grip.

'Enjoy it, Carlo has an amazing wine cellar, he is very proud of it. I imagine that will be the first of many he makes you try!' he laughs with obvious fondness for his godfather.

I am quietly pleased to have the excuse to drink on my own, which I wouldn't normally do — on a date at least! I really need to loosen up and relax. It is such a strange thing to feel completely at ease in someone's company and yet still feel so nervous. We read the menu together.

Luca points out some of his favourite dishes and translates where the Italian is unfamiliar to me. After much deliberation we are ready to order. Carlo takes our order personally, even though there are several waiters and waitresses tending to the other tables. He doesn't write anything down; he just nods as we tell him what we want. I order prawns in garlic butter to start and homemade ravioli with pumpkin, sage and cream. Luca decides on the parmesan and truffle oil risotto and a fillet steak.

As we wait for the food to arrive I sip my Prosecco and sit back in my chair, the warmth of the evening air and the alcohol are starting to relax me but they can't stop the near constant fluttering in my stomach. We talk easily, Luca's family are on my mind, being here in a place so obviously close to them.

'Have you ever tried to contact any of your father's family?' I ask him, hoping that I am not being too personal.

'Never!' Luca is short at first but then he softens. 'To be honest, I have little interest in them, they disrespected my mother and I won't do the same by inviting them into my life. They have never had any interest in me and I have very little in them.'

I sense the anger in his voice and I don't want to push the subject but I am curious. 'What about Roberto?' I ask. 'Sylvie said he was different to the others.'

'I think he is,' Luca admits. 'I had a letter from him once. It was only short but he apologised for not supporting mum and me more and for the way his family treated us. He asked to see us again.'

'Did you see him?'

'No. I was too young to do anything about it really and mum didn't think that she could cope with seeing Roberto. She said it would remind her of my father too much and she didn't want to cause any more tension in the family. She was always thinking of other people. I think she wrote to him but I'm pretty sure she never saw him.'

I sense that he would have liked to meet his father's brother but I don't push the point. I don't want to dwell on sad subjects tonight and clearly neither does Luca because he changes the subject.

'So, tell me everything about the house. How is it all going?'

And then we are off. I tell him about the work and the launch party, reeling off the people who have said that they will come. 'You will come, won't you?' I suddenly realise that I haven't actually sent him an official invite. 'And Sylvie, of course.'

'Wouldn't miss it.' He smiles that smile again.

Our starters come out and we eat them quickly, pausing only to swap mouthfuls and to compliment the food, which is truly delicious. I am pleased to have something to soak up some of the alcohol and wish there had been more on my plate. Luckily we don't have to wait too long before Carlo brings our main courses and a bottle of Amerone which he opens and pours for Luca and me. It's a lovely wine, warm, rich and fruity. I won't pretend I can taste the actual flavours, I am really not a wine connoisseur, but I know what I like and I really like it. A sommelier probably wouldn't say this, but it tastes a bit like grown up Ribena and I love Ribena!

The food is, if at all possible, even better than the wine. I would like to have left some. I read somewhere that it makes a woman more feminine and fanciable if she can't finish her meal, but it was too good to leave. We both clear our plates and talk intently about our lives and the things that we want to do. I tell Luca about my dreams for the hotel and how I want to prove to my parents that I made the right decision leaving Morgan Stanley.

He tells me the places in the world that he still wants to see and the plans to expand his business into the Asian market where there is currently a high demand for Italian arts and antiques. He talks about Aunt Sylvie and how much he has enjoyed staying with her the last few weeks, how he wants to see more of her now his mum is gone and eventually how he wants to give her grand-nieces or nephews, which sends my stomach into overdrive.

As the night draws in, the air around us hangs heavy with heat and darkness, broken only by the moon, stars and the soft candlelight in Carlo's garden. I feel almost magnetically attracted to Luca; I have to control every part of my body just to sit still opposite him. My hand wants to reach out and touch his, to intertwine my fingers with his. As we talk, we lean into each other across the table and he looks directly into my eyes when he speaks to me. Normally this would make me uncomfortable but tonight I can't draw my eyes away from his so I just look straight back.

We are deep in conversation when Carlo comes back to our table with a huge plate of thick, creamy tiramisu in one hand and a bottle of limoncello and two shot glasses balanced in the other hand. As if woken from a dream, I draw my gaze from Luca and sit back again in my chair. I look around and smile as I am reminded of the beauty that surrounds us. I'm surprised to see that we are the only people left outside. Even the staff has gone, except for Carlo. I am full to bursting now but the pudding looks so good and I have never been able to resist something sweet. Carlo hands us both a fork and urges me to eat.

'Try, try, bellissimo.'

I scoop up the creamy cake and put it in my mouth. It is divine. Absolutely, completely delicious. Luca and Carlo watch me waiting for a reaction and are clearly pleased at what they see. Carlo slaps Luca on the back, laughs loudly and says something in Italian that I don't understand.

'This is Carlo's signature dish,' Luca explains. 'Everyone who tries it falls in love with it!'

'It is wonderful!' I'm blushing at my obviously overt enjoyment of the pudding.

'You see,' Carlo says in a very thick Italian accent, 'The ladies, they love-a my tiramisu!' he laughs loudly and pours two limoncellos. He hands one to me and takes the other for himself. 'Cheers! Bellissimo!' he knocks his glass against mine. I have to admit that after white wine, Prosseco and most of the bottle of Amerone, I don't really want another drink, but it is difficult to refuse it without offending him, which is the last thing I want to do.

'Cheers!' I close my eyes and throw it back, the sharp lemon catches in my throat and I cough. Carlo makes me drink one more before Luca steps in to save me and enters into what I think is a verbal fight over whether he should pay the bill or not. In the end I'm not sure who won, Carlo doesn't bring one to the table but Luca leaves a large wad of cash on it anyway before he helps me up from my chair.

At the gate, we both embrace Carlo again and promise to come back soon. I'm lightheaded and a little unsteady on my feet so I hold on to Luca's arm tightly. When we reach the car he bends down to open the passenger door for me.

As he straightens his face is directly in front of mine. I can feel his breath on my mouth. It is soft and warm and smells faintly of Ribena. I want to kiss him so much it hurts. He is looking directly into my eyes and I am still holding his arm.

'Thank you for such a lovely night,' I say softly.

'You're welcome, thank *you*.' his voice is soft too and moving closer to me. I close my eyes as his lips touch mine, softly at first, gently caressing them, teasing me, teasing my lips. Then as he senses I want more, he kisses me properly, harder but still so soft, he explores my mouth with his tongue and pulls me into him, pressing me hard against his body with one strong arm around my waist and back. I had been leaning backwards into the car to keep upright but his grip is strong and it pulls me away, deeper into him, deeper into the kiss.

I'm completely lost in the moment. I feel like I will never be able to kiss him enough to satisfy me, like it should never end, because if it does it can only leave me wanting more. His free hand caresses the back of my neck and moves around to my cheek, stroking it gently as his kiss softens. He pulls his face back just for a second and cups mine in his hand, he looks straight into my eyes and then his hand moves back around to my neck and gently he pulls me in again. I push my body against him, trying to satisfy the tingling I can feel in every part of me. As we mould into each other he takes his hand from my face and reaches it down to find mine. Our fingers meet and he lifts our intertwined hands into the empty air then wraps my hand around his back, still holding onto it. I am giddy with lust.

As the kiss slows and I come back to earth, my head feels like it is spinning. We are standing close now, our lips barely touching, still looking at each other. I should have been regaining my composure but my head is refusing to let me. The spinning is getting faster and my vision is blurred. I try to stand straighter and shake the feeling but my stomach is lurching, and this time it doesn't feel like the contained flutters of excitement. In fact, I don't think that I can contain it at all. Oh God. Oh, please, no. My head is dangerously out of control now. The giddiness has tuned to full on dizziness. Oh please, please, please, please, no. Like pulling an anchor from the seabed, I draw back from Luca and close my eyes. Our noses are still close, skimming each other. I can't see the look on his face because I'm too scared to open my eyes again. I stand very still and take a deep breath.

'Are you OK?' Luca whispers, and I can hear a mixture of concern and lust in his voice. I nod fractionally, still afraid to move or speak. Luca steps back and takes my face in his hands. 'Sophie.' His voice is louder and more concerned now. I open my eyes to look at him and catch a glimpse of worry in his otherwise perfect face, before it spins out of my line of vision and I lurch to the side, throwing up all over the back door of his car. I crumple to my knees and lean into the car's wheel, clutching it, groaning in dismay. I can't bear to see the look on his face, so I keep mine planted firmly in my hands and huddle as closely as I can to the safety of the metal frame of the car. Luca doesn't speak. He makes a soothing, hushing noise and scoops me into his arms and onto the back seat. I feel him reach across and pull the seat belt over me and then mercifully everything phases out and I'm pretty sure I pass out.

Chapter 28

What on earth is that banging? I put my hands to my head, not sure if it is inside or outside. Outside where? I am not even sure where I am. Painfully I open my eyes and wait for my vision to clear. It's a few minutes before I work out that I am in fact in my own bed, in my own cottage, and the banging in my head is the noise from the builders outside. I groan and turn over, burying my head in my pillow and squeezing my eyes tightly shut again.

What had I done? I feel horrific. Nothing short of horrendous. My head is pounding, my throat is parched, I have a horrible taste in my mouth and my stomach is churning, a feeling which intensifies a million fold when I remember what happened last night. Or what I think happened. I remember dinner and I remember being kissed. Amazingly. And then I remember being sick. Oh the shame. Please, God, don't let it have got worse than that.

Cursing and hating myself, I pull the curtains back and wince at the brightness of the light outside. There are two men moving a large wheelbarrow full of turf to the outer edge of the pool, and talking with intolerable loudness. I let the curtain fall back to ease the pain in my eyes but it does nothing for my throat, which is so dry I can barely swallow. I sit up gingerly, desperately trying to piece together the end of the night. I have no recollection of getting back to the cottage or into bed. Luca must have carried me in. I put my head back in my hands. Slowly I lift the sheet that covers me and I'm relieved to see that my underwear is at least on. Jen's dress is on the floor next to my bed but I have no idea if I took it off myself or if Luca had to do it.

Water, I need water.

I pull myself off the edge of the bed and stumble, head still in hands, over to the bathroom. I turn on the tap already anticipating, almost tasting the water running down my parched throat. To my horror the tap makes a clunking noise, shudders and spits out a trail of green muck, which reminds me cruelly of the last thing to come out of my mouth.

I make it downstairs and open the fridge in the kitchen in the hope that some non-existent person would have filled it with water for me. Of course they haven't, because they don't exist.

Hating myself even more, I quickly slip back into Jen's dress and head over to the main house. The sun nearly blinds me as I open the front door and I step out into the oppressive heat. I just have to make it to the kitchen, get some water, then get back to the cottage and back to bed. Work will just have to wait today.

If only it were that easy. To my utter dismay, the kitchen tap at the main house does exactly the same as the one in my bathroom. I let out a long, painful noise, which is clearly loud enough for one of the builders to hear, as for the next few minutes I am subjected to a long, loud, Italian rant which is peppered with expletives. In my delicate condition it takes me a while to work out that his problem is the same as mine. It is thirty degrees plus outside and there is no water.

I look at my watch, it's only ten a.m. but the builders would have been here since at least seven. I check the kitchen fridges and they too are out of water. We had been due two crates of bottled water the previous morning but they didn't arrive and it is on my 'to do' list today to chase it. In very broken Italian, I try to soothe the irate builder in front of me. There is nothing for it, I'm going to have to go and get some water.

With a worrying sense of déjà vu I go back to my room in the cottage, grab my sunglasses and wheelie case and, remembering to take off last night's dress and replace it with my denim shorts and vest, I head off on foot to the village. As I walk down the hill in the searing heat, the memories from the night before flood back. The beauty of the restaurant, the food, Carlo, Luca, that kiss. That incredible, mind blowing, world altering kiss. And then the rest. I can barely even bring myself to think about it. I am beyond mortified. Perhaps this is punishment for my behaviour. It certainly feels like it. Why didn't I just say no to the limoncello?

In the village I pick up as many bottles of water as I can fit in my case plus an extra carrier bag full and head back up the dusty road to the house. The sun is behind me now and it is burning my neck. I can feel beads of sweat dripping down my stomach and my thighs are rubbing inside my shorts with moisture. I'm probably sweating out all of the alcohol from last night. My feet have swollen so much they are hanging over the edge of my rubber flip flops.

As I trudge up the hill and round the corner I see a tall, dark man with black sunglasses walking towards me. He is wearing white linen trousers, camel loafers and a pale blue short-sleeved shirt with the top couple of buttons undone. Even in my state and from a distance I can see that he is good looking, in a very polished way. He carries himself in a way that suggests that he knows it too. He also looks vaguely familiar. As he gets closer he removes his sunglasses and flashes a disarmingly dazzling white smile at me. For the second time that morning I think I am going to pass out. It is Max Carter. *The* Max Carter, from the 'Agent Carter' movies. Carter is a bona fide Hollywood superstar who writes, produces, directs and stars in his own mega movies. What on earth is he doing here?

'Hey, you look like you could use a hand, can I help?' he asks, in an easy American drawl. I stare at him agog, practically incapable of responding and excruciatingly aware of my sweaty red face and un-brushed teeth laced with the aroma of sick.

'No thanks, honestly, I'm fine.'

I stare at my swollen feet hanging over the edge of my mismatching flip flops.

'Oh, come on, those bags look heavy, I'm just having a wander, it's no trouble.' He is making it very difficult to say no and to be honest I do feel on the brink of passing out.

'Well, if you're sure, that would be really kind of you, thank you.'

I still refuse to meet his gaze; God knows what he must think of me.

'Sure I'm sure.' He sounds delighted actually as he takes the bag and case off me. It feels amazing to walk without the extra weight but my blood is pumping so fast with shame and embarrassment that I still think I might pass out. Spontaneously I groan again.

'Are you OK?' Max Carter asks. I can't believe Max Carter is walking next to me and asking me a question, this is way too surreal. 'I hope you don't mind me saying, but you look a little worse for wear.'

And that is how I end up walking home with a Hollywood movie star telling him all about my wonderful, disastrous date. It feels good to tell someone about it actually, and it helps that he finds it absolutely hilarious. Once he has stopped laughing at my sad fate he smiles kindly at me.

'Hey, kid, don't worry about it. I've done far worse in my time. And trust me, I have definitely seen a lot worse.'

I smile at him gratefully and look at him properly for the first time. It is very strange looking at a face that I know so well but have never actually seen before. All I can think about is how white his teeth are.

'If he is really worthy of you, he will laugh at this like I am,' he adds kindly and I feel a rush of gratitude to this famous stranger for making me feel a little better.

'Do you live here?' Max asks. 'I'm having a place built just up the road and thought I would try to get to know the neighbours.'

'I do, I'm renovating the old manor house just up the hill on the left, you must have passed it on your way down.'

'Oh yes,' he responds enthusiastically. 'Beautiful place, looks really something from the outside, how far along in the works are you? I would love to look around one day, get some inspiration for my place?'

'Oh you must! It's the least I can do. We are scheduled to finish in just a couple of weeks. You must come to the opening party if you're here.'

He smiles. 'I have filming commitments abroad for most of the summer,' he tells me. 'But I'll be popping back and forth as and when I can, so if I'm here that would be wonderful, thanks, kid.'

I smile to him and myself. Normally I would feel patronised if someone called me kid but I liked it coming from him. It's a shame that he probably won't be able to make the opening party. I could just imagine the look on Fi's face if Max Carter turned up. And my parents! What would they say? It would certainly give them something to talk about back home at the Golf Club.

As we approach the gates to the house, Max hands me back the case and bag full of water. 'If it's OK with you then, I'll pop in before I leave and have a look around?'

'Of course.' I take the bags and am grateful that I don't have to show him around now. At least I will have a chance to brush my hair and teeth before I see him again. 'Pop in anytime and thanks again for your help.'

'Sure, kid. Good luck with the guy!' he lowers his glasses and gives me wink before setting off back up the hill.

In the house I put out the water on one of the kitchen surfaces and let the builders know that it is there. I take a bottle for myself, go back to my cottage and crawl back into bed. What a surreal morning. I down half of the water, pull the curtains shut and, vowing to text Luca as soon as I wake up, and never to go out again without checking that I have water at home first, I go back to sleep.

Chapter 29

I feel a little better after some more sleep, though my head is still mushy and I am delicate to say the least. I wonder if this morning actually happened or if I dreamt it, but then I see my flip flops and an empty carrier bag next to my half-drunk bottle of water and decide that, bizarrely, it really must have happened. It takes about thirty seconds before the now familiar stomach lurch accompanies my renewed memory of last night.

I reach for my mobile. There is a message from Jen asking how the date went and saying she will be here by midday, but nothing from Luca. I have a shower and brush my teeth whilst I try to compose a message to him in my head. By the time I look half presentable I'm still stuck on 'thanks and sorry'. There isn't really much else I can say. I ponder whether to try and blame a stomach bug or mystery illness but, given that he sat opposite me and watched me consume and mix vast amounts of alcohol, I don't think that is going to work. Nope. I am just going to have to face up to this one. I pick up my phone and type:

'Thank you so much for such a wonderful evening. I don't know what else to say except that I am so sorry about how it ended. I hope you feel better than I do this morning. Love Soph x'

I re-read the message before I send it and delete the 'love'. I'm feeling far too vulnerable to put myself out there this morning. We did have an amazing kiss last night but then I pretty much threw up all over him so God only knows what he thinks of me now. The time on my phone says nearly midday. Jen will be here soon. I will re-live the story one more time for her and then try to put it to the back of my mind. Jen will make me feel better about it, I'm sure.

As predicted, Jen does indeed make me feel better. OK, so she does laugh her head off at first, just as Max had, but she is sympathetic too and she recounts some of her worst ever date moments for me, which cheers me up no end. Although I'm worried when we realise that from all of her stories not one of the bad date moments resulted in a second date!

Still, at least we have a laugh as we clean out the newly installed bathrooms in the house, put curtains up and bed linen on, which is about all that I can manage in my fragile state. As we stuff the huge pillows on the bed in the main room into pistachio-coloured cases, I tell Jen about my encounter with Max Carter this morning. Once she has got over her initial surprise and actually believes me, she laughs almost as much as she did at my misfortune from last night.

'Only you, Soph!' she is crying with laughter now, tears are actually rolling down her cheeks. 'The one time you don't want

270

to see anyone and you bump into one of the biggest stars on the planet!' I grimace but laugh with her.

'At least it wasn't Luca; that really would have been too much!' I say.

'Well, I guess you should be grateful for small mercies. Anyway, last night's clothes and sick in the hair is probably run of the mill in Hollywood!'

Even though the laughing is at my expense it is very much needed and I am reinvigorated for the afternoon. We crack on with work upstairs for another hour or so before our rumbling stomachs remind us that we haven't had lunch. We go downstairs to see if there is anything left from Katarina's lunch delivery. As we examine what's left, which is not a lot, my phone beeps in my back pocket. Jen hears it too and urges me to see who it is. Tentatively I take it out, half of me, or maybe a little more, is desperate to hear from Luca but the rest of me is terrified to know what he thinks of me now. I'm right to be worried. It's him:

I'm glad you had a good time and I am really sorry that you feel that way. I had a lovely evening. Hope you feel better soon.'

OK. So it isn't the most damning reply in the world but let's be honest, it isn't particularly encouraging either. I was hoping for something more than polite. Even anger would have been better than polite. At least it would suggest that he cares about me, that the kiss was everything that I think and hope it was. I read the message to Jen.

271

'Well, he does say that he had a lovely evening.' Jen tries to find the best in the message as she does in everything. 'That's something isn't it?'

'I guess so,' I agree. 'But no kisses, no "love", and no mention of seeing me again. I think he has made his feelings pretty clear.' I'm trying to sound nonchalant but inside I'm breaking. I can't believe that after the evening that we spent together, after that incredible kiss, that he really doesn't feel anything. All at once my tiredness and my hangover hit me and I think that I am going to cry. I know that I drank too much and made a fool of myself, but does that really mitigate everything that had happened before. I feel like an idiot for letting myself believe it was more than it really is.

Jen takes my hand. 'Stop thinking about it so much.' Her voice is kind. 'He'll be in touch again, I'm sure of it. It's a nice message, you're just tired and over thinking it.' She smiles and squeezes my hand. 'And if he isn't, then what kind of a man is he? Who gets put off by a little sick?' She's trying to make me laugh but I'm not in the mood now. I half-smile and squeeze her hand back. I know that she's right but I am unfathomably close to tears. 'Why don't you go back to the cottage? Take the rest of the afternoon off and you will feel better tomorrow. You're tired and emotional today, you need to rest. I can finish up here. Go on,' Jen urges. I hate not pulling my weight but I am exhausted. The hysteria of earlier has worn off and now I am just drained. I desperately want to see and speak to Luca but in the absence of being able to do that the only other thing I want is my bed.

I hug Jen, grateful for my best friend, and head back to my little cottage. I make myself a cup of tea and a piece of toast, and decide to have a quick check through my emails as I eat and drink before I go back to bed.

I am surprised to see the laptop is open and on, the little green light flashes incessantly in the corner of my eye. I pull it across the table and look at the open email. As I read the opening line my heart sinks even lower. It's the email from Andrew. I remember that it's the last thing that I read before I got ready last night. I must have forgotten to switch it off. I read it again and remind myself to do something about it when I have my strength back tomorrow. It crosses my mind that it would have been terrible if Luca had seen the email, it would definitely have given him the wrong idea about Andrew and me. I ponder it for a moment but dismiss the idea. There are no signs of him having come into the sitting room and why would he have done? No. I'm sure that he hasn't seen it.

I re-read the text message that he sent me. Jen is right. He does say he had a lovely evening. Perhaps if I go back to bed and sleep this nasty hangover off everything will feel different in the morning. I close the laptop and head back upstairs to bed for the second time since I woke this morning, but this time I sleep right through to the following morning.

Chapter 30

The next day is busy but uneventful. I feel considerably better of body and a little better of mind. There is still no more contact from Luca so I immerse myself in another day's hard toil. Jen and I finish what we started the previous day upstairs and then set to work cleaning downstairs in the few rooms where the building and decorating work has been finished. I must check my phone twenty times by the time we have finished work and every time I do, my spirits dip further.

'You have to relax, it's not good for you to look at your phone so much,' Jen chastises. 'He will be in touch; he probably just doesn't want to seem too keen.'

I hope she's right but I have a bad feeling about it all. Obviously it is a reaction to the way the date ended, but I just feel like everything is up in the air and I really want some kind of confirmation, preferably positive, as to whether this is the start of something or the end of something.

'You're probably right.' I put on a brave face. 'Do you fancy getting some dinner in the village tonight?'

'I can't tonight.' I can hear a tinge of guilt in Jen's voice. 'Jake is coming over. You're welcome to join us,' she offers sweetly.

The lovely thing is that I know that she really means it, she wouldn't mind if I did join them for a while, but, no offence to them, the last thing that I want to do is spend a night in with a loved-up couple.

'Thanks.' I am genuinely grateful for the offer. 'But I think I'll give it a miss. I could probably do with an early night anyway. It's been a long week.'

'If you're sure. How about I come over for breakfast in the morning and we can finalise the plans for the launch party?'

'Great.'

We agree a time and go our separate ways.

Jen comes over as promised, laden with croissants and homemade jam. We work hard making calls, finalising food, drink and decorations and confirming the guest list for the party. When we have done all that we can, we meet Pauline and Frank at the main house and show them around all of the work that has been done. They are impressed with the progress and when they have seen everything they take us for an early dinner in the village. It's nice to sit outside and enjoy the food and their company, but my heart is not really in it and when we finish our meal Pauline and Frank stay on for a drink, while Jen goes to her cottage for another evening with Jake, and I go to mine for another early night.

By Sunday lunchtime I am desperate for news from Luca, for any kind of connection. Before I can stop myself, I pick up the phone and dial Aunt Sylvie's number. As the phone rings, I have a sudden panic that Luca might answer it and I consider hanging up but just before I do I hear Sylvie's soft voice at the other end of the line: 'Pronto.'

'Sylvie?' I check. 'It's Sophie.'

'Sophie!' she sounds pleased to hear from me. 'How lovely, how are you?'

'I'm great, thanks,' I lie, and there is a moment's silence while she waits for me to explain why I am calling and I try to come up with a reason. Just before it gets uncomfortable, a flash of inspiration hits me. 'Sylvie, I was wondering if I can come and see you tomorrow, if you are free? I am meeting a friend in Florence to choose some artwork for the house and I would really like your advice before I go.'

'Of course I'm free! I would be delighted to help.' Sylvie sounds pleased. 'I will be at home all day tomorrow, please come by whenever you can.'

I smile at how wonderfully accommodating she is. 'Thank you, I'll come in the morning. I look forward to seeing you.'

'And I you, my dear. See you then.' Sylvie replaces the receiver.

I didn't ask anything about Luca and she didn't tell me anything. I have no idea if he is there or not, but at least now there is a slight possibility that I might run into him tomorrow.

Chapter 31

Sylvie greets me warmly at the door with a hug and two kisses. She invites me into her cottage, which is small and neat. It feels homely and rustic. There are dried flowers hanging from the ceiling, terracotta tiles covering the floors and photographs of her family in every room. She takes me through to the kitchen where there is a small Aga in one corner and a pine table with three matching chairs in the other. There is no sign of Luca.

In the kitchen, Sylvie fills an old-fashioned kettle with water and stands it on the Aga. I sit at the table in the corner and watch her fuss around, pulling out cups, saucers and plates. She takes a large tin down from one of the cupboards on the wall and pulls a huge fruit cake out of it. She places it on a plate in front of me. I skipped breakfast in my hurry to get out this morning and it looks so good that I don't refuse when she cuts me a large slice.

'So,' she pushes the plate towards me and walks back over to the Aga to remove the now whistling kettle from the stove. 'Tell me what it is that you are looking for. How can I help you?'

I am desperate to ask about Luca, but instead I tell her about my meeting with Michael and what it is that I want to do. 'I would really love to find some replicas of the original artwork in the house; I know how much the paintings meant to you and your sister.'

Sylvie pours the tea and looks nostalgic as she thinks about them.

'Obviously we could never get the originals back but we have tried so hard to be true to the house and its heritage. I want to follow that through to the end, so I was wondering if you can remember some of the names of the paintings, or if you can describe them to me. Maybe you have some photos from inside the house that have some of the paintings in them?' Sylvie is sitting opposite me now, cradling her tea; her face is thick with emotion.

'Oh, my dear, you are so very sweet. I would love to help you and I think that I probably can.'

'Thank you!' I'm relieved and excited. 'Luca has told me how much the paintings meant to all of you, it's so important to me to get them right.'

Sylvie smiles kindly again and I feel a bond between us.

'How is Luca?' I ask. 'I was hoping that I might hear from him after we had dinner last week.'

For the first time Sylvie looks a bit uncomfortable. She shifts in her seat and looks down at the cup in her hands. 'I wondered,' she says, 'If you had a nice time with Luca. He was so happy when he left to take you out. I think perhaps he has a little soft spot for you, but he hasn't said very much since then. I thought that he might tell me about the dinner but he didn't want to talk about it.' Sylvie must be able to see the bitter disappointment on my face because she smiles at me reassuringly. 'He did mention that perhaps there is another man in your life.' Sylvie is making a statement but asking a question at the same time with the tone of her voice. 'He seemed upset by that.' She takes a sip of her tea and waits for me to talk.

'There's no other man in my life. Why would he think that?' As I say the words, it dawns on me exactly why he would think that. The laptop. The email from Andrew. He must have seen it, there is no other explanation. I think back to the text message that I sent him, I had gone over it a million times in my head the last few days to try and work out how I might have caused offence.

'I don't know what else to say except that I am so sorry about how it ended.'

If he thinks that I have a boyfriend then perhaps he thought that I was referring to the kiss, that I thought it was a mistake. I am equally horrified that he thinks I have a boyfriend or that I could ever be sorry for the most amazing kiss that I have ever had, and also immensely relieved that there is an explanation for his silence and that if I can just see him again, I might have a chance to clear this whole mess up.

Sylvie is watching me, she looks concerned and I realise that I haven't spoken while I process everything in my mind.

'Are you OK, dear?' she asks. 'Luca said that you have a boyfriend, I thought you must have told him?'

'No!' I explain the whole story about Andrew and the email and leaving the laptop open. When I have finished Sylvie takes my hand across the table.

'Just tell him, dear, it will be a relief to see him smile again. He has been miserable all week!'

I never thought I would be so ludicrously happy for someone to tell me that Luca is miserable!

'Will he be home soon?' I ask, eager to see him and explain.

Sylvie looks apologetic. 'He won't be back for a while, I don't think, dear. He got a job in Rome with one of his big clients and he left last night. I think he plans on going back home to Florence afterwards, but he did say he will pop back and see me in a week or so.'

A week! She might as well have said forever, it feels so long. Still, at least I can still clear up the confusion. I forge a smile.

'I'll text him tonight and clear everything up.'

'Good girl,' Sylvie nods her approval. 'Now, let me go and dig out the rest of my photos and we can get to work.'

We spend the next hour looking through her pictures and writing down her memories of the paintings in the house. She knows the names of some, the artists of others and just descriptions of a few, but by the time I leave I have a pretty comprehensive list of the things that I am looking for. I give Sylvie a big hug before I go and promise to let her know how I get on, then I head into Florence to meet Michael.

Michael is waiting for me in a small coffee shop next to the university. He stands up when I walk in and greets me like an old friend with a warm 'buon giorno' and a kiss on each cheek. We order lattes and get straight down to business.

I show him the photographs and the information Sylvie has given me and we work our way through it together.

'This was a really special collection.' Michael is impressed. 'The Russo family are well known for their art collection but I didn't realise that they had owned all of these. Rialto must have had an exceptional eye for art.'

It's ridiculous, I know, but I actually feel a strange sense of pride. 'So do you think that we might be able to get prints of any of them?' I ask, looking at the list of paintings that Michael has written down.

'I think there is a good chance. Some of these paintings are actually in galleries in Florence, they should be easy to get. Others are not in Florence any more, some are not even in Italy, but many of them are well known and on show for the public, so we should be able to get hold of prints from somewhere. There are a couple that are still in private hands, they will be difficult to get hold of but I think we have a good shot at getting about eighty percent of these at least.'

I am thrilled. 'That's amazing! You are so clever to know all of this! I have studied art and I only recognise the name of one of the paintings.'

'Well, this is my job,' he laughs. 'Luckily the Russo collection consists largely of Italian artists, so most of them are well known to me. We may not have been so lucky if their collection had been more international.'

'All the same, I am very impressed, and very grateful!' I add.

Michael smiles, pleased by the compliment. 'Do you want to leave it with me and I'll get back to you in a few days with what I can find?' he asks me.

'That would be amazing, but it seems like a lot of work, I don't want to take up too much of your time.'

'Not at all, it should only be a matter of a few phone calls and some internet research. It will be a nice little project for me. I'm happy to do it.'

I am touched by the generosity of this person that I hardly know. 'This really is so kind of you, thank you.'

'You are very welcome. There is a small frame shop not far from here, I know the owner. Once the prints come through I can arrange for him to frame them for you if you would like?'

'Oh, yes!' Stupidly I haven't actually thought about getting them framed, but of course they would need to be if they are going to hang on the walls!

'We can walk there now if you would like?' Michael offers. 'You can get an idea of what you want?'

We finish our second lattes and walk the short journey to what turns out to be a small, old shop with no sign or name outside to indicate as to what might be going on inside. Michael pushes the door, which hits a small bell as it opens, alerting the owner to our presence.

An elderly man comes through from the back room; he takes off his glasses and rubs then on his dusty white shirt, which I can't imagine makes them much cleaner. He looks pleased to see Michael and they exchange pleasantries warmly before Michael introduces me.

'Mario makes most of the frames here himself but he also has a large stock out the back,' Michael explains. 'If you tell him what you are looking for, then when I get hold of the prints I can bring them straight here for you. Or would you like to see the prints first and then decide on the frames?'

'No, that sounds like a good plan to me. I would be grateful for your advice actually, Michael, I wouldn't really know where to start,' I tell him. We go into a small workshop set back from the main shop, it smells musty and the sunlight coming in from the dirty windows at the back shows millions of dust particles lingering in the air around us. In every corner, against every wall and on every surface is a frame of some description. There are magnificent, hand-carved works of art, sleek modern frames, small intricate ones and shiny metal ones. I am so pleased that I have Michael's guidance when I see the array of options on offer.

With Mario's help, we decide on a range of thick, gilded, extravagantly designed frames that look just like some of the ones I could see in Aunt Sylvie's photographs. If there had been one on a wall in my Clapham flat it would have looked ridiculous, but they are clearly exceptional pieces of art in their own right and I am absolutely sure that they are right for the paintings in the house. Michael makes the necessary arrangements with Mario and we agree to leave it to his discretion as to exactly what shape and size of frame will best fit each print. I am so grateful to them that I hug them both when we are finished, which definitely takes Mario by surprise. I while away the journey home trying to compose a message to send to Luca. This is what I come up with:

'Hi Luca, Sylvie told me today that you might have seen something that makes you think I have a boyfriend. Please get in touch. It is not what you think. Thanks again for Wednesday night, I really had a lovely time and would love to see you again soon. Love Sophie. X*

I send the message once I am back at the cottage and relaxing in the bath with a glass of wine. As soon as I click send I put my phone down on the bathroom floor next to my glass and sink my head under the water, luxuriating in the hot bubbles that I am submerged in. I don't have to wait long for a reply. I hear the muffled beep of my phone through the water and bubbles washing around in my ear. Grabbing a towel to dry my hands, I pick up my phone. It's from him! I open the message and hold my breath as I read it, feeling sick with anticipation:

'Hi Sophie, I'm away on business until Friday. I'm really glad you had a good time, I did too. If you are in I could pop by the house and check out the progress on my way home? Luca x

I breathe out a long and exaggerated sigh of relief. It isn't exactly a love poem but it is a start and I am going to see him again. I will see him on Friday and already I can't wait. It dawns on me that my parents will be arriving on Friday, but nothing is going to stop me from seeing Luca. I send a simple reply:

'I would love that. See you then x'

The next few days just can't go quickly enough. Jen is at college almost full time for the last week of her course, which at least means that I have to be on hand all of the time in the house and am literally run off my feet. Jen has exams and demonstrations nearly every day, but she still comes by the house every evening to catch up on the latest developments and sign off on all of the joint decisions that need making on a daily basis.

By the time Friday arrives we are both shattered but the house is looking wonderful. All of the major work has been finished inside and outside the grounds are starting to look really spectacular. New lawns have been laid beyond the patio and around the pool, which are a rich, bright green. The gardens beyond the pool have been cut, pruned, revived and restored and are looking magnificent. The pool shines luminously under the bright, Tuscan sun and the new outdoor furniture sets everything off to perfection.

As I walk around the house and grounds on Friday morning, awaiting my parents' arrival, I can't help but swell with pride as I take everything in. It is unrecognisable compared to the derelict house that I found and fell in love with just weeks ago and yet it still has the same feel as it had then. I am so delighted with the transformation; I could never have even wished that it would look so fantastic and that it would be mine. Mine and Jen's to love and to nurture and to build together. I don't know who I'm more excited to show it to — my parents or Luca. Either way, my parents are going to be first. Pauline and Frank are picking them up from the airport and they are due to arrive at about ten a.m. By nine thirty, I have set one of the tables on the patio by the pool with tea, coffee, pastries and some fresh fruit and I am pacing the entrance hall waiting for them. A long forty minutes later I see Frank's car pull into the driveway. I watch from the hall window to see my parents' faces as they get out of the car. The look of awe and excitement in my mother's eyes is validation itself for every decision I have made. I run out to the car and throw my arms around mum first and then dad as he walks up behind us grinning from ear to ear.

'Come here, love.' He envelops me in a massive hug and squeezes me hard, slapping me on the back in a way that only a man can. 'This is wonderful. I am so proud of my little girl!'

'Thanks, dad.' I well up at the praise and at their obvious delight. 'Wait till you see inside!'

I let him go and they follow me in. Mum and dad could not have loved the place more. They ooh and aah at everything from the cornicing and the domed windows, to the fully stocked shelves in the library and the beautifully decorated, elegantly grandiose bedrooms. Once I have given the full tour, we sit on the patio and enjoy the food and drink that I prepared earlier. It's lovely to all sit together and catch up after such a long time apart.

'Isn't it beautiful?' Pauline is talking to mum.

'Oh, it is.' Mum is barely able to draw her eyes away from the beauty around her. 'It really is something special. We are very proud of you, love.' She pats my hand. It's a simple gesture but I can't tell you how much it means. I have spent the last two years, well actually, the last twenty seven years, waiting for this moment. I smile at mum, trying hard to hold back the tears.

We sit for a couple of hours recounting stories of the last few weeks and discussing plans for the week ahead, before I suggest that mum and dad might like to go up to their room and have a rest before the evening.

'I am a little tired.' Mum sounds apologetic. 'Your father and I were up at four to catch our flight this morning,' she explains.

Almost on cue, dad yawns and then laughs at his timing. 'I could certainly do with a little siesta. What time is dinner?' he asks.

'We'll come and pick you all up at seven thirty,' Frank answers.

'Excellent. We can all celebrate our girls' success together.' Mum exchanges a proud glance with Pauline, 'And who knows, it might be an extra special celebration.'

She winks at dad like they are in cahoots about something. I have no idea what she is talking about and I am just about to ask her when Frank stands up and scrapes his chair loudly on the patio floor.

'We'll make a move too then. See you all at seven thirty.' He helps Pauline up and in a flurry of hugs and kisses we say our goodbyes until later.

Feeling happy and relaxed, I work in the cellar for the next few hours clearing out the rest of the storage space and taking inventory of the stock that we are already storing. I go back to the cottage earlier than I usually would so that I can get ready for Luca's arrival before dinner. I am so excited to see him I can barely concentrate on getting ready. I contemplate having a large glass of wine to ease my nerves but decide against it. I want to be completely sober when I speak to him and I definitely don't want to be smelling of alcohol after our last encounter! There will be plenty of time for drinking later!

I don't want to look too overdressed so I put on my white trousers and a navy, silk vest top that has been sitting in my wardrobe unworn since I arrived in Italy. I do the best I can with my hair and make-up in the time available, then decide to wait for Luca at the main house.

I don't have to wait long before I hear the sound of a car pulling up on the gravel outside. My stomach flips, which I'm used to by now, and I walk slowly to the front door. I take a few deep breaths and try to compose myself. As Luca knocks on the door I close my eyes and take one last deep breath before opening it.

'Hi,' I say brightly and then stop in my tracks.

Luca isn't standing in front of me. Andrew is. I am lost for words so I just stand there looking at him. He beams at me and comes straight through the door, gathering me up in a hug so that my feet actually leave the floor.

'Hi, Soph. God I've missed you! This place is great.' He puts me down and looks around him.

'Thanks.' I still don't know what to say. I'm sure I emailed my parents and told them not to bring Andrew. I try to think back. I did. I definitely emailed them. But, oh God, I forgot to email Andrew. I meant to do it so many times but things kept cropping up and I kept putting it off until, eventually, it completely went out of my mind. My parents so rarely check their emails they probably still haven't even seen the one I sent them.

I have an awful, sinking feeling in my stomach as I take it all in. Poor Andrew has come all this way for nothing. What am I going to do?

Buying some time, I invite him in to the house.

'Come through, it's great to see you.' I try to sound sincere. Andrew follows me through to the morning room.

'Soph, it's lovely,' he says again, as I lead him to the patio. 'You knew I was coming, right?' he asks. 'You got my texts and my email?'

'Oh, yes. I did get them, I'm sorry I didn't reply to them all, it has been so manic here I have barely had a second to myself.' Andrew smiles and stands in front of me. He takes both of my hands in his

'There's no need to apologise, I can only imagine how hard you must have been working. The house looks beautiful.' I smile at him, grateful for the compliment.

'So, did you come over with my parents?' I ask, trying to find some safe conversation ground.

'I had to catch a later flight so I came straight here in a taxi from the airport. I couldn't wait to see you.'

'Oh,' is all I can muster in response. I know I need to say something else but I feel so bad I don't even know where to start. Andrew keeps talking at me.

'The thing is, Sophie, I really wanted to see you before dinner with your parents tonight.' I wonder how he knows about dinner but of course he must have been speaking to them and of course they would have invited him. This is not going to be an easy evening. 'I wanted to see you because whilst we have been apart I have spent a lot of time thinking about you.' He goes on, 'About us and about what I want for us.'

I shift uncomfortably in front of him as he looks me straight in the eyes. He let's go of one of my hands and gets something from his pocket.

'I have been thinking,' he repeats himself, 'and I want you to know that I support you.'

'I know you do, Andrew.' I am starting to feel nervous at where this is heading.

'And I want you to know that I want to be here with you, to support you, by your side.'

To my horror, still holding one hand and looking into my eyes, Andrew goes down on one knee in front of me and holds up a small, black velvet box.

'Sophie.' He is very serious all of a sudden. 'I love you and I want you to be my wife.'

I stare at him, completely dumbfounded. I can't believe that this is happening. I feel so many things all at once that I don't know what to respond with first. I'm angry at myself for not telling him sooner and more clearly how I really feel; I'm embarrassed for me and for him; more than anything I feel so sorry for him. As I look at him kneeling below me, looking into my eyes, so trusting, so loving and so desperate to please me, I just feel truly awful. Tears are pricking the back of my eyes as I realise what I have put this poor man through and what I'm going to have to do now.

To my horror, Andrew is welling up too, though not for the same reason.

He smiles at me. 'So, Sophie, will you marry me?'

As the words come out of his mouth I clasp his hand with both of mine in a gesture of sympathy. Just as I do, the door to the morning room opens and, as if things could possibly get any worse, Luca walks in.

I watch, unable to speak, as Luca takes in the scene in front of him. Andrew on bended knee, holding up a ring with one hand, the other hand clasped in both of mine, both of us crying.

Luca stops in his tracks. He looks at me and then at Andrew. He is clearly confused and then embarrassed, but he turns and leaves too quickly for me to know what he is thinking. More than anything I want to run out after him and explain, but Andrew is still sitting on the floor in front of me, obviously confused himself by Luca's arrival and then sudden departure. I owe it to him to finish this now, once and for all. I hear Luca's car pull away and this time I can't stop the tears from falling.

'Don't cry, Sophie, please don't cry.'

I can tell Andrew is confused, not so sure that the tears are happy ones any more.

'Oh, Andrew,' I pull him up from the floor. 'Please, sit down.' I lead him over to a couple of wooden chairs that are being used while we wait for the rest of the furniture to be delivered, and I sit facing him.

'I can't believe that you are here, that you are doing all of this. I feel so terrible.' I take his hand.

'Why do you feel terrible?' His voice falters slightly like he is afraid of the answer and I hate myself all over again for doing this to him.

'I am so sorry, Andrew. I should have told you this before. I should have made it clear. I don't love you any more. I think you are wonderful and that you deserve someone equally as wonderful, but that person isn't me. I'm not in love with you and, though I am so touched to be asked, I can't marry you.'

He lowers his eyes to the floor and his body crumples in the chair. I feel sick.

'I'm so sorry.'

I am at a loss for anything else to say. We sit in silence until Andrew regains his composure. It feels like a lifetime. I don't deserve it, but much to his credit and testament to what a good person he is, Andrew makes everything very easy for me.

'I understand. I just wish you had told me earlier, Soph.'

'I know. So do I. I am truly sorry, Andrew.'

'It's OK. I suppose if you had told me earlier then I wouldn't have got to see you again or this beautiful house. I am proud of you, Sophie. I can't say that I'm not devastated that you don't want to marry me, but I'm proud of you all the same and I hope that we can be friends.'

'Of course we can.' I reach over and put my arms around him. I hold him for a while with real affection, relieved and grateful for his generosity of spirit.

'Well.' He gently pushes me away. 'I suppose I should start looking for a hotel and try to get myself a flight back home.'

I realise uncomfortably that Andrew had been planning on staying with me in the cottage. Obviously that isn't going to happen, but now that I have finally told him that we are over and he has so graciously accepted it, I don't see any reason why he shouldn't stay on in the house for a night or two. It is, after all, a hotel and it is so nearly finished now. It's the least that I can do after he has come all the way out here to propose to me.

'Why don't you stay here for a night or two before you go home? I'm sure Jen would love to see you and you have only just arrived.'

Andrew hesitates in his reply

'If you want to, that is. I understand if it will be too strange for you, staying here.'

Andrew smiles warmly at me, 'That would be wonderful, Soph; I would love that, if you're sure?'

'Sure I'm sure. Let me show you to your room, sir.' I put on my most official voice.

'Why, thank you, madam.' Andrew responds in his best 'guest' voice and we laugh, glad to be comfortable together. I settle Andrew in his room and, having agreed that he will still come for dinner tonight, I tell him to meet me downstairs in five minutes when he has freshened up. I go ahead and try to call Luca before Frank and Pauline arrive. His phone goes straight to answer phone. I can see Frank's car pulling into the driveway so I send him a quick message:

'Luca, please call me. I am so sorry about what you saw. I really need to talk to you; it is not what you think. Sophie x'

Clicking send, I put my phone in my bag and call up the stairs to mum and dad. Mum looks like she is going to spontaneously combust as she walks down and sees Andrew standing beside me.

'Hello, darlings,' she smiles and winks at us to let us know that she is in on our 'little secret'.

Jen is clearly not in on anything because when I open the door to her she looks completely shocked to see Andrew next to me.

'What's going on?' she mouths as my mum envelops Andrew in a huge hug. I roll my eyes and shake my head. I can't explain in front of everyone so I mouth 'later' to ensure her that I will fill her in on everything as soon as I get a chance.

'So, any news from you two?' mum trills at us, lacking any subtlety whatsoever. To spare Andrew's feelings I cut mum off before she can say any more.

'Andrew is just staying for a night or two. He wanted to see the hotel and to wish Jen and I luck before he goes home.'

Now it is mum's turn to look confused.

'Wasn't it lovely of him to come, Mum? He is such a good friend.' I squeeze Andrew's hand briefly to let him know that I mean it. He smiles at me gratefully and with mum spluttering and desperately trying to whisper questions in my ear, we all walk out of the house and leave for dinner.

With Andrew in Frank and Pauline's car I take the opportunity to drive with my parents and Jen so that I can explain everything to them en route. Jen finds the whole thing quite funny, though I can tell that she is mortified for Andrew too, she has always been quite fond of him. My mum is almost as devastated as Andrew but, after a few stern words from my dad, she manages to croak out, 'Whatever makes you happy of course, love,' though she can't resist adding, 'Such a shame though, such a lovely boy.'

I catch dad's eye in the driver's mirror and he gives me a reassuring smile which fills me with love and gratitude for him. After strict instructions not to mention the non-engagement for the rest of the night, we arrive at the restaurant and manage to have a really lovely evening. Mum and dad are super excited for the launch party, and I am delighted to be able to distract them with the details.

I don't check my phone again until I'm back in my room at the cottage. I so desperately want to but I know that I won't be able to engage in any kind of conversation, text or otherwise, with Luca whilst I'm at dinner with my parents and Andrew, so I think it best not to even try. If I saw something from him I would only think about it constantly until I could reply, which would be too much of a distraction. I had been right not to look because there is a message from Luca and it isn't a good one:

'No need to explain, Sophie. Congratulations, I am really happy for you.'

I start to type a reply but there is no way I can get everything that I need to say into a text message. I need to talk to him. My heart thumps heavily in my chest as I dial his number but it needn't have as I don't even hear a ring, just a recorded voice message in Italian that I don't understand. I feel sick to my stomach, completely exhausted, emotionally drained and totally deflated. It is too late to call Sylvie's house but I will do it first thing in the morning and please, God, Luca will be there. I climb into bed and, not able to face thinking about the events of the day, I close my eyes and try hard to blank everything out until exhaustion takes over and I fall asleep.

Without the noise from the builders I wake late in the morning and the first thing I do is try and call Luca. I dial his number but am met with the same Italian voicemail message. I scroll through my numbers until I find Sylvie's.

'Pronto,' Sylvie answers after a couple of rings.

'Hi, Sylvie, it's Sophie.' I try to sound jolly. How are you?'

'Sophie! I'm good, thank you, how can I help you?'

'Actually, I was wondering if Luca is there.' I cross my fingers and squeeze my eyes shut. 'I just need to talk to him about something.'

'I am sorry, dear,' Sylvie's words deflate me immediately. 'He left early this morning, I'm not sure when he is planning on coming back. Perhaps you could try his mobile?' I hold the phone away from my face as I breathe deeply, trying to keep the tears from falling.

'Is everything OK, dear?' I hear Sylvie say at the end of the line. Suddenly, in the absence of Luca, I desperately want to see her.

'Yes, of course.' I manage. 'Actually, I want to talk to you too. The paintings and the last of the furniture are being delivered on Wednesday, I wondered if you would like to come and see it all.'

'I would love that.' Sylvie sounds thrilled and I am pleased to have asked.

'Great,' I try to match her excitement. 'Why don't you come in the morning and stay for lunch?' We make plans and say our goodbyes.

As the phone goes dead I let the tears spill and once they start I can't stop them. I bury my head under the duvet and have a really good cry. It is therapeutic and I am tempted to stay here for the rest of the morning but I have lunch with Jen and our parents and with the launch party less than one week away, every moment counts.

I wipe my eyes and haul myself out of bed. Only yesterday I had been so excited about this weekend and preparations for the party next weekend. Now it just feels like such a lot of work. Luca has been so much a part of everything so far, it doesn't seem right that he won't be here to see it all come to fruition. I can only hope to speak to him and sort everything out before the end of the week.

Chapter 32

As it happens I am actually quite grateful for the distraction of my parents over the weekend. They are so enthusiastic about the house and helping for the party that it is hard not to get caught up in their excitement.

Andrew turns out to be pretty good to have around too. He is a great help come Monday morning when the food and drink supplies start to arrive alongside deliveries of cutlery, crockery, pots, pans, vases and just about everything that you could imagine a hotel kitchen would need. Between them Andrew, Frank and dad lug the heavy boxes into the house. They sweat heavily in the intense heat and the number of boxes goes on and on, but still they smile and work with good humour. I watch Andrew pick up the smaller boxes and pass them to my dad so that he doesn't have to carry the heavy ones inside and I feel a pang of sadness that I can't love him as much as I like him.

I push aside the ever invading image of Luca's face in my mind and try to focus on the task in hand. Pauline, mum, Jen and I have set up an assembly line to open, unpack and put away the various contents of the boxes that are quickly stacking up all around us. We work happily, chatting and singing along to music on Jen's iPod. By the time the last box is unpacked and put away it is dark outside.

I look at my phone to check the time and try to ignore the ache in my heart that gets worse every time I realise that Luca still hasn't called. 'It's ten o' clock,' I say out loud to everyone. 'I think we have all done enough work for one day, how about I call for a pizza?'

'Lovely,' Pauline agrees as she and mum dust off their clothes from their final run to the cellar with giant bottles of olive oil.

'Sounds good to me too, dad likes anchovies on his.' Mum reels off a list of things that dad does and doesn't like. The men walk into the room while she is still deciding if it is pepperoni or meatballs that gives dad indigestion.

'Did I hear meatballs?' dad asks. 'I'm starving.'

I laugh as the three men banter about working up an appetite and being able to eat a horse. We clear a space on the floor, which is still awaiting the furniture arrival on Wednesday.

Jen brings up a box of beer and a bottle of wine from the cellar and when the pizzas arrive, the seven of us sit around them in the middle of us and enjoy our well deserved food and drink. It is nearly midnight when we stack up the empty boxes and bottles and say our goodnights.

On the walk over to my little cottage, I ponder how amazing it is that it isn't awkward being in the house alone with Andrew, and think again how easy life would be if I loved him. But I don't. I love Luca and he isn't here. When I get inside I suddenly feel very alone and I long for morning to come again and for the bustling activity in the house to keep me company. I go straight to bed, barely running a toothbrush over my teeth, and fall asleep while trying to imagine a scenario where Luca might turn up tomorrow with a forgiving smile and open arms.

Much to my disappointment but not to my surprise, Luca doesn't turn up on Tuesday. Nor does he call me or switch on his phone. We do, however, have an extra pair of hands in the house in the form of Jake, who has come to help us in the morning while Jen takes her final exam. I feel awful when Jake turns up. I had completely forgotten she had her exam.

'Poor Jen! She was here so late, she should have said something.'

Jake smiles kindly and dismisses my worry. 'She was very well prepared, we practised everything over the weekend, and she will be fine.'

I can tell that he means it and I can see the warmth in his eyes when he speaks about her. I would have thought that Jen has fallen on her feet with this one, but so has Jake, so instead I think how lucky they are to have found each other. Ignoring the dull ache in the pit of my stomach I set Jake up with my dad on the patio. Dad is struggling with a stack of huge boxes that contain large, teak, cream umbrellas and is grateful for help unpacking them and putting them up in the centre of each of the new patio tables. I leave them to get on with it and go to oversee the hanging of the newly refurbished chandeliers. It is another long day, with people coming and going all the time. Jen turns up late in the afternoon full of end-of-term excitement and thrilled at how her exam has gone. Jake was obviously right.

By the end of the day things are really starting to come together. As well as the chandeliers, the cleaned and repaired curtains have been hung up and the remaining outdoor furniture is set up, umbrellas and all.

As everyone leaves in the evening, earlier than the one before, we can all sense that the end is in sight. Even though I still haven't heard from Luca, I go to bed feeling slightly brighter at the progress that we have made and at the thought of seeing Sylvie tomorrow, who I hope might at least have some news from him.

Wednesday arrives hot and sunny, as every day before it has, and I am up even earlier than usual, excited for the arrival of the paintings and the last of the furniture. Sylvie is at the house at nine a.m. looking fresh and lovely in a pale green summer dress and flat tan sandals. She is blown away when she walks into the morning room resplendent with its pristine curtains and shining chandeliers, twinkling in the morning sunshine.

'I can barely believe it.' She looks around her, walking in a circle on the spot and taking it all in. 'It looks wonderful.'

I think that she wants to say something else but I can see her eyes welling with tears and her voice is choked. Holding back the tears that are pushing at the back of my own eyes, I rally us both.

'The reception desk is being delivered in an hour and then the paintings will be here by lunchtime! Let me show you around everything else before it all starts happening!'

I show Sylvie the rooms upstairs and Jen joins us for a quick stroll around the pool and gardens, which are thick with the scent of newly planted roses and jasmine. We are just about to show Sylvie inside the cottage when we hear the delivery lorry pulling up outside. We head back to the front of the main house and watch as the driver unloads the furniture from the back of the truck. While we stand there, Frank and Pauline arrive to pick up Andrew and drive him back to the airport.

As Frank helps the delivery driver take everything inside, Andrew comes out to say his goodbyes. By the time he has hugged everyone and is ready to go, it is just him and me on the driveway, and Frank waiting patiently in the car.

'So, this is it,' he smiles at me. 'I'm really proud of you, Sophie. Good luck with everything.'

I smile gratefully back at him. 'Thanks, Andrew. Are you sure I can't convince you to stay on for the party?'

He shakes his head. 'It's time for me to go.'

'I really am sorry about how this has all turned out,' I start, but he waves his hand to save me the trouble and holds out his arms for a hug. I walk into them happily and he holds me tight.

We stand there for a moment or two, silently saying our goodbyes. He lets me go and, with a little wink, walks over to the car. I wave him off and, pushing aside the sadness I feel at our final goodbye, I go back into the house where the delivery driver and my dad are sweating profusely and struggling to get the reception desk into the room on the right of the entrance hall.

A lot of blood (as the corner of the desk hits my dad in the nose), sweat and swearing later, the desk is in and we set about putting everything around it in the right place. There is a swivel chair with a green leather cushion that goes behind it, a tiffany style desk lamp that we picked up with Sylvie in Florence and an old fashioned telephone. Sylvie is just as excited as we are to see the final result and claps her hands together as I plug the phone in the wall and then sit on the chair behind the desk and spin myself around like a child.

Only seconds after it is plugged in, to our combined amazement, the telephone rings. We all look at it.

'May I?' Sylvie asks.

'Be our guest!' I gesture at the telephone and she picks up the receiver.

'Good morning. How can I help you?' Jen and I look on in surprise and excitement as Sylvie takes what sounds like our very first booking. 'Thank you so much, we look forward to seeing you then.' She replaces the receiver.

We stare at her in anticipation.

'Well?' Jen asks impatiently.

'Congratulations, girls, you have your first booking! Mr and Mrs Chase will be staying for a week from this Friday.' She is beaming with pleasure.

'Mr and Mrs Chase,' Jen repeats. 'You have just taken our first booking from our best friend Fiona's parents.'

'Well, a booking is a booking, friend or no friend!' Sylvie is defiant and she is right.

Our first booking! Jen and I have a quick hug to celebrate the milestone.

'You're a natural.' Jen turns to Sylvie and hands her the booking sheets to fill in. 'You know,' Jen looks at me now, 'We will be needing a receptionist, someone to help out when we are busy.'

I nod, reading her thoughts. 'I don't suppose you would be interested in working a couple of days a week, would you?' I ask Sylvie.

Well, if she was excited before she is way beyond that now. She throws her arms around both of us. 'Is that a yes?' I laugh when she finally lets us go.

'Yes! Oh yes, girls, I would love to!' She looks at us both closely. 'Do you know, I think you two might just be my guardian angels. I have been so lonely since my husband and my sister died, and you two have come along and I feel like new life has been breathed into me. And being back in the house as well, I can't quite take it all in.'

We all have tears in our eyes now. This house just seems to have a way of making people cry. I don't think I have ever been as emotional in my life as I have been since we got it.

We are disturbed by the arrival of the second delivery of the day. This time it is a large white van and I am surprised to see Michael get out of the front. 'Ciao.' He walks over and kisses Jen and me on both cheeks, and then Sylvie too, once we introduce them. 'I thought you might need some help getting the pictures up so I collected them this morning and picked up some extra supplies in case any of the old hooks need replacing.'

'Thanks!' Jen and I speak at the same time, pleased to see him and even more excited to see the pictures. Dad helps Michael carry them in and one by one they walk some of the most beautiful pictures I have ever laid eyes on past us. Jen and

I follow Michael and dad in with the last frame and I turn to ask Sylvie if she can help us choose where to place the pictures in the house.

I am surprised to see that she is still standing alone in the hallway.

'Are you OK, Sylvie?'

I walk back to her and see that she is crying, properly crying now. Thick and heavy tears are rolling down her kind face.

'Sylvie, what's wrong?' I ask, concerned.

'Nothing is wrong, dear,' she smiles through the tears. 'I'm sorry, I am such a silly old thing,' she wipes her face with a lace hankie from her pocket. 'It's just seeing those paintings. I haven't seen some of those pictures in years. I can't believe that you have managed to find them all.'

'Well, they are only prints,' I explain. 'But they look good, don't they?'

'They look wonderful. I wish Luca was here to see them. It would mean so much to him to see the pictures that his mother loved so much.'

'So do I,' I admit. It feels good to talk to her about him. 'I did it for him really,' I tell her. 'And for you and the house, of course, but he told me how much the paintings meant to your sister and I thought this would be a lovely way to pay homage to her.'

Sylvie puts her hand on my arm and squeezes it gently. 'What a lovely girl you are. Luca is very lucky to have someone like you care so much for him.'

I try to smile but this time it is my turn to cry. Embarrassed, I quickly wipe away the escaped tears. Sylvia looks so worried for me I actually feel guilty.

'What is it, dear?' she asks, still holding her hand on my arm. I take a deep breath and tell her what happened with Andrew, what Luca saw and how I haven't been able to speak to him to explain anything since. By the time I have finished my tears are falling freely. Sylvie hands me her hankie. 'Take heart, child, all hope is not lost. He will come back and when he does you can explain everything. Now dry those tears. We've got pictures to put up!' She gives me a little shake and takes me by the arm back into the house.

It is only lunchtime but it has already been a long and emotional day. I leave Sylvie and Jen to help Michael and my dad put the pictures up, and set to work cleaning the mess caused by all of the deliveries. I am glad to lose myself in the dusting and polishing for a few hours, breaking only to direct new deliveries and give instructions. By the time it is dark all of the furniture is in place and, but for one final clean, the house is ready for the party preparations, which means it is nearly ready to officially open. We all go home to our beds exhilarated and exhausted, ready for one final push tomorrow.

Chapter 33

It is all hands on deck on Thursday morning as Jen and I are joined early by our parents and Jake for a final clean and prep. We scrub, dust, polish and sweep for what feels like hours. Well, actually it is hours. Five to be exact.

It is back-breaking work and we are all shattered by the time Katarina arrives with our final lunch delivery. This time, as well as the cold meat, cheeses, breads and pastries, she also has a huge black sack over her shoulder that we soon discover contains a thick pile of sheer white organza and several rolls of pistachio green satin ribbon. After joining us for lunch she sets about covering every dining chair inside the house and out, tying them with the ribbon at the back of the seat so that they drape elegantly to the floor. Jen and I line the pools and gardens with the glass lanterns from the garden centre and set up large trellis tables, which Katarina then covers in organza, around the pool to put food, drink, glasses and plates on.

Mum and Pauline had been up at five a.m. to go to the flower market and pick up the fresh flowers already ordered. They are busy arranging gorgeous bouquets of white roses and great displays of white and cornflower blue hydrangea in large urns. Despite being exhausted, I am relaxed, and the atmosphere is busy but calm. The house looks pristine and, against the odds, everything is under control and should be done in time for tomorrow.

In the afternoon a couple of Jake and Jen's friends from college arrive. Lisa is English but lives and works in Rome and has spent her summer learning to cook. Geoff is retired and has come over from Warrington to indulge his new passion of cookery. They both seem lovely and very happy to be involved with the launch. After introductions, they set to work in the kitchen with Jake and Jen at the helm. I work my way through the house and gardens, perfecting as I go and putting the finishing touches to everything.

At dusk I walk back from the far gardens, where I have swept the paths and straightened the solar light lamps that run along the front of the flower beds. The air is hanging thick and heavy around me and, for the first time since I arrived in Tuscany, a cluster of dark clouds has gathered in front of the deep red residue left by the setting sun. I hope that it isn't a bad omen.

Perhaps the clouds have come out in sympathy for the dark sadness that lingers at the back of my mind and the bottom of my heart. I still haven't heard from Luca. I had hoped that he might call, or text at least, to wish us luck for tomorrow but so far, nothing. I hate myself for feeling so miserable when this is such an amazing moment for Jen and me. I am so excited about the launch and so proud of everything that we have achieved, but somehow it doesn't feel right to be excited about the future when I don't know if Luca is going to be in it. I wish so much that I had stopped him from walking away when I had a chance but it is too late for that now, the moment has passed and there is nothing I can do to change it.

As I approach the house, my spirits are lifted by the incredible smells that are wafting outside and being held by the dense evening air. I go into the kitchen to see how everyone is getting on and can't help but smile as I take in the sights and sounds and the enticing smell of warm, buttery pastry. Geoff is stacking up piles of the most delicious looking cannoncini, little pastry horns filled with chocolate cream, on a huge silver platter that sits beside another plate covered in a batch of perfectly cooked pizelle cookies. Jake is soaking biscuit fingers in espresso for a huge tiramisu layer cake he is building, and Lisa is standing next to him rolling cold meats for the canapés. Jen has decided to make a range of traditional oven bakes and she is preparing them to cook in the morning. She is also going to make two huge risottos, a seafood one and a meat one, but she will prepare them tomorrow. It is a hive of activity and it is wonderful to see it all up and running.

'It smells amazing in here! Can I try one?' I'm standing over the platter of cannoncini and the temptation is just too much.

'Of course.' Geoff sounds pleased to be asked and hands me one of the little horns that is edged with dark chocolate and tiny crunching nuts. I bite into the crispy shell and the rich chocolaty cream oozes out into my mouth. It tastes divine.

'Wow! This is amazing! You're a pastry genius!' Geoff looks embarrassed but I see his chest puff out with pride. 'I can't thank you all enough for helping us. Will you be working much longer?'

'Not much.' Jen places a huge lasagne in the fridge. 'The canapés are pretty much done,' she looks at Lisa who nods.

'Yep, that's the last one.' Lisa puts a small roll of rare beef on a puff of pastry and dots it with horseradish.

'Jake is just finishing the last dessert and that was the last al forno to go in the fridge. Everything else can be prepared in the morning. How is it going in the house?' Jen asks. 'What else do we need to do tonight?'

'I can't quite believe it but I think that we are nearly finished!' I tell her. 'I'm just going to help our mums put the flowers in the storage shed to keep them cool until the morning and then I'll make sure they go and get some rest. They definitely deserve it, they've worked so hard!'

'I know,' Jen agrees. 'They have been wonderful. We really must do something to thank them.'

'Definitely, let's talk about it in the morning when you come over. I think we should all get an early night tonight.'

'Sure.' Jen starts to wipe down the work surfaces that are covered in grated cheese and splodges of béchamel. I leave them to it and go outside to help put the flowers in storage but dad and Frank are already on the case and are lifting the final large urn between them. When it is safely locked away for the night, I order them all to bed via the kitchen to grab a cannoncini and they don't argue.

I wave them off and notice that the clouds are thickening and moving closer. I hope that tomorrow won't be a freak bad weather day but pretty quickly dismiss the idea. Bad weather doesn't seem to exist here in the summer.

By nine p.m. the kitchen has been cleared and cleaned. Jen and Jake leave hand in hand at the same time as Geoff and Lisa, and all of a sudden the activity has stopped and the house is quiet again. I lock up the main house before walking slowly back to my own little cottage. On my way I turn around to look back at my beautiful house on the eve of its opening, now shrouded in darkness and illuminated only by the solar lights that are dotted around the garden.

This is my life now. I can't believe how drastically everything has changed in just two months. If I had been able to write down my dreams and hopes just a few months ago I don't think even they would have been as wonderful as this. Inevitably my thoughts turn to Luca and I remember a line from Bridget Jones' Diary. I know it off by heart. I must have watched the film at least twenty times.

'It is a truth universally acknowledged that when one part of your life starts going okay, another falls spectacularly to pieces.'

I smile at the eternal wisdom of Bridget. I suppose it really is too much to expect Luca to be here with me. Life just isn't that perfect. I hear a low rumble of thunder in the distance, like the gods are groaning at me. I can just hear them. 'You are never happy, Sophie, we give you all of this and you still want more!' A shiver runs down my spine as a breeze lifts the air around me and it ushers me back to the cottage.

I lie in bed awake for at least an hour, uncomfortable in the intense humidity that is settling around me and offered no comfort from my wide open window. Eventually I drift into a deep sleep lulled by the deepening rolls of thunder in the distance.

Chapter 34

I am relieved to see the sun shining brightly through my bedroom window when I wake early in the morning. I get up quickly and pull on my trusty cut-offs and white vest. I will come back and get ready for the party later before the guests start to arrive.

As I pop some bread into the toaster, I suddenly realise that I don't have anything to wear for the party! Of all of the things to forget, how on earth could I have forgotten that? What with Luca going, and then getting everything ready, I haven't even thought about what I am going to wear. I bound back up the stairs, two at a time and fling open my wardrobe, but it is no use, the dress fairy hasn't been to deliver a sparkling new gown. I have the coral dress that I bought in Florence for the dinner party and a couple of pretty little floral dresses but that's it. I can't wear the coral one again, not least because everyone who was at the dinner party will be here tonight, and the other ones just aren't special enough for such a big night!

I grab my phone and dial Jen's number. She answers after a single ring.

'Morning, I'm leaving in a minute, everything OK?'

'Don't leave!' I shout in panic, which is perhaps a little over the top and it frightens Jen.

'What's wrong?' she sounds panicked now too.

'I don't have anything to wear!' I blurt out. 'I can't believe I forgot to get a dress!'

Jen is surprisingly calm about the situation given what I know she would be like if the roles were reversed. 'Don't worry! Just borrow something of mine; you will look lovely in anything.'

'How can you say that?' I cry. 'This is possibly the biggest party, the biggest day and night of my life and I have to dig something out from the back of my friend's wardrobe! What are you wearing?' I ask her.

'Oh, I got something ages ago. Now listen, you need to calm down. There is nothing we can do it about it now. I'll bring over my dresses and you can wear one of them. You will look lovely.'

Still not happy but without any other choice, I thank her and hang up the phone. I don't feel like eating any more so instead I go straight outside to make my way over to the house.

The grass in my front garden is wet; I can feel it over the edges of my flip flops. It must have rained last night.

As I get nearer to the house, there is no question that it has rained.

All of my worry about not having a dress pales into insignificance as I take in the scene in front of me. It is utter chaos. The pool is filthy. It is covered in leaves, bugs and debris from what must have been a big storm last night. There is even a table cloth and two lanterns floating in it. More table cloths are strewn around the patio and the edge of the pool, a few of the chairs have been knocked over and one has been swept right over to the other side of the pool. Automatically I lift my hand to my mouth and I hold it there as I walk around inspecting the damage more closely. Thankfully it seems like most of the damage is aesthetic. The pool can be cleaned and we have plenty of spare linen to replace the dirty table cloths. The organza drapes are damp but they will dry quickly under the hot sun.

It had all been so perfect when I went to bed, I can't believe the state of it. I didn't even hear the storm; I must have been in such a deep sleep. Relieved that the damage is repairable I go to check out the side and front of the house.

As I reach the trellised patio area at the side, my relief instantly disappears. To my horror I can see that half of the trellis roof has collapsed and is hanging to the floor across the entire middle section, much of the beautiful wisteria has been pulled down with it and the floor is covered with leaves, mud and smashed glass from the broken lanterns that were only bought and hung last week, and now lay shattered across the floor.

Treading my way carefully over the glass, too shocked to cry, I keep going around to the front of the house. Thankfully it isn't anywhere near as bad. Some of the mud from the newly-created flower bed around the fountains has been washed onto the gravel and the flowers are looking a bit bruised and battered but it is nothing that can't be fixed with a little TLC.

The problem is that we don't have the time to give the flower beds a little TLC, let alone clean up everywhere else and fix the broken trellises. I sit on the edge of the fountain, put my head in my hands and allow myself a little sob. That is exactly how Jen and Jake find me a few minutes later when they pull into the driveway. Jen gets out of the car like lightning and runs to me. She puts her arm around my shoulder.

'Don't cry, Soph. Please, it's going to be fine. I have brought all of my dresses for you.'

I look up at her and manage a weak smile. 'I wish that was the problem.'

'Is it Luca?' she looks concerned.

'No! It's the house! I didn't hear it but there must have been a storm last night.'

'There was.' Jen looks surprised that I didn't hear it. 'I don't know how you slept through it, it was deafening! I thought that the pool and tables might be a bit of a mess, but we can clear them up.' She looks around her and takes in the dishevelled flower beds. 'And mum will be able to fix all of this.'

She rubs my back. Jake comes over, weighed down with what looks like a huge bag of dresses.

'Everything OK?' he asks Jen and she explains.

'The storm has made a bit of a mess. I think we might need to get our parents here to help clear up.'

'It's made more than a bit of a mess,' I tell them. 'Come and see.' Jake and Jen follow me to the side of the house with worried faces. Jen gasps when she sees the destruction in front her.

'Wow, I see what you mean.' Jake looks and sounds horrified.

Ever the optimist, Jen rallies quickly. 'Don't worry! We have hours before people will start to arrive. We can fix this. There are still a couple of lanterns left; at least they will provide some light. I am sure our dads can do something to fix the trellising.' I marvel at her positivity.

'Do you think so?'

'Well, what's the alternative? Cancel the party?' She asks the question but in a way that makes it clear that it's not an option.

I shrug my shoulders, not as confident as she is.

'No way, that is not going to happen!' she is defiant. 'We have come too far and have too many people coming to let a little storm damage get us down. Jake,' she turns to face him. 'Can you take those dresses to the cottage for me, please, and leave them where I told you to, then come back and we can crack on with the clean up. I'll call my mum,' she turns to me now, very bossy all at once. 'You go and get your mum and dad up. There's a lot to do!'

Buoyed by her spirit, I pull myself together and go into the house to wake my parents. As they quickly get dressed to come down and help, I start at the back of the house. I scoop the linens that are within reach out of the pool and lean over the edge to fish out the lanterns that are floating near the steps. We have a giant net in the storage room for cleaning so I go to get it to clean out the leaves and bugs. I'm relieved to see the vases of flowers we stored away last night are still perfect and am thankful that we hadn't left them outside as well.

As I fetch the net from the side wall, I catch sight of the original lanterns that Jake and Luca took down after one of them nearly fell on my head. I wonder if we can put some candles in them and re-hang them properly. Just for tonight. It would be so beautiful outside all lit by candlelight if we can fix the trellising. Even if they can't be hung we can line them up on the ground to light the patio area and to replace the new ones that were broken last night. Perhaps this is a blessing in disguise, I think, and surprise myself with my sudden optimism. Grabbing the net I take it outside to the pool and start to drag it through the heavy pool water, catching as much dirt and debris as I can.

My change in mood doesn't last for long. Jen is running from the morning room, followed by an ashen-looking Jake.

'Soph!' she wails. 'They've gone, they've all gone!'

'What have?' I shout across the garden, dropping the net in the water and going to see what on earth can be the matter now.

'It's the electrics! The bloody electrics have gone! The storm must have knocked them out. All of the food is ruined!' She slumps on the floor. 'The fridges are out. There isn't any power in the kitchen. The lights don't even work. It's no use.' She looks defeated. 'We really are done for now, we can't possibly throw a party for over fifty people without any food or any place to cook or store food.' Jake stands behind her and puts his hands on her shoulders, rubbing them gently in an attempt to soothe her. I walk past them both into the morning room and flick a light switch. Not because I don't believe Jen but for some reason I just need to see it for myself.

Surprisingly, despite the fact that the electrics have indeed gone, I don't feel like crying. For once I am going to be the optimistic one.

'There must be something we can do.' Jen looks at me like I'm mad. 'Come on!' I coax her. 'You said it yourself, Jen, we are not cancelling the party now. There are loads and loads of candles in the garage. And the old lanterns are all in storage, I'm sure there is enough to light the house.'

'What about the food?' Jen isn't convinced. 'We can't possibly cater for everyone without power!' I rack my mind for an answer and, as if on cue, the door bell rings. I open it and find Katarina and Sylvie standing there.

Katarina walks straight past me into the house. 'Are my chairs bad? I have new organza to re-do if I need,' she shouts over her shoulder as she goes outside to inspect them.

'Katarina called me this morning, she was very worried about the storm, so was I,' Sylvie explains. 'We have come to see if we can help with anything.'

'Thank you.' I am touched at the gesture.

'Is there much damage?' Sylvie asks.

'Come and see.' I lead her through the entrance hall. 'Have you heard from Luca?' Even amidst the morning's disasters I am still thinking about him.

'He's travelling, dear,' her voice is kind. 'I'm sorry, but I don't think I will be able to talk to him today.'

The disappointment is almost as crushing as the devastation in the house. At least I can do something about that.

'Of course.' I swallow a painful lump that has quickly formed in my throat. I want to ask where he is travelling to but we are at the back door and there are more pressing things to talk about. Jen and Jake come over to greet Sylvie.

'Cheer up, girls!' Jake takes on the role of optimist. 'I'm sure we can fix this. We can't let Katarina down; she is already recovering the chairs. She is a determined young thing!'

Katarina is systematically stripping each of the wet and dirty chairs and recovering them with fresh organza. I am cheered by her kindness and diligence.

'I think we can fix most of this,' Sylvie agrees with Jake.

'It gets worse,' I say grimly. I take her to see the side of the house and explain about the electrics. 'All of the food Jen and her friends made last night is ruined and we can't possibly make more without electricity.'

'Do you know an electrician?' she asks the obvious question.

'We did have one working on the house last week but he is on a job in Florence now. Even if I can get hold of him I doubt he can come back at such short notice. I don't know any others and even if I did, I can't imagine we could get them here in time to have everything fixed for the party.'

'We can help!' Katarina pipes up from behind us where I didn't even realise she has been standing. 'I ask my mother for food, for pastry and dessert. And I bring food like I do for lunch, bread, meat, cheese.' It is a statement not a question and I'm overwhelmed with the determination, kindness and generosity of this young soul.

'You are just so kind, Katarina, and I am so, so grateful for the offer but we have to feed nearly sixty people tonight. I don't think that will be enough.'

'So I get Paulo to help.' She is undeterred. 'He can make food at cafe and bring it here.'

I look at Jen to gauge her reaction. It is an option, if he would agree to do it. But it doesn't feel right, catering the launch from somewhere else when we are supposed to be showcasing the food as a major part of the hotel and what it has to offer. As we discuss the options, Frank and Pauline arrive. My parents are downstairs now too, and we all stand under the broken trellising at the side of the house exploring our options.

'I saw some Calor gas canisters in storage,' my dad tells Jen. 'Could you cook the risotto over them? There are paella pans in the kitchen that would be perfect.'

'I've never done it before.' Jen looks unsure. 'But I can certainly give it a go. I'll need new meat and fish though; our supplies are all bad now.'

'It's fine!' Katarina is on the phone but she covers the mouthpiece and interrupts our discussion. 'Paulo close cafe, he bring meat from butcher and fish too. He have large prawn, maybe for barbecue?'

'Do we have a barbecue?' Jen asks me.

'I don't know. Have you seen one in storage, Dad?'

'Fraid not, love. I might be able to make one, though, if we can find some bricks and coal?'

'I have a giant barbecue you can use if you throw a shrimp or two on it for me.' A loud American voice behind us makes me jump and we all turn around in surprise.

'I hope you don't mind,' Max Carter flashes those big white teeth at us through his lovely smile. 'The front gate is open and I was passing, thought I would pop my head in to see if I'm still invited to the party tonight? Hiya, Sophie,' he adds and winks at me. Dad and Frank stand together with their mouths hanging wide open. They stare at me and then back at Max. Mum and Pauline discreetly smooth their hair and clothes, casting amazed glances at each other. Katarina drops her phone and looks like she is going to cry.

'Max!' I'm thrilled to see him. 'Of course you're invited! We would love that! I didn't think you would be back.'

'Even I don't know where I am from one day to the next,' he laughs. 'But it turns out I'm here. Looks like you guys could do with a bit of help too!'

He looks at the broken trellis above us and the mess at our feet. I explain the whole sorry story.

'We are just trying to find a way to go ahead with the party,' I tell him when he has learnt about our predicament in full.

'I'll tell you what,' Max speaks to the group in his smooth American drawl. 'I hate to miss a party, if you let me bring a guest tonight, how about I send a couple of my builders over to fix this mess?' He waves his hand above his head at the broken trellis. 'They can bring my barbecue with them, it's a monster! You could cater for an army on it! I'll even stay and help you clean if you like. I'm a dab hand with a broom! What do you say?'

We all look at each other in amazement. I laugh in disbelief at the turn of events.

'I say I think I want to kiss you! Thank you! All of you!' I look to Max and then Katarina who is still staring at him agog.

'Steady on!' Max laughs. 'If I can get a kiss for a barbecue and a bit of sweeping I'll have to see what else I can do to up the stakes!'

Mum giggles and blushes. Jen pitches in, back to her old self

'Right!' she calls us to attention. 'Katarina, if you are sure that Paulo can bring the food and you can help us out from the patisserie, we will pay you both obviously, then that would be wonderful and, Max, you are too kind, thank you! Builders and barbecue and you can definitely bring a guest!' she laughs. 'I'm Jen by the way.' She holds out her hand, very coy all of a sudden. He shakes it and Jen quickly introduces everyone else. They all try very hard to be casual, except for Pauline who asks if he knows Tom Cruise and mum, who I actually think does a little curtsey. Max Carter kisses her on the cheek, which immediately turns bright pink. That's where I get it from!

'Well, that's settled then,' he says in his American drawl. 'I better get on the phone.' He takes out his mobile and steps away from the group as he makes a call. As soon as he is out of earshot there is a flurry of whispers as everyone descends on me.

'Max Carter! I can't believe it! How do you know him, love?' dad asks. 'Are you friends?'

'Isn't he even more handsome in real life?' Pauline says and gets chastised by Frank. I laugh and shush them so that Max can't hear, though I'm sure that he is used to this sort of reaction. I briefly explain about our meeting a few weeks ago, although I leave out some of the less attractive details from the morning.

'I can't believe you didn't tell me you are friends with Max Carter.' Mum overlooks the fact that I have only met him once before. 'You should have told me, I could have told everyone at home. Sheryl and Bob would be so jealous if they knew!'

'All sorted.' Max walks back over to us. 'The boys will be here within the hour and they are trying to get an electrician in for the morning.'

'Thank you so much!' Jen and I speak in unison. We are both completely overwhelmed by everyone's kindness and support.

'Sure. I guess we should get to work.' He pushes up his shirt sleeves. 'Where shall I start?'

And with that we all get on with the jobs in hand. Katarina finishes re-covering the dirty chairs then goes back to the patisserie to talk to her mum about supplying the pastries, cakes and canapés, as well as several large baskets of bread. Mum and Pauline work on the gardens, cleaning up the flower beds and the areas around them. Dad and Frank remove the glass and other debris from beneath the broken trellis and Jen and Jake go to salvage what they can from the kitchen and change their plans for the afternoon's catering activities. Max and I set to work out the back. We pick up the mess, clean the pool, sweep the floors and re-lay the tables. I wish I had my camera on me to take a picture of the international movie star sweeping my floor! Max is actually really great company. He takes my mind off the job in hand and keeps me entertained with amazing stories about his famous friends. Against all odds I am actually having fun! I could listen to him for hours. But of course, today, I can't!

In no time at all, the house is back to its beautiful self. The mess has been cleared and Max's builders are working hard to fix the trellising. I bring the candles up from the cellar and Max retrieves the old lanterns from the shed. We put a candle in each of them and leave them at the edge of the side patio.

'If you can hang these safely in the trellis when it is fixed, that would be great,' I tell one of the builders, who is holding up a huge piece of vine and trying to attach it to a new piece of wood for the trellis. He looks at me blankly and, to my surprise, Max speaks to him confidently and quickly in perfect Italian.

'They don't speak much English,' he winks at me, clearly enjoying my surprise.

Mum and Pauline are inside the house now. They have finished tending to the broken flowers and are collecting all of the empty wine bottles, jam jars and vases that they can find to put candles in.

'Where's dad?' I ask, picking up a candle and squeezing it into the top of an empty red wine bottle.

'He's gone into town with Frank. They are under orders from Jen to buy up all of the ice in Tuscany!'

Sure enough, dad and Frank return at about three p.m. with a backseat and a boot full of ice!

'We must have gone to ten different places,' dad huffs and wheezes as he walks past holding three bags stacked up one on top of the other. 'Out of the way! This is freezing!' he rushes past me. 'Where do you want it?'

'In the storage shed please, Dad, Max has cleared out a couple of the old tin troughs from the garden, you can empty it into them.'

'Okey dokey,' dad calls back, quickening his pace as the freezing ice burns his arms. We all muck in carrying and emptying the ice. Just as I get the last bag from the boot, Paulo and Katarina turn up.

'Paulo.' I put the ice down and go over to greet them. 'Thank you so much for everything, you are a saviour!' I give him a big hug and he smiles shyly.

'I am glad to help!' He opens his boot, which has three large ice coolers in it. He takes one out and hands it to Katarina. 'This is the fish for the risottos and a whole sea bass I think you can barbecue.'

'Amazing, thank you!'

He hands me the second cool box. 'This is the meat for the risotto.' I take it from him and, balancing the last of the ice on top, carry it all into the kitchen.

Paulo follows with the third box, which is full to the brim with prawns, langoustine and more sea bass. Katarina goes back to the car and returns a minute later with a giant wicker hamper full of every kind of bread that you can imagine and another cool box which she hands to Jen before she collapses under the weight and size of the two containers. Jen opens it and looks inside.

'Wow! Katarina, this is wonderful. I can't believe that you have done all of this for us.' She kisses her on both cheeks.

In the cool box is a huge zabligone, a tiramisu layer cake, almost exactly like the one that Jake had made the night before, a whole stack of strawberry tarts, cannoncini and amaretto cream meringues.

'You two are simply amazing, I don't know what we have done to deserve this or how we can possibly repay you!' I feel quite emotional at how much everyone has done for us.

'You are friends,' Katarina is matter of fact. 'Neighbours now too! We help each other.' I hug her warmly.

Paulo disappears and comes back carrying four huge platters, stacked on top of each other.

'Where shall I put these?' he asks.

'More food,' I gasp. 'You have done so much, you can't have stopped all day!' I take two of the platters from him and place them on one of the large work counters.

'Well, you will be needing canapés. I hope these are OK.'

'They are more than OK.' Jen admires the mounds of canapés that include mini ciabattas with sun-blushed tomatoes and pesto; asparagus rolled in Parma ham; goats cheese crostini; and ricotta figs. 'They are incredible!'

Paulo and Katarina grin, they are clearly pleased with the praise and obviously thrilled to be able to help. What wonderful people.

Max puts his head around the kitchen door. 'It's four p.m. guys.' He looks at his watch. 'The trellising is finished so if it's OK with you, I'll head home and get my glad rags on.'

'Of course, we can't thank you enough for everything, Max,' I say.

He waves off my thanks. 'Anything for a good party! See you in a couple of hours'.

Guests will be arriving from six p.m. and we all need to start getting ready. Katarina and Paulo leave, promising to be back in an hour with Katarina's friends, who are going to help with the serving. Jen and Jake store the canapés that need refrigerating on top of the ice troughs that have been filled with wine, champagne, beer and an array of soft drinks by dad and Frank. They lock the storage room and go back to Jen's cottage to get ready. They will pick up Lisa and Geoff on their way back in an hour, who will be surprised to be cooking the risottos on gas in the garden and the seafood on a barbecue. Mum and Pauline are fiddling with the vases of flowers that have been put out on the tables, and Sylvie is putting the last of the candles in their various holders around the pool area. Everything looks spectacular. The side of the house is perfect, with the original lanterns hanging ready for the candles to be lit at dusk, and most of the wisteria salvaged and dripping below and between them. The barbecue and gas stands are set up at the far end of the pool ready to be cooked on, and the buffet tables are covered in white linen and lined with glasses for every imaginable drink, as well as stacks of plates and piles of gleaming cutlery, perfectly rolled in white linen napkins.

'You have all done so much.' I am choked.

Mum puts her arm round me. 'Come on, love, no time to be soppy, you have to make yourself look beautiful and so do I. A movie star is coming to the party, you know!' she laughs and I give her a quick hug then usher her upstairs and send Sylvie, Pauline and Frank home.

There is nothing left for me to do except get ready myself so I take a final satisfied look around and quickly go back to my little cottage.

Chapter 35

Realistically, I have about an hour before I need to be back at the house to light the candles and get the music going before guests arrive. Jen has arranged for a saxophonist to come and serenade the guests during dinner but he won't be arriving until seven p.m. so we have put together a special playlist on her iPod to play as people arrive. Luckily the iPod dock can run on batteries so another potential disaster is averted!

With all of the things I still need to do running through my mind, I jump in the shower. It is such a relief to feel the warm water powerfully hitting my back. I shut my eyes and put my head back so that it runs over my face, taking just a moment to myself before the madness starts again. Feeling immeasurably better just for being clean, I wrap myself in a towel and sit on the floor in front of the full mirror with my make-up bag.

What with everything going on this morning I have barely had a chance to think about Luca but, now that the party is so close and I am alone again, he is back in my mind and I'm sad that he isn't here to see everything that we have achieved. To see me. A tiny part of me had still hoped that he might show up but Sylvie has put paid to that. Even with all of the great things that have happened this morning, and everyone's amazing kindness, I still feel a tinge of sadness at Luca's absence. I can't wait to see Fi and other friends and family but being the life and soul of the party, keeping everyone entertained all night, is going to be hard work when the one person I really want to be there to share it with, won't be. It doesn't help that I am going to be surrounded by happy couples: Fi and Jackson, Jen and Jake, Katarina and Paulo. Even our parents are super happy out here. I look at myself in the mirror. The extra pounds that I put on when I arrived have melted away from all of the hard work on the house. My seven for all mankind jeans would probably fit me again now! My hair is streaked golden blonde from the sun and my skin has turned a rich brown. Probably for the first time in my life I actually think I look nice. Italy suits me. Everything in my life is perfect. Everything except for the fact that Luca isn't in it. My phone beeps on the floor next to me. It's Jen.

'Leaving to pick up Lisa and Geoff now, should be there in 20 minutes'

Twenty minutes! I have wasted half an hour brooding. What am I doing? I have all day every day to be sad about Luca, tonight I have a party to host and I owe it to myself and Jen and to all of our wonderful friends and family, who have done so much to help us, to be the best host that I can possibly be. Quickly but expertly, I apply my make-up. I flick my head upside down and blast my hair with the hairdryer to create as much body as possible, then when it is nearly dry I flick it back and smooth it over so that it hangs long and sleek over my shoulders. I just need to choose a dress and I am ready.

I open my wardrobe expecting to see a selection of Jen's dresses hanging in front of me but to my surprise there is just one dress hanging up, zipped in a white dress bag. Jen must have chosen one for me. I pull the zip down and look inside. I don't recognise it at first but as I open the bag up and finger the flowing cream chiffon, the gold beading and the band of crystals around the waist I can't believe what I am seeing. It can't be. Pulling the zip to the bottom, I take the dress out of the bag completely. It is! It's the dress from our very first shopping trip to Florence. The dress that cost 1000 euros!

I hold it up against me and stand in the mirror. It is even more beautiful than I remember. I'm stunned. Jen must have bought it for me. Very carefully, so as not to catch any of the beautiful beadwork, I step into it and bend my arm as far as I can behind my back to pull the zip up. It is exquisite. It looks even better than it did the first time against my tanned skin. I twirl for myself in front of the mirror and, as I do, I see something else in the bottom of my wardrobe. On the floor underneath the now empty dress bag is the most beautiful pair of silver and crystal peep-toe heels. This is too much. I can't believe that Jen has done this for me. I slip my feet into the shoes, which fit perfectly. They feel amazing. I feel amazing.

Barely able to contain my excitement, desperate to show myself off and to thank my wonderful friend I grab my clutch bag, throw in my phone, hairbrush and a couple of make-up essentials and make my way quickly but carefully down the stairs. As I walk down the path, through the gardens to the main house, I feel like I have never looked so beautiful in my life. I can't even believe that I am using that word about myself, but I really do feel beautiful. I wish so much that Luca were here to see it but my fickle mood is not going to change again. I have to be grateful for everything that I see in front of me and for the wonder and kindness of human nature, which has exposed itself in the best possible way, and in so many ways today.

The house looks magnificent. The pool is ethereal in its elegance as the lights shine up through the water, illuminating its sapphire splendour. The white organza on the chairs ripples romantically in the slight, warm breeze and the soft glow from the solar power fairy lights can just be seen twinkling through the wisteria above the patio and framing the cypress trees that flank the garden. It is magical. Standing in my incredible gown, looking at my dream house in all its elegant beauty, basking in the rose-coloured warmth of the early evening sun, I vow to always remember how wonderful life can be and the power of hope. Silently, I thank the universe for the incredible blessings that it has bestowed upon me and promise to try to give back to it in every way that I can.

I will enjoy tonight for everything that it is and everything that it represents and in the hope that it may lead to even better things tomorrow and that maybe one day soon, I might be able to share those things with Luca.

Chapter 36

Jen and Jake are already in the kitchen with Lisa and Geoff when I go inside the house. Jen looks stunning in a long, plunging black lace dress which is covered by a not-quite-so-stunning white apron. Jake looks very dapper too in tuxedo trousers and a white shirt, also covered with an apron.

'Oh wow!' Jen gasps when she sees me. I grin widely at her, my eyes threatening to cry for about the hundredth time this week. 'You look in-cred-i-ble.' She emphasises every syllable.

I throw my arms around her. 'Thank you, thank you so, so much. I can't believe you did this for me!'

'You deserve it! You're the best friend ever.' She hugs me back.

'I love you!' I tell her, overcome by just how much I really do love my best friend.

'I love you too. Now come on, we've got a party to throw!' she grins at me.

Our parents are resplendent in their best suits and dresses, beaming from ear to ear, barely able to contain their excitement.

'Is everything ready, love?' mum asks once she has stopped crying at the sight of Jen and me in our dresses.

'Nearly! I just need to light all the candles in the house and in the lanterns outside.' I suddenly realise that I am going to have to get up a step ladder in my dress to light the hanging lanterns and, as if hearing my thoughts, my dad steps in.

'Not looking like that, you don't! Come on, Frank.' He nudges his friend's arm. 'Let's do the candles outside, then we can get started on the serious work and grab ourselves a couple of drinks!'

They set off in good cheer. Jen goes back to preparing food in the kitchen and mum and Pauline run around the house lighting the candles that are in every possible corner, nook and cranny. Leaving them to it, I press play on the iPod and, to the uplifting sounds of Stevie Wonder singing cheerily alongside me, I take several bottles of now nicely chilled champagne from one of the tubs of ice and open them.

Just as I am pouring the third glass, Katarina and her friends arrive looking smart in black skirts and white shirts. Taking her job very seriously, she takes over the pouring of the champagne and her friends set the glasses on round silver trays so that they can greet the guests with them by the door as they arrive. They don't have to wait long as just moments later Paulo and his parents, Maria from the village shop and her husband, Katarina's parents and the couple who run the village delicatessen (who also kindly supplied Katarina with food for the canapés tonight), arrive in quick succession. They have clearly all dressed in their finest for the occasion and come in with warm smiles, eager to look around the house and see the changes that we have made. Their entrance is accompanied by an array of appreciative noises as they take in the soft, candlelit beauty of the house that would once have been such a huge part of their village life. Their exaggerated and animated Italian tones can still be heard coming through from the house as Sara and Michael arrive a few minutes later, followed quickly by one of Jen's tutors and a few friends from her cooking school. I show them through to the garden where the other guests are now mingling happily as the girls serve the champagne and the first of the canapés.

I hear a familiar voice from the front door and turn back to see our very first official hotel guests ever, Fi's parents, Sue and John. As soon as Sue sees me, she throws her arms open and runs towards me.

'My darling Sophie!'

Jen has heard them arrive too and comes out to greet our other best friend's parents. Sue opens one arm beyond the hug that I am in with her and scoops Jen into it. 'You girls!' she exclaims. 'Look at this place. It's wonderful! I'm so proud of you, you clever things!'

Jen and I have always loved Sue and John, Sue particularly is always full of joy and laughter. She is young and trendy for her age and we have spent many a long afternoon with her and Fi celebrating a successful shopping trip with cocktails in Covent Garden. Once she has finally let us go and we have given John a hug too, they go through to the garden and another flurry of excitement and hugs takes place as they meet my parents and Pauline and Frank. Jen and I are so caught up with Sue and John's arrival that we have barely noticed Fi and Jackson getting out of the same car and coming in just behind them.

'Fi!' I scream and run as fast as I can on the cobbled stones in my new heels. I fling my arms around her, then pull Jen into yet another group hug as she reaches us a second later. We stand together, hugging each other and skipping on the spot until Jackson interrupts.

'Don't I get one?' he laughs. 'Share the love!' I break free and give Jackson an equally enthusiastic hug. He looks tanned and gorgeous in fitted black trousers and a pale blue shirt which is slightly crumpled and open at the collar, messy in a way that only he can pull off. When Fi stands next to him in a beautiful bodycon dress of the same blue with a low neck that shows off her perfect décolletage, they are an achingly beautiful couple.

'It's so amazing that you are here! I can't wait to show you around. I've missed you so much!'

'I've missed you too!' Fi takes my hand in one of hers and Jen's in the other. 'This place looks phenomenal.'

'Awesome,' Jackson agrees, looking at the main fountain, restored to its former splendour and shining magnificently as the rushing water is lit from within. 'Looks like I did the right thing!' he winks at Fi.

'What do you mean?' I catch their conspiratorial glance.

'Well.' Fi speaks slowly, teasing us. 'Jackson has been in Rome this week shooting for the Sunday Times.' She looks at him. 'Go on, you tell them.'

Jen and I look at each other and then back at Jackson.

'What?' we both ask impatiently. 'Tell us!'

Jackson laughs. 'OK, OK! Well, what Fi hasn't told you is that I was actually shooting for the Sunday Times Travel supplement and I have convinced the editor to let the team stay on a couple of days so that we can do a special for you. On the hotel,' he clarifies. Jen and I are too gobsmacked to speak. 'I hope you don't mind,' Jackson goes on, 'But I invited them to the party, it's just another two people: the European editor and the luxury hotel editor. They should be here soon. My camera's in the car, if it's OK I thought I would take a few shots of the party.'

Still speechless with gratitude for our best friend and her lovely boyfriend, Jen and I have to hold back the tears for the one hundred and first time this week. We drop Fi's hands and throw our arms back around Jackson, almost knocking him over, and thanking him until he has to prise us off him.

'Control yourself, girls!' he laughs. 'You'll want to look professional, at least when they arrive!'

He is right of course. Anyone could arrive at any minute and we have to look the part. We show them into the house and they are gratifyingly impressed.

'Louise is just going to love this place,' Fi says, as we briefly show them the library and dining room before taking them out through the morning room to the patio.

'Who's Louise?' I ask.

'*Trend*'s travel editor. I did tell you she's coming, didn't I? I gave her the invite. She is bringing one of the junior editors from *Vacation*. Vacation is the luxury travel magazine that is owned by the same publishing group as Trend magazine. Fi has clearly been working hard on our behalf.

'Fi, that is amazing. How did you get them to come?'

She shrugs her shoulders as if it's no big deal. 'They're friends. It wasn't hard to convince them of a free trip to Italy to stay in a beautifully renovated luxury hotel!' she laughs. 'I spoke to a lady called Sylvie a couple of days ago and told her they would be needing rooms, she said it wouldn't be a problem so I asked her not to mention it. I wanted to surprise you!'

'You are the best, Fi! We owe you big time!' Jen says, still smiling in disbelief.

'Well, don't thank me yet, you won't necessarily get editorial, but it's a start and I'm pretty sure they will fall in love with this place.' She looks around her at the gardens and pool, which are now set against a darkening sky and glowing from the light of hundreds of fairy lights and candles. The soft sounds of Kenny G are floating around the still air from the saxophonist who stands on the steps in front of the morning room. It mingles with the chatter and laughter from the guests who sway to the melody as they sip their champagne in the beautiful surroundings.

Behind the pool, Geoff mans two giant gas canisters, on top of which the risottos are bubbling away nicely, giving off the seductive scents of warm butter and garlic into the night air. Jake has taken charge of the barbecue where line after line of giant langoustine are turning a luscious pink over the smoking heat.

Everything is going well. It looks, sounds and smells wonderful. The guests continue to arrive, including a reporter and photographer from the local newspaper who walk around enthusiastically taking pictures all over the house, and the editor of an Italian travel website who lives in one of the local villages. By eight p.m. there must be nearly seventy people in the house and gardens. Most of them are on the patio and around the pool enjoying the hot food that is being served up onto the long tables for everyone to help themselves to. Some of the older guests sit quietly talking in the library or relaxing on the sofas in the morning room, where George, Jen's bank manager and his wife, Marion, have also positioned themselves whilst they tuck into huge plates of seafood risotto topped with the langoustine from the barbecue. I smile, happy to see them so clearly enjoying the food and George puts his finger and thumb together, holding them up to show his approval.

'Everything seems to be going well.' Jen comes up and stands next to me in the morning room. 'I've just finished prepping the desserts. They will be ready to go as soon as people have finished with the mains.'

'Wonderful. You've done such an amazing job,' I tell her. 'Have you seen Sylvie?' I ask, realising that I haven't seen her arrive.

'Not yet.' Jen doesn't seem concerned. 'I'm sure she'll be here soon. Is that the door again now?' We hear more noise coming from the hallway. 'Perhaps that's her.'

I turn to go and invite our guests in. It isn't Sylvie, it's Max Carter, looking extremely dapper in a perfectly tailored navy suit with an open white shirt and gold rimmed aviator glasses that are totally unnecessary at this time in the evening but certainly look the part, and if anyone can pull them off, he can!

'Girls!' he greets us loudly as he walks in. 'The place looks great! Congratulations! This is Kirsten,' he introduces the stunningly beautiful woman who is standing behind him.

He didn't need to. I put my hand out to introduce myself and realise I am face to face with Kirsten Stone. The Kirsten Stone who just happens to be the hottest thing in Hollywood right now. Kirsten Stone is standing in my house looking exquisite in a flowing gold silk gown that is split to the thigh.

'Kirsten.' I desperately try to keep my cool but fear that I am giving my excitement away as badly as mum did with Max earlier in the day. 'It's a pleasure! Thank you for coming!'

I know I'm gushing but I can't stop myself. Jen is just as bad as I am but Kirsten is graceful and modest in receipt.

'Thank you for having me. Your hotel is really beautiful.'

'Thank you!' I guide them through to the back where the rest of the guests are and whisper to Max, 'Thanks for the warning! You didn't tell me your guest is Kirsten Stone!'

'You didn't ask, kid!' He laughs at me. 'You look beautiful by the way,' he adds seriously, and I blush a deep crimson, thrilled to have finally redeemed my looks from our first fateful meeting. As Max and Kirsten go outside, the excitement and the noise level rises tangibly. Max introduces Kirsten to my parents and to Pauline and Frank, who are clearly thrilled to be singled out by him and love being at the centre of everyone's staring eyes. Looking around I can see one of Jackson's colleagues fiercely scribbling in a small leather notebook and the editors from Trend and Vacation magazine are looking at Max and Kirsten like they can't believe their eyes. I watch as they slowly edge their way closer to them, desperate to catch their attention.

'How the hell do you know Max Carter and Kirsten Stone?' Fi runs over to me. 'And why on earth do I not know that you know them! This is insane! They have to be the hottest couple in Hollywood right now. This party is going to be much more than the talk of the town when my editor gets home!'

I realise that I haven't actually read a magazine or newspaper in weeks, which explains why I wasn't expecting Kirsten to arrive with Max. I explain the story of our meeting to a gobsmacked Fi.

'Well, I think we can say that this hotel is going to be well and truly on the map. What is it called by the way?' she asks.

'Hotel Rialto,' I say, and we clink champagne glasses.

'To Hotel Rialto,' she says. Her eyes wander over my shoulder. 'Who's that?' She asks, nodding towards someone behind me. 'He's gorgeous.' I turn around to see who she is looking at but I can't make anyone out. I do see Sylvie though, who has clearly just arrived on the arm of Luca's godfather, Carlo.

'Sorry, Fi, I just have to go and say hi to someone quickly, I'll catch you in a sec.'

'Sure,' she says easily.

Sylvie looks lovely in an aubergine skirt and matching top edged with black sparkles and sequins. She smiles widely when she sees me.

As I make my way through the now crowded garden over to her, someone behind her turns around and places their hand on her shoulder.

I stop and catch my breath.

Luca is standing behind Sylvie and he looks more handsome than ever. His eyes are scanning the garden eagerly, but they come to rest when they find mine, already locked on him. I stand still looking at him, glued to the spot.

Not taking his eyes from mine, he takes his hand from Sylvie's shoulder and comes across the grass towards me.

His face is serious. My stomach is in knots. Everything around me is a blur. I want to move but I seem to have lost control of my limbs. He reaches where I'm standing and stops in front of me.

'Hi.'

The sound of his voice hits me like a shot of adrenalin, sending my heart crazy in my chest.

'Hi,' I just about manage to croak back. We stand looking at each other for what feels like an eternity but is probably only a few seconds, then we both speak at the same time.

'I'm sorry for what you saw,' I mumble, not catching what he has said.

'Sorry,' he speaks again. 'Go on'.

I stumble on my words and try to gather myself. 'I was just saying sorry. Sorry for what you saw last time you were in the house.' I can feel tears pricking the back of my eyes already and I desperately try to think clearly so that I can explain everything before he goes anywhere again.

'Sophie, please don't apologise.'

'But you don't understand.' I can hear the urgency in my own voice. 'It isn't what you think.'

'I know,' he interrupts. 'I know it isn't.'

'You do?' I look at his face.

'Sylvie explained everything to me, she told me what happened. It's me who should be apologising. I took off so quickly after I saw you and Andrew because I was embarrassed and hurt, and because I didn't want to ruin a special moment for you. I didn't know what else to do so I just got back in my car and drove until I found myself back home in Florence. I should have spoken to you. I should have given you a chance to explain but I didn't think that I could muster the false enthusiasm to be happy for you. I didn't want to spoil everything for you so I just switched my phone off.'

I can vaguely make out a small crowd drawing closer to us. I see Jen and Fi standing with our parents and Sylvie in front of them with Carlo. I am still trying to take in what he is saying.

'But Sylvie said you were going away, she said you were travelling,' was all I could think to say. I want to be sure that I am understanding him, that he is back for good and not just passing through.

'I was travelling,' he is smiling at me now. 'I was travelling back here to see you. As soon as I spoke to her and she explained everything I felt like such an idiot and I felt so bad for not calling you. I just wanted to get back here and see you. I am so sorry, Sophie. Can you forgive me?'

He picks up my hands and holds them in both of his.

'Forgive you?' I repeat, wanting so much to believe what I am hearing but hardly daring to.

'If you can. I know I've been an idiot and that I should have let you explain, but if you let me I will make it up to you.' He smiles hesitantly and the skin by his beautiful eyes crinkles in that way that makes him totally and utterly irresistible. 'What do you say?' he asks.

Before I can answer my arms have found their way around his neck and I am leaning in and kissing him. I have no control over my body at all, I'm locked into him, our mouths connect in a warm, soft embrace and I am powerless to do anything else but to keep kissing him. We kiss on and on until he gently pulls away from me.

'So I'm forgiven then?' he smiles tenderly.

I smile too and nod my head. 'There is nothing to forgive.' I lean in to kiss him again but am interrupted by a small whoop from behind us where Jen is standing with Fi, who bursts into a spontaneous round of applause, which is quickly taken up by the rest of the group. Embarrassed, I bite my lip nervously and dip my head laughing.

Luca takes my chin in his hand and lifts my face back to his. 'We mustn't disappoint our audience.' He kisses me, tenderly and then passionately, until once again I have totally forgotten where we are.